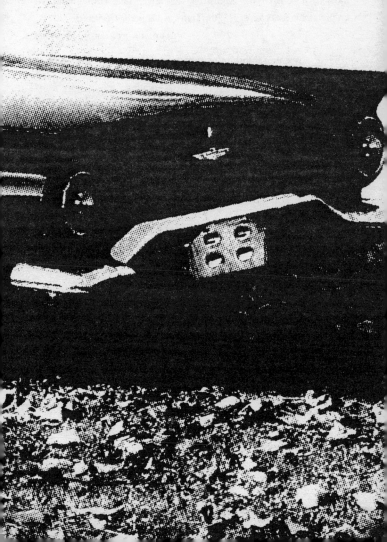

THE LADY IN THE CAR
WITH GLASSES AND A GUN

"Japrisot's story is detailed, substantial, full-blooded. It combines huge intellectual grasp with fascinating narrative, fine writing and an unforgettable protagonist . . . [this] rates as a superb achievement"

EDMUND CRISPIN, *The Times*

"Full of suspense, absorbing, fast-moving . . . this is Japrisot's finest suspense thriller" *L'Express*

"A cordon bleu mixture of suspense, sex, trick-psychology and fast action" *Publishers Weekly*

"Another success . . . Sébastien Japrisot has a very personal way of evoking fear" MARTINE MONOD, *Humanité Dimanche*

"Japrisot writes with warmth, and has a gift for rendering almost every character instantly likable" *New Yorker*

Sébastien Japrisot's talents as a storyteller have something magic about them. You have to wait until the last page to be liberated from his grasp"

JEAN-MARIE GUILLAUME, *Quotidien de Paris*

Sébastien Japrisot

THE LADY IN THE CAR
WITH GLASSES AND A GUN

*Translated from the French
by Helen Weaver*

THE HARVILL PRESS
LONDON

First published with the title *La dame dans l'auto avec des lunettes et un fusil* by
Éditions Denoel, Paris, 1966

First published in Great Britain by Souvenir Press, 1968

This paperback edition first published in 1998 by
The Harvill Press
84 Thornhill Road
London N1 1RD

1 3 5 7 9 8 6 4 2

Copyright © Sébastien Japrisot, 1966
English translation copyright © Souvenir Press, 1967

A CIP catalogue record for this book is
available from the British Library

ISBN 1 86046 439 4

Designed and typeset in Minion at Libanus Press, Marlborough, Wiltshire

Printed and bound in Great Britain by Mackays of Chatham

Half title illustration: by Newell and Sorrell

The Lady in the Car
with Glasses and a Gun

The Lady

I have never seen the sea.

The black-and-white-tiled floor sways like water a few inches from my eyes.

It hurts so much I could die.

I am not dead.

When they attacked me – I'm not mad, someone or something attacked me – I thought, I've never seen the sea. For hours I had been afraid, afraid of being arrested, afraid of everything. I had made up a whole lot of stupid excuses and it was the stupidest one that crossed my mind: don't hurt me, I'm not really bad, I wanted to see the sea.

I also know that I screamed, screamed with all my might, but that my screams remained trapped in my throat. Someone lifted me off the ground, someone smothered me.

Screaming, screaming, screaming, I thought again: it's not real, it's a nightmare, I'm going to wake up in my room, it will be morning.

And then this.

Louder than all my screams, I heard the cracking of the bones of my own hand; my hand being crushed.

Pain is not black, it is not red. It is a well of blinding light that exists only in your mind. But you fall into it all the same.

* * *

Cool, the tiles against my forehead, I must have fainted again.

Don't move. Above all, don't move.

I am not lying flat on the floor. I am kneeling with the furnace of my left arm against my stomach, bent double with the pain that I would like to contain and that invades my shoulders, the nape of my neck, my back.

Very close to my eye, through the curtain of my fallen hair, an ant moves across a white tile. Further off, a grey, vertical shape must be the pipe of the basin.

I don't remember taking off my glasses. They must have fallen off when I was pulled backwards – I am not mad, someone or something pulled me backwards and stifled my screams. I must find my glasses.

How long have I been like this, on my knees in this tiny room, plunged in semi-darkness? Several hours or a few seconds? I have never fainted in my life. It is less than a hole, it is only a scratch in my memory.

If I had been here for very long someone outside would have become worried. I was standing in front of the basin, washing my hands. My right hand, when I hold it against my cheek, is still damp. I must find my glasses, I must get up.

When I raise my head quickly, too quickly – the tiles spin, I am afraid I will faint again, but everything subsides, the buzzing in my ears and even the pain. It all flows back into my left hand, which I do not look at but which feels like lead, swollen out of all proportion.

Hang on to the basin with my right hand, get up.

On my feet, my blurred image moving when I do in the mirror opposite, I feel as if time is starting to flow again.

I know where I am: the bathroom of a petrol station on the main road to Avallon. I know who I am: an idiot who is running away from the police, a face towards which I lean my face almost close enough to touch, a hand that hurts and that

4

I bring up to eye level so I can see it, a tear that runs down my cheek and falls onto this hand, the sound of someone breathing in a world strangely silent; myself.

Near the mirror in which I see myself is a ledge where I left my handbag when I came in. It is still there.

I open it with my right hand and my teeth. I look for my second pair of glasses, the ones I wear for typing.

Clear now, my face in the mirror is smudged with dust, tear-stained, tense with fear.

I no longer dare look at my left hand. I hold it against my body, pressed against my badly soiled white suit.

The door of the room is closed. But I left it open behind me when I came in.

I am not mad. I stopped the car. I asked them to fill the tank. I wanted to run a comb through my hair and wash my hands. They pointed to a building with white walls at the back of the station. Inside it was too dark for me, I did not shut the door. I don't know now whether it happened immediately, whether I had time to tidy my hair. All I remember is that I turned on the tap, that the water was cool – oh, yes, I did do my hair, I'm sure of it! – and suddenly there was a sort of movement, a presence, as of something alive and brutal behind me. I was lifted off the floor, I screamed with all my might without making a sound, I did not have time to understand what was happening to me, the pain that pierced my hand shot through my whole body, I was on my knees, I was alone, I am here.

Open my bag again.

My money is there, in the envelope with the office letterhead. They didn't take anything.

It's absurd, it's impossible.

I count the notes, lose track, start again. A cold shadow passes over my heart; they didn't want to take my money or anything else, all they wanted – I am mad, I will go mad – was to hurt my hand.

I look at my left hand, my huge purple fingers, and suddenly I can't stand it any more, I collapse against the basin, fall to my knees again and howl. I will howl like an animal until the end of time, I will howl, weep, and stamp my feet until someone comes, until I see daylight again.

I hear hurried footsteps outside, voices, gravel crunching. I howl.

The door opens very suddenly onto a dazzling world.

The July sun has not moved over the hills. The men who come in and lean over me, all talking at once, are the ones I passed when I got out of the car. I recognize the owner of the garage and two customers who must be local people who had also stopped for petrol.

While they are helping me to my feet, through my sobs my mind fastens on a silly detail: the tap of the basin is still on. A moment ago I didn't even hear it. I want to turn off that tap, I must turn it off.

Those who watch me do not understand. Nor do they understand that I don't know how long I have been here. Nor that I have two pairs of glasses: as they hand me the ones that have fallen, they make me repeat ten times that they are mine, really mine. They tell me, "Calm yourself, come now, calm yourself." They think I am mad.

Outside, everything is so clear, so peaceful, so terribly real that my tears suddenly stop. It is an ordinary petrol station: petrol pumps, gravel, white walls, a gaudy poster pasted to a window, a hedge of spindle and oleander. Six o'clock on a summer evening. How could I have screamed and rolled on the floor?

The car is where I left it. Seeing it reawakens my old anxiety, the anxiety that was latent in me when it happened. They're going to question me, ask me where I am from, what I have done, I will answer all wrong, they will guess my secret.

In the doorway of the office towards which they lead me, a woman in a blue apron and a little girl of six or seven are watching me with curious, serene faces, as if at the theatre.

Yesterday afternoon, too, at the same time, a little girl with long hair and a doll in her arms watched me approach. And yesterday afternoon, too, I was ashamed. I can't remember why.

Yes, I can. Quite clearly. I can't stand children's eyes. Behind me there is always the little girl I was, watching me.

The sea.

If things go badly, if I am arrested and must furnish a – what is the word? – an alibi, an explanation, I will have to begin with the sea.

It won't be altogether the truth, but I will talk for a long time without catching my breath, half crying, I will be the naïve victim of a cheap dream. I'll make up whatever I need to make it more real: attacks of split personality; alcoholic grandparents; or that I fell down the stairs as a child. I want to disgust the people who interrogate me, I want to drown them in a torrent of syrupy nonsense.

I'll tell them I didn't know what I was doing, it was me and it wasn't me, understand? I thought it would be a good opportunity to see the sea. It's the other one who's guilty.

They will answer of course, that if I was so anxious to see the sea, I could have done it a long time ago. All I had to do was buy a train ticket and book a room at Palavas-les-Flots, other girls have done it and not died of it, there are such things as paid holidays.

I'll tell them that I often wanted to do it but that I couldn't.

It's true, for that matter. Every summer for the past six

7

years, I've written to tourist bureaus and hotels, received brochures, stopped in front of shop windows to look at bikinis. One time I came within an inch – in the end, my finger refused to press a buzzer – of joining a holiday club. Two weeks on a beach at Baleares, return air fare and visit to Palma included, orchestra, swimming teacher and sailing boat reserved for the duration of the visit, good weather guaranteed by Union-Life, I don't know what else; just reading the description gave you a tan. But, figure it out if you can, every summer I spend half my holiday at the First Hotel of Montbriand (there is only one) in the Haute Loire, and the other half near Compiègne at the home of a former classmate who has "a husband of her own" and a deaf mother-in-law. We play bridge.

It's not that I am such a creature of habit or that I have such a passion for card games. And it's not that I am particularly shy. As a matter of fact, it takes a lot of nerve to overwhelm your colleagues with memories of the sea and St-Tropez when you are fresh from the forest of Compiègne. Well, I don't know.

I hate people who have seen the sea, I hate people who haven't seen it, I think I hate the whole world. There you are. I think I hate myself. If that explains something too, okay.

My name is Dany Longo. Marie Virginie Longo, to be exact; I made up Danielle when I was a child. I have lied all my life. Right now I wouldn't mind Virginie, but to explain it to others would be silly.

My legal age is twenty-six, my mental age eleven or twelve; I am five feet six inches tall, I have dirty blonde hair, which I tint once a month with hydrogen peroxide, I am not ugly but I wear glasses – with smoked lenses, dear, so no one will know I am short-sighted – and everyone realizes, stupid – and the thing I am best at is keeping my mouth shut.

I have never said anything to anyone but "Please pass the salt," except twice, and both times I suffered. I hate people who don't understand the first time you slap their hands. I hate myself.

I was born in a village in Flanders, of which I remember only the smell of the coal mixed with mud that the women were allowed to gather near the mines. My father, an Italian refugee who worked at the train station, died when I was two years old. He was run over by a freight wagon from which he had just stolen a box of safety pins. Since it is from him that I inherit my short-sightedness, I assume that he had misread what was printed on the box.

This happened during the Occupation, and the convoy was on its way to the German army. A few years later my father was rehabilitated in a way. As a memento of him I still have somewhere in my dresser a silver or silver-plated medal embossed with the image of a slender girl breaking her chains like a carnival strong-man. Every time I see a strong-man performing in the street I think of my father. I can't help it.

But there are other heroes in my family. At the Liberation, less than two years after the death of her husband, my mother jumped from a window of our town hall just after her head had been shaved. I have nothing to remember her by. If I tell this to someone one day I will add, not even a lock of her hair. If they give me a horrified look, I don't care.

I had seen her only two or three times in two years, poor girl, in the visiting room of an orphanage. I couldn't possibly tell you what she looked like. Poor, with the manner of poverty, probably. She came from Italy too. Her name was Renata Castellani. Born in San Appolinare, province of Frosinone. She was twenty-four when she died. I have a mama younger than myself.

I read all this on my birth certificate. The sisters who

9

brought me up always refused to tell me about my mother. After graduation, when I was released, I returned to the village where we used to live. I was shown the part of the cemetery where she was buried. I wanted to save my money and do something, buy her a tombstone, but there were other people with her, they wouldn't let me.

Well, I don't give a damn.

I worked for a few months in Mans as a secretary in a toy factory, then in Noyon for a notary. I was twenty when I found a job in Paris. I have changed jobs, but I am still in Paris. I now earn 1,270 francs a month, after taxes, for typing, filing, answering the telephone and occasionally emptying the wastepaper bin, in an advertising agency with a staff of twenty-eight.

On this salary I can have steak for lunch and yoghurt and jam for dinner, dress just about the way I like, pay for a two-room apartment in rue de Grenelle, and improve my mind twice a month with *Marie-Claire* and every night with a wide-screen TV on which I only have three more payments to make. I sleep well, don't drink, smoke in moderation, have had a few affairs but not the kind that would shock the landlady – I don't have a landlady but I do have the respect of the people down the hall. I am free, without responsibilities, and utterly miserable.

Those who know me – the layout men at the agency or the woman who sells me groceries – would probably be amazed to hear me complain. But I must complain. I realised before I learned to walk that if I didn't do it, no one would do it for me.

Yesterday afternoon, Friday July 10. It seems like a century ago, another life.

It couldn't have been more than an hour before the agency

closed. The agency occupies two floors of what was a private house until recently, all volutes and colonnades, near the Trocadéro. It is full of crystal chandeliers that tinkle with every breath of air, marble fireplaces, and tarnished mirrors. My office is on the third floor.

There was sunlight beating on the window behind me and on the papers that covered my desk. I had checked the plan for the Frosey campaign (the toilet water that is fresh as dew), spent twenty minutes on the phone trying to get a weekly to lower the price of a badly printed ad., and typed two letters. A little earlier I had gone out as usual for a cup of coffee at the nearby coffee bar with two copy girls and a gay guy from Space Buying. He was the one who had asked me to call about the botched ad. When he handles it himself he lets them get away with murder.

It was an ordinary afternoon, and yet not completely so. At the studio the craftsmen were talking about cars and Kiki Caron, lazy bitches were coming into my office to bum cigarettes, the assistant to the assistant to the boss, who works hard at seeming indispensable, was braying in the hall. There was nothing to distinguish the climate of this day from other days, but everyone gave off that impatience, that suppressed jubilation, that precedes long weekends.

Since July 14 fell on a Tuesday this year, it had been understood since at least last January (that is, the time when we received our schedules) that we would be given a four-day holiday. To make up for the lost working day we worked two Saturday mornings at a time when nobody was on holiday except me. I took my holiday in June. Not to accommodate someone else who wanted to take their holiday in July, but because, may God damn me if I lie, even the First Hotel of Montbriand in the Haute Loire was full for the rest of the season. People are mad. This, too, will have to be explained if

I am arrested: my return from an alleged Mediterranean holiday, well tanned (I bought myself an ultraviolet lamp for my birthday, 180 francs, they say they give you cancer but I don't give a damn), to a bunch of excited people who were getting ready to leave. For me it was over, *kaput*, until the eternity of next year. And as far as I was concerned, my holiday had at least this advantage, that I could put it out of my mind simply by crossing the threshold of my office. But, excuse me, they made it their job to prolong the agony. It died only by inches.

For the boys it was Yugoslavia. I don't know how they swing it, but they sell drawings of canned goods to the Yugoslavians, they always have money tied up down there. They say that it doesn't amount to much, but that for very little a day you can live like a king on beaches that take your breath away, with your wife, your wife's sister and all her kids, and if you're clever about going through customs, you can even bring back souvenirs – alcohol, or a peasant's pitchfork that you can use for a hatstand. I was sick of hearing about Yugoslavia.

For the girls it was Cap d'Antibes. If you go there, come and see me, I have a friend with a swimming pool, he puts a special liquid in it for the density of the water, and even if you're a terrible swimmer you can't help floating. On their lunch hour they would comb the department stores with a sandwich in one hand and their holiday pay in the other. I would see them come back to the office with eyes that were already looking at the sea, flushed from running and dishevelled from the bargain counters, their arms loaded with their finds: a nylon dancing dress that fits into a pack of cigarettes; or a Japanese transistor with a built-in tape recorder to record all the songs on *Europe I* as they are broadcast – two free reels as a bonus and you can use the wrapper as a beach bag; when you blow it up it becomes a pillow. May God damn me if I lie, one afternoon one of them even called me into the bathroom to ask my opinion of her new bikini.

I celebrated my twenty-sixth birthday on July 4, last Saturday, after the excitement of the big departure. I stayed at home, I did a little housework, I didn't see anyone. I felt old, left out, sad, short-sighted, and stupid. And too jealous to live. Even when you think you've stopped believing in God, to be that jealous must be a sin.

Yesterday afternoon things were not much better. There was the prospect of that interminable weekend for which I had no plans, and also – especially – the plans of the others, which I had heard from the next-door offices, partly because their voices are loud, partly because I am a miserable masochist and was listening.

Other people always have plans. I can't plan anything ahead. I always call at the last minute and nine times out of ten they don't answer or they have something else to do. Worse still, once I arranged a dinner at my place with a woman journalist with whom I have a working relationship and a rather well-known actor who was her lover, plus a craftsman from the agency so I wouldn't look too stupid. We made the date two weeks in advance, I wrote it down in my engagement book, and when they arrived I had forgotten all about it, all I had to give them was yoghurt and jam. We went out to a Chinese restaurant and I had to go through a big scene just to get them to let me pay the bill.

I don't know why I'm like that. Maybe because for the first eighteen years of my life I never had to think for myself. My plans for holidays or for Sundays were made for me, and they were always the same: I would repaint the chapel with other girls who, like me, had nobody outside the orphanage (I love to paint anyway), or hang around the deserted playgrounds with a ball under my arm. Sometimes I was taken to Roubaix where Mama Supe, our Superior, had a brother who was a pharmacist. I would stay for a few days minding the till, they would give me a dose of tonic before every meal, then Mama Supe would come and get me.

When I was sixteen, during one of those trips to Roubaix, I did or said something that made her sad – I don't remember what, that wasn't important – and at the last moment she decided that we would miss the train that was to take us back. She treated me to shellfish in a brasserie and we went to the movies. We saw *Sunset Boulevard*. When we came out Mama Supe was sick with shame. She had chosen this film because she cherished a deathless memory of Gloria Swanson as a pure young girl; she certainly did not suspect that in less than two hours there would parade before my eyes all the depravity that she had always tried to conceal from me.

I cried, too, on the way to the station (we had to run like mad to catch the last train), but I was not crying from shame – rather from wonder. I was in the throes of a delicious sadness; I was breathless with love. It was the first film I had ever seen and the best in my whole life. When she fires at William Holden and he staggers to the swimming pool, when Erich von Stroheim directs the cameras of the newsreels and she walks down the staircase thinking she's creating a new role, I thought I would die there, on my seat, in a cinema in Roubaix. I was in love with them, I wanted to be them, all three of them, Holden, Stroheim, and Gloria Swanson. I even loved Holden's little girlfriend. When they walk through the scenery of the empty studio, I longed desperately to live inside that story. I wished it would play again, endlessly, and that I would never have to leave it again.

To console herself on the train, Mama Supe kept repeating that, thank God, the most painful of this tissue of aberrations was merely implied, that it was too deep for her, and that

14

certainly I had not been able to understand it. But I have seen the film again several times since I came to Paris and I know that the first time essentially nothing escaped me.

Yesterday afternoon, as I was sealing the two letters I had just typed, I thought I might go and see a film. This is probably what I would have done if I had a tenth of the good sense that is attributed to me on my best days – and that isn't saying very much. I would have picked up the phone a few hours in advance, for a change, and I would have found someone to accompany me. After that (I know myself), a hydrogen bomb falling on Paris would not have kept me away, and none of this would have happened.

And yet, who knows? The truth is that yesterday, today, or six months from now, something like this would have happened to me anyway. I am jinxed.

I did not pick up the phone. I lit a cigarette and I took my two letters to the post basket in the hall. Then I went down to the floor below and spent a few minutes in that mare's nest where newspapers (referred to pompously as "documents") are filed. Georgette, the girl in charge, was cutting out advertisements with her tongue sticking out. I looked at the film programmes in that morning's *Figaro*, but found nothing that appealed to me.

When I went back up to my office the boss was waiting for me. When I opened the door and found him standing there in a room I had thought to be empty, my heart jumped.

He is a man of forty-five or so, rather tall, and he weighs over 200 pounds. His hair is cut short, very close to the head. His features are coarse but pleasant, and they say that when he was younger and slimmer he was handsome. His name is Michel Caravaille. It was he who founded the agency. He has a talent for advertising; he knows how to explain exactly what he wants, and in a business where it is just as important to convince the client who pays us as the buying public, he is a first-rate salesman.

His relations with and interest in the personnel are confined to business. I hardly know him. I see him only once a week, on Monday mornings, at a half-hour meeting in his office where he goes over current business. I am only there to take notes.

Three years ago he married Anita, a girl my age, whose secretary I was in another advertising agency. We were friends, in as much as you are when you spend forty hours a week in the same office, have lunch together every day in a cafeteria in rue La Boétie and sometimes meet on Saturday to go to the music hall.

When they got married it was she who suggested that I come and work for Caravaille. She had been working there for a few months. I do just about what she did, minus her talent, which was considerable, her hunger for success, and, obviously, her salary. I have never met anyone who was so desperately and selfishly eager to get ahead. She worked from the principle that in a world where most people learn to bend before a storm, you must create storms in order to walk over people. They called her Anita Screw-You. She knew it and she signed her memoranda that way when she was letting somebody have it.

About three weeks into her marriage she had a little girl. After that she stopped working, and I hardly ever see her. As for Michel Caravaille, I thought (until yesterday afternoon) that he had even forgotten I knew his wife.

He looked tired or preoccupied, with that sallow look he sometimes gets when he has been on a diet for a few days. He called me Dany and said he had problems.

I saw that there were some files piled on the visitors' chair facing my desk. I removed them, but he did not sit down.

16

He was looking around as if he had come into my office for the first time.

He said he was taking a plane to Switzerland the next day. We have an important client in Geneva: Milkaby, powdered milk for babies. To sell the next campaign he could take along layouts, sample prints on glossy paper, colour photographs – enough material to hold his own respectably for an hour or two among a dozen directors and subdirectors with frozen faces and manicured gestures. It was our literary striking force that was in danger of missing the plane. Soberly, he explained (if I've heard this kind of explanation once, I've heard it a hundred times) that a whole report had been drafted on the strategy of the competition and our own, but that at the last moment he had had to change everything, that it was in very rough form and that, for all intents and purposes, he no longer had anything to show.

He spoke quickly without looking at me, because he was embarrassed to have to ask me a favour. He said he couldn't leave empty-handed, nor could he put off his meeting with Milkaby – he had already done that twice. The third time even the Swiss would realize that we were a bunch of idiots and that it would be better to deliver their powdered milk to people's houses free of charge.

I had a fair idea what he was driving at, but I didn't say anything. There was a silence during which he played unconsciously with one of the tiny toys lined up on my desk. I had sat down. I lit another cigarette. I pointed to my pack of Gitanes, but he did not want one.

At last he asked me whether I had plans for the evening. He often talks this way, in a sophisticated and slightly insulting manner. I think he is incapable of imagining that I could do anything at all with my evenings except sleep, so as to be fresh for the office the next day. Poor idiot, I didn't know what I wanted to do, and in a voice that tried to be impersonal I asked, "How many pages are there to be typed?"

"Around fifty."

I exhaled the smoke I had in my mouth in a pretty reproachful cloud, all the while thinking (which spoiled everything), you exhale like a movie star, he'll see that you're trying to make an impression.

"And you want me to do it this evening? But that's impossible! I do six pages an hour, and that is top speed. Take Mme Blondeau, she may get it done."

He told me that his plane tomorrow did not leave until noon. And there was no question of entrusting this job to Mme Blondeau. She typed quickly but would not be up to a text full of corrections, cross references, and incomplete sentences. I was familiar with the material. Then he said – and I think this is what decided me – that he did not like, he never liked, anyone to stay at the office after hours, especially for a long stint of typing. There are people living on the upper floors, and the agency retains its lease only through obscure administrative negotiations. He told me that I would come and work at his house. I could sleep there, and that way I would not waste any time if I did not finish that evening. I would finish the job the next morning, before he left.

I had never been to his house. This and the prospect of seeing Anita again made it impossible for me to refuse. For a second or two, while he fidgeted and said, "Good, it's all settled", I don't know what I imagined. I am an idiot. The three of us at dinner, in a big room with soft lights? Muted laughter as we talked about old times? Have some more crab, do! Anita leads me by the hand to my room, a little mellow and sentimental from the wine we have drunk. A window is open to the night and the curtains swell in the breeze.

He brought me down to earth immediately. Looking at

18

his watch, he said that I could work undisturbed, since his servants had gone back to Spain for the holidays, and he and Anita had a tiresome function to attend, a festival of commercial films at the Palais de Chaillot. He added, however, "Anita will be happy to see you again. You were her protégée in a way, weren't you?" But he said it without looking at me, walking to the door, as though I did not exist, not as a human being, anyway – no more than an IBM electric typewriter with "Presidential" typeface.

Before going out, he turned around and made a vague gesture towards my desk. He asked if I had anything important still to do. I was planning to read the proofs of an industrial brochure, but that could wait, and for once I said the right thing,

"Collect my pay."

I was talking about the extra month's pay of which we are given half in December, half in July. Those on holiday have already received their envelope along with their June pay. The others receive it for July 14. As with the end of the month, it is the head bookkeeper who goes through the office and hands it to everyone personally. He usually comes to my office within half an hour of the end of the day. First he goes to copywriting where he unleashes a kind of storm, but yesterday afternoon I had not yet heard the copy girls pouncing on the poor man.

The boss stood motionless with his hand on the door handle. He announced that he was going home and that he would like to take me with him straight away. He would give me my envelope himself, which would give him the opportunity to add something to it, say three hundred francs, if that was agreeable to me.

There was a kind of relief in his look, and of course I was pleased too, but for him it was brief, as if I had simply made it possible for him to settle an embarrassing matter.

"Get your things, Dany. I'll meet you downstairs in five minutes. My car is out at the front."

He left, closing the door behind him. Almost immediately he opened it again. I was putting the toy he had moved back in line with the others. It was a little hinged elephant, candy pink. Noticing the care with which I did this, he said, "I beg your pardon." He said he was counting on me to say nothing to the others about this work outside the office. I understood that he did not want me to talk about the late report, that he felt a little guilty. He wanted to say something else, maybe to explain that he felt guilty, but in the end he just glanced at the little pink elephant and left, this time for good.

I sat in my chair for a moment, wondering what would happen if I was unable to get those fifty pages typed before he left. Even if I had to work late I would find the necessary time, that wasn't what worried me. But I can't count on my eyes over a period of several hours. They get red and watery, I see stars, and sometimes they hurt so much I can't see at all.

I was also thinking about Anita. Stupid things. Had I known that morning that I was going to see her again, I would have worn my white suit; it was absolutely necessary that I stop at my apartment and change my clothes. Before, when I worked with her, I was still wearing skirts that I had made myself at the orphanage. She used to say, "You make me sick with your unhappy childhood and your home-made things." I wanted her to find me different, in my very best. Then suddenly I remembered that the boss had given me five minutes. With him five minutes meant three hundred seconds. His punctuality would put a cuckoo clock to shame.

On a sheet of my pad I scrawled, "Gone for the weekend. Back Wednesday. Dany." But as soon as I had written that, I tore the page into little pieces and wrote on the next page, carefully this time, "Must catch a plane for the weekend. Back Wednesday. Dany."

Now I felt like telling my life story. A plane was not enough. How about a plane for Monte Carlo? But I looked at my watch. The big hand was almost at half past five, and anyway, I must be the only one in the agency who had never taken a plane, nobody would be impressed.

I clipped the note to the shade of my desk lamp. Anyone who came in could see it. I think I was happy. It is difficult to explain. It was as if I now felt that impatience I had sensed all afternoon in the others.

As I put on my summer coat, I remembered that Anita and Michel Caravaille had a little girl. I took the pink elephant and put it in my pocket.

I remember that there was still sunlight on the window and on the papers piled on my desk.

In the car, a large black Citroën with leather seats, he suggested that we stop by my place first so I could pick up a nightdress and my toothbrush.

It was not yet the rush hour, so he drove rather quickly. I told him he seemed tired. He answered that the whole world was tired. Then I praised his car, but this did not interest him, and silence fell again.

We crossed the Seine at the Pont de l'Alma. He found a parking place on rue de Grenelle in front of the camera shop across the road from my building. When I got out of the car, he followed me. He did not ask whether he could come up or anything. He walked into the building behind me.

I am not ashamed of my apartment – at least I don't think I am – and I was sure I hadn't left any underwear to dry over the radiator. Still, I was annoyed that he came up. He would take up all the room and I would have to change in a bathroom where when you tap one wall the sound reverberates from the other three. Besides, it's a four-flight walk up.

I told him he did not have to come with me, that I would only be a few minutes. He answered that of course he would, that it was no trouble. I don't know what he had in mind. Maybe that I was going to bring a suitcase.

There was nobody on my floor, which was all to the good. I have a neighbour whose husband treated himself to a holiday at the Boucicaut Hospital by getting smashed up on a one-way street. She carries on something awful if you don't ask after him, and if you do she can go on all day. I went ahead of Caravaille to my apartment and closed the door as soon as he was in. He looked around, but said nothing. It was obvious that he did not know what to do with his big body. He seemed to me much younger and – how should I say? – more real, more alive than at the office.

I took my white suit out of the cupboard and shut myself in the bathroom. I heard him walking right next to me. As I undressed I told him through the door that there was some drink in the chest under the window. Did I have time to take a shower? He did not answer. I did not take a shower, I gave myself a quick sponge bath instead.

When I came back into the room – dressed, made up, hair done, but barefoot – he was sitting on the sofa talking on the phone to Anita. He told her that we would be there in a few minutes. As he talked he looked at my suit. I put on some white shoes, sitting on the arm of a chair without taking my eyes off him. In his own eyes I saw only boredom.

He was talking to Anita. He was saying Yes Anita, no Anita, I knew it was her. I don't even remember now what he was saying to her: No, I hadn't changed, yes, I was rather tall, yes, rather slim, yes, I was pretty, yes, and blonde, very blonde, and tanned, yes – things like that, anyway, things that should have been nice, that were nice, no doubt, but that his voice distorted. I can still hear that voice – dutiful, monotonous, the voice of an usher. He was answering Anita, he was patiently giving in to a whim of Anita's. She wanted him to describe me, so he was describing me. She is a human being. As for me, Dany Longo, I might just as well have been a washing machine on sale in a department store.

He said one other thing. Oh, it wasn't just a turn of phrase to indicate to his wife, without annoying me, that I am more fantastic than ever. It was the most accurate possible description of what he saw, an unedited observation. He said that my glasses concealed the colour of my eyes. I laughed. I even took off my glasses to show the colour of my eyes. They are not blue and changeable like the sea, like Anita's were when she would let me carry her tray along with mine at the cafeteria in rue La Boétie, but dark, steady, and unexpressive like a dreary northern plain. And blind without glasses.

I don't know if it was because of that, because of my eyes, or because suddenly I realized that for them I would never be anything but a rather limited subject for amusement on the telephone; but even as I laughed, I was sad. I was sick of it all. I wished that this evening were already over with, that the two of them were already at their damned commercial film festival, that they had never existed, that Anita had never existed – in short, that we could go.

We left. I put a nightdress and my toothbrush in my bag, as he had suggested. We followed the quays along the Seine as far as the Pont d'Auteuil. Before he got to his house, he remembered something and double-parked his car in a shopping street.

He gave me a fifty-franc note, saying that neither he nor Anita ever ate at night, and that there probably would not be anything for me in the house. If I had had the slightest sense of humour, I would have burst out laughing at the thought of my idyllic little intimate dinner with soft lights and the breeze swelling the curtains. Instead, I blushed. I told him that I did not eat either, but he refused to believe me and insisted that I take the money.

While he waited at the wheel of his car, I bought two brioches in a bakery and a chocolate bar. He had also asked me – "as you're there" – to go to the chemist and pick up some medicine for him. While they were filling out the prescription, I read on the box that it was drops for the heart. He starves himself and to keep from feeling faint he dopes himself with digitalis. Brilliant.

In the car, as he pocketed his change, he asked without looking at me where I had bought my suit. He is one of those husbands who can't stand to see a becoming outfit on any woman except his wife. I told him that I had bought it for nothing at the agency after we had taken some photographs for a client in faubourg Saint-Honoré. He nodded his head as if thinking, Yes, that's what I thought, and to me, trying to be pleasant, he said something like, "For ready-to-wear, it's very effective."

I had never been inside Villa Montmorency at Auteuil. Because my mood was detracting from my surroundings no doubt, it reminded me, in the middle of Paris, of some village for provincial pensioners, with its staid and symmetrical paths. The Caravailles lived on avenue des Trembles. There was also an avenue des Tilleuls and, I assume, an avenue des Marronniers. Their house was as I had imagined it: beautiful, big, surrounded with flowers. It was a little after six o'clock. The sun moved in dazzling flashes through the foliage.

I remember our arrival, the sound of our footsteps in the

silence of that late afternoon. In a red-tiled entrance hall with a huge rug woven with unicorns, all the lights on in spite of the daylight, a stone staircase rose towards the upper floors, and on the first step, in patent-leather shoes, one sock higher than the other, dressed in lace and pale-blue velvet and hugging a bald doll to her heart, stood a little girl with blonde hair who was staring at me with a forlorn expression.

As I went towards her, I hated myself for not being able to take things as they come, simply. I bent down to kiss her and to pull up her sock. She submitted silently. Her eyes were large and blue, like Anita's. I asked her what her name was: Michèle Caravaille, which she pronounced "Cwavaille." I asked her how old she was: "Thwee." I thought of the little pink elephant that I had meant to give her, but it was in the pocket of my coat, and the coat was in my apartment.

Just then her father called me into a huge room which I hardly left again. The sofa and chairs were of black leather, the furnishings sombre, the walls lined with books. A rearing horse supported a huge lamp.

I changed my glasses and tried the typewriter. It was a 1940s Remington semiportable with an English keyboard, to make everything perfect! Still, you could type six readable copies, but Caravaille said that four would be enough. He opened the Milkaby report, page after page covered with tiny handwriting (I have never understood how a big brute like him could write so small), and explained the difficulties that I might encounter. He had to see a printer for some damn reason before going to the Palais de Chaillot. He left, saying that Anita would come, and wishing me luck.

I worked.

Anita came down half an hour later, her blonde hair pulled behind her head, a cigarette in her hand. She said, "Hi, it's been ages, how are you, I have a horrible headache", all very fast, studying me from head to foot, with the same tense look she always had.

She opened a door at the back of the room and showed me my bedroom. She explained that her husband sometimes slept there when he had to work late at night. It contained an enormous bed covered with white fur and on one wall an enlarged photograph of Anita sitting naked across an armchair; a very fine photograph which showed the grain of her skin. I laughed inanely. She turned the picture, which was mounted on a wooden frame, to the wall. She told me that Caravaille had installed an amateur studio in the attic, but that she was his only model. Meanwhile she opened another door near the bed and showed me a black-tiled bathroom. Our eyes met for a second and I realized that all this bored her to death.

I returned to my work. While I typed, she laid a place on a low table and brought in two slices of roast beef, some fruit, and an open bottle of wine. She was not dressed to go out yet. She asked me whether I needed anything else, but without waiting for the answer she also wished me luck, said goodbye, and disappeared.

A little later, she paused in the doorway wearing a black satin coat fastened with a big brooch at the neck and holding her little girl by the hand. She was taking her to her mother, nearby in boulevard Souchet (I've been there two or three times), she was then meeting her husband at Chaillot. She told me that they would be home early because of the trip to Switzerland, but that I did not have to wait up for them if I felt tired. I could see that she was trying to find something friendly to say before leaving me alone and that she was not succeeding. I got up so that I could see the little girl better and say Good night, Michèle dear. As she walked away she turned around and went on looking at me. She was still holding her bald doll to her chest.

Then I hammered away. Two or three times I lit a cigarette, and since I don't like to smoke while I'm typing, I walked around the room, looking at the backs of the books. There was something rather pretentious but fascinating on one wall: a twelve-by-sixteen sheet of ground glass in a gilt frame on which a built-in lens projected colour transparencies from behind. Caravaille had probably used one of those machines designed for advertising in shop windows. The photograph changed every minute. I saw several fishing ports drenched in sunlight, the reflections in the water multiplying the colours of the boats. I don't know their names. Idiot that I am, all I know is that it was Agfacolour. I've been in this rat race too long not to recognize the quality of a red.

Once too, when my eyes were beginning to tire, I went to bathe them with cold water in the black-tiled bathroom. Not a sound came from outside. Paris seemed very far away, and I felt the weight of the empty house with its dark rooms pressing on me.

By half past twelve I had typed thirty pages. I couldn't stop making mistakes, my brain was like powdered milk. I counted the remaining pages: about fifteen. I put the cover back on the machine.

I was hungry. I ate one of the brioches I had bought, a slice of roast beef, and an apple, and drank a little wine. Not wanting to leave a mess, I looked for the kitchen, which was vast and furnished like a room in a farmhouse, with a stone sink in which two big piles of dishes were gathering mould. I know my Anita. Since her servants had gone on holiday, she had certainly not bothered to make a piece of toast.

Taking off the jacket of my suit, I washed my plate, glass, fork, and knife, turned out the lights and went to bed. It was warm but, God knows why, I did not dare open a window. I couldn't go to sleep. I thought of Anita, of the old days when

27

I worked for her. While undressing I had not been able to resist peeking at the photograph that showed her naked in an armchair. I was angry at myself for that stupid laugh of mine. I don't mean that it's stupid to laugh at a guy who displays his wife's charms on the walls of his house; it was the sound of my laugh that was stupid.

When I had worked for Anita, she had spent the night with me several times. She was living with her mother at the time and she had asked me – as only she could, with large doses of affection, threats, and the prettiest persistence – to lend her my apartment to entertain a boy. She changed boys, but not meeting places and, having given in once, I lost the courage to refuse. During the festivities I would go to the movies. I would find her later, undressed and flushed, reading or listening to the radio and smoking, with her legs over the arm of a chair a little like she is in the photograph. It would never have occurred to her to remake the bed. My most vivid memory is of those rumpled, messy sheets in which I would have to sleep beside her the rest of the night. When I said something she would call me a "disgusting little virgin" and tell me to go back to the convent and die of envy. Or she would put on a terribly penitent look and promise that next time she would do it on the kitchen table. The next day at the office she would become Anita Screw-You again, dressed like an innocent girl from a good family, her eyes clear, her gestures efficient, and her heart buttoned up to the neck.

In the end I must have dozed off, for a little while later I heard them come in. The boss was complaining that he had drunk too much and talked to too many idiots. Then he came and asked in a low voice from the other side of my door, "Asleep, Dany? How's it coming on?" I answered that everything was fine, that I had fifteen pages to go. With a kind of mimicry, I suppose, I said this in a whisper, as if I were afraid of waking someone in that infernal barn. Then I went back to sleep. The next moment, it seemed, someone was scratching at the door and it was morning – this morning. The sun was already coming into the room, and the boss said, "I've made coffee. There's a cup on the table."

After making the bed and having a bath, I dressed, drank the cold coffee sitting beside the typewriter, and went back to work.

The boss came in two or three times to see how I was getting on. Anita appeared later in a white petticoat. She was looking for something that she did not find, with one hand clutching her headache from the day before and the other flicking her first cigarette of the day. She had to go and get her daughter in boulevard Suchet. This meant that they were taking advantage of the meeting with Milkaby, all three, to spend the weekend in Switzerland. This departure was making her nervous, and in this respect, at least, I found her changed. Before, it had been her principle that clients, like lovers, respect you more for making them wait, and that it is stupid to make yourself sick over a plane when you can easily take the next one.

Everyone was nervous in fact – her, me, and Caravaille. I typed the final pages like those typists whom I can't abide, without even trying to understand what I was reading. I must have made a thousand mistakes, for I was hitting almost all the keys with my left hand (I am left-handed, and when I go fast, when I want to go fast, I forget that I have a right hand) I wasted an enormous amount of time telling myself, "Think about what you're doing, your right hand, idiot, your right hand," like a boxer who has just taken a punishing blow. The blow I had had – I can't help it if it's stupid, I'll have to tell this too if I'm questioned – was that weekend in Switzerland.

I went to Zurich once, a frightful memory. I have never seen Geneva, but I assume that it must have – at least for the Caravailles and people like them – plush hotels, big moonlit terraces with the melancholy sweetness of violins, luminous days and illuminated nights, in short, hours such as I will never know, and not just because they can be purchased with hard francs or dollars. I hate myself for being this way – it's true, it's true, it's true – but I am what I am, I don't know how to say it.

I finished my work at about eleven. I was sorting the pages and collating the four copies when Caravaille came to release me. He was wearing a navy-blue summer suit and an ugly white polka-dot tie, and he overwhelmed me with his size and his energy. He had made a trip to the agency to pick up the layouts. He had brought me my pay envelope. With the promised 300 francs, I counted more than 1,000 francs, almost a whole month's pay. I said – I never fail – "Thank you very much; it's terrific, it's too much by far."

He put what I had typed into a black leather suitcase. He asked me in a breathless voice if I had a driving licence. It was not a question. Anita knows that I have one, she had probably told him so. When she bought her first car, a second-hand convertible, she was so afraid, that it was I who drove it out of the garage for her. Later, I reparked it for her four or five times a day in the blue zone.

Nevertheless, I have really driven only one car in my life, a van belonging to the orphanage. It was Mama Supe who bought my licence ("because it's useful, and it will force you to pick a husband with his feet on the ground, not a good-looking pauper"), and I was the only one to drive her around on her errands. It was my last year at school. There were two similar vans and they gave me the oldest. "Smash it up," Mama Supe used to say, "It'll give you experience, and after that we'll snare Sister Mary of Pity's beauty." But at twenty miles an hour she would cling to her seat for dear life, and at twenty-five she would scream blue murder. One day she was so afraid that she pulled the handbrake and we both just missed going through the windscreen.

Bending over his black bag, Caravaille said in one breath that it was hell finding a taxi on a Saturday morning, that he had had his phone disconnected so that I would not be bothered, that he did not want to get reconnected, that he still had his daughter to pick up, and that I would be doing them a great favour if I came to Orly with them. I did not understand. He straightened up, red-faced, and explained: that way, I could bring back his car.

He was insane.

I told him that there were places to park at Orly, but he merely shrugged his shoulders and answered, thanks, he knew that.

"Come along Dany."

I told him that it was impossible.

"Why?"

He was looking right at me now, bending over slightly. He seemed full of power and impatience. When somebody stands too close to me, I lose the thread of what I want to say.

After several seconds I replied, "I don't know! Because!"

The stupidest answer possible. He shrugged his shoulders again, said that I mustn't be silly, and carried his suitcase into the hall. For him the matter was settled.

I couldn't go to Orly with them. I couldn't bring back his car. I had to tell him that I had never driven anything but a broken-down van, and that Mama Supe felt reassured only when there was a church in sight, because that gave us a chance of receiving extreme unction. I followed him into the hall. Anita was coming down the stairs. I didn't say anything.

31

They had three suitcases. I carried one of them into the garden. I looked around for the Citroën, but what I saw appalled me. They weren't taking the Citroën, but an enormous American convertible, which Anita was driving out of the garage. A tank.

I went back into the hall, then into the room where I had worked. I couldn't even remember what I had come back for. My bag. I picked up my bag. I put my bag back on the desk. I could not drive that car.

Caravaille was hastily locking up the house. When he saw me rooted to the spot, he must have realized at last that something was the matter. He came over. He put his hand on my arm,

"It's Anita's car," he said. There's an accelerator and a brake, that's all. It's very easy to drive." He paused and then added, "Don't be that way."

I turned to him. I saw that his eyes were blue, a very light blue, and rimmed with fatigue. Blue, I had never noticed before. At the same time I noticed for the first time that I existed for him. I existed as a rather silly girl, but one he was fond of. At least I think so. I did not understand what he meant by "Don't be that way." I still don't understand it. He was too close to me. As he had been a moment ago, he seemed very tall and very strong, I felt myself melting. He added after a long silence – or at least a silence that seemed unbearable – that if I did not want to come with them he would manage, he would leave the car in a car park. It wasn't important.

I bowed my head, and said I would come.

I was in the back seat with the little girl. She was wearing a red coat with a velvet collar, and she sat very straight with her warm hand in mine, not saying a word. Anita and her husband did not talk either. It was twenty minutes to twelve when we left the Péripherique at the Porte d'Orléans and took the Autoroute du Sud. He was driving.

I asked where I should leave the car. In the garden. We were forced to shout, for he was speeding and the wind carried our words away. He said that the papers were in the glove compartment and that the key to the front gate was with the car keys. With his index finger he jiggled the bunch of keys that hung from the ignition. I asked him where I should leave them. He thought about it and then said that I should just hold onto them; I would give them to him at the office on Wednesday afternoon, on their return from Switzerland.

Anita turned around, impatient, with the same expression she would have when I worked for her.

"Do you think you could shut up for a minute?" she said. "It's not that complicated, is it? Do you know how fast we're driving?" The little girl, seeing that her mother was displeased with me, withdrew her hand from mine.

At ten to twelve – the plane left at five past – Caravaille stopped at the kerb of the pavement outside the terminal. They dashed out of the car. Anita, in a beige coat lined with green silk, lifted her little girl and, holding her against her breast, bent over to kiss me. My boss was finding a porter. He held out his hand, which I longed desperately to hold onto, for suddenly I thought of a thousand things to ask him. What if it rained? It might rain before Wednesday. I could not leave the car uncovered. How did you put the top up? Confused, he looked at the luminous sky, then at me, then at the dashboard.

"I don't know anything about it! It's Anita's car."

He called Anita, who was waiting impatiently at one of the doors to the terminal. When she understood what I wanted, she flew into a rage. She told me what she thought of me in one word. Meanwhile she waved – she was wearing summer gloves – at a button that seemed to be very low, well under the

33

steering wheel. But she did it so angrily that I did not see which one it was. She was still holding her little girl, who must have been heavy for her and whose shoes were dirtying her coat. Caravaille led them into the terminal. Before they disappeared, it was he who turned and made a vague gesture of farewell.

I was alone in the back seat of a monstrous machine. I felt as if there were a great silence in my head.

It must have been several minutes before I noticed that the engine was still running and that people were looking at me. Then an official came and told me that I could not stay there. For something to do until he was gone, I took off the scarf I had put on when we left Caravaille's house and folded it carefully. It is a scarf of turquoise silk that I bought in Mans the first year I worked, the day I got the telegram informing me that Mama Supe was dead. I keep it in my bag almost all of the time.

Through the silence that filled my head Mama Supe told me, "Don't worry, take the car to the car park, it's only fifty yards away. Afterwards you will have plenty of time to think about it."

I got out of the car, which was white and gleamed in the sun, and because I did not want to, could not, take the wheel immediately, I gave myself time to go and look at the name on the front of the bonnet. It was a Thunderbird, a big white bird under the summer sky, a Bird of Thunder.

I got in. The door seemed to close by itself. The leather seats shone the colour of golden sand, everything around me was sand and glittering chrome. There were handles and knobs all along the dashboard and even between the seats. I forced myself not to look at them. As Caravaille had said, I did not find a clutch under my feet. I leaned over to study the gearshift. Besides park and reverse, there were only two positions:

one for starting and one for driving. My forehead was damp and my throat dry, but what I was feeling was not only fear; I don't know what it was. I was sure that I would always remember this moment, that I would regret not being able to live it again. I took off my right shoe – the heel would make it awkward to drive. I told Mama Supe I was ready, I went into drive and I was off.

At first the car gave a leap forward because I accelerated too hard, but it calmed down immediately and carried me straight ahead smoothly, at a dignified speed. After that, things got complicated. The lanes in front of the airport led me in all directions and unfailingly into the wrong ones. I passed the same spot four or five times, four or five times I found myself facing the negative gesture of the same policeman, a driver behind me called me an idiot because I did not use my flicker and before I found it – right under my nose – I turned on the windscreen wipers, the hot-air fan, radio Monte Carlo, and the button that operated the front right window. I was near hysteria when I finally drove into the car park that I had been aiming for desperately each time I had passed, and if I could still stand on my legs when I got out of the car, it was only because I had no choice but to do so.

But I was also proud, in a way, and although I still trembled with nervousness, I knew that my fear had passed. I felt capable of driving miles in that car. Now I heard the roar of the planes on the runways. I put two twenty-centime pieces in the parking meter. I took the keys that hung from the ignition, my handbag, and my scarf, and went for a walk to calm my nerves. As I crossed the road that runs beside the terminal, a Swissair Caravelle was climbing into the sun. It might have been the one that was carrying Anita away.

I took a visitor's ticket from a terminal official. The place was full of people and noise and I felt detached from myself. I went up the escalator to the terraces. I watched a blue-and-white Air France Boeing cover the length of the runway and some men in canary-yellow scurry around on the ground. I watched some travellers walk in an orderly line towards a huge machine. One of the pilots paced up and down with his hands in his pockets, kicking a pebble with his toe.

I went downstairs. Through the bay windows I looked for my soccer-playing pilot, but he must have got back onto the plane; I could not find him again. I lingered a moment in front of some display cases of curios, the most curious of which seemed to me that fleeting reflection of a girl in a white suit with golden hair who wasn't really me. I bought *France-Soir* and tried to read the headlines at the bar. Ten times I read that someone had done something, but I still don't know who or what. I drank a Dubonnet with vodka and smoked a cigarette. I saw people get up, collect up their change from their tables, and leave for the other end of the world. I felt good, I felt bad, I don't remember any more; I had a second drink and a third, telling myself, You poor girl, you'll be ready for the stock-car races after this, just what do you want? And I think I already knew what it was I wanted.

It was not very clear, it was still only a kind of mental itch, a vague uneasiness that resembled anxiety. I was listening to a woman's voice with a sweet and almost confidential tone repeating endlessly into the loudspeaker what gate to go to for Portugal or Argentina. I promised myself that one day I would come back to the very same table, and that, I don't know, I don't know. I paid for my drinks. I told myself that I had been drinking to the health of my beautiful Bird of Thunder. And that's all. I got up, picked up my change from the table, and left, to see the sea.

* * *

Oh, I didn't admit it right away. I am an old hand at compromising with myself. All I thought, as I got back into the car, was that it didn't matter if I kept it for an hour or two, and that even if Caravaille found out about it I was certainly entitled to stop for lunch. I would take a drive through Paris, I would stop somewhere for steak and coffee, I would drive quietly through the Bois de Boulogne and, at about four o'clock let's say, I would return the car to his garden. Right? Right.

I took my time, I studied all the mechanisms on the dashboard. When I found the one that controlled the top, I thought with disgust of Anita's fit of rage. The speedometer, which was very wide with big metallic numerals, indicated a maximum speed of 120 miles per hour. I calculated that this was close to 200 kilometres per hour and I thought, Not bad, my dear. I made an inventory of the glove compartment. It contained nothing but parking tickets, garage receipts and road maps. The car registration and insurance, which I found in a transparent plastic envelope, were, I supposed, in the name of one of Caravaille's firms, care of his home address on avenue des Trembles. They say that he has four, more or less fictitious, companies which he uses to juggle the agency's books, but I don't know anything about that and the head bookkeeper is very reticent on the subject. I was reassured to learn that the car's papers were not in Anita's name. What does not belong to anyone – at least, not to one person – is easier to borrow.

I got out to see what was in the boot: some rags, a sponge, and a Thunderbird advertising brochure. I took the brochure, just in case. As I returned to the wheel – it moved to the right so you could get in easily and locked as soon as the engine started, it was sublime – I realized that travellers were turning around to look at me. The look was not exactly the one I usually get, even if I took into consideration that my skirt was tight and I may have showed more of my legs than you're supposed to. I told myself that all this would not last, but that to be admired by others was a pleasant sensation. Right? Right.

I backed up expertly, left the car park, executed a graceful curve in front of the airport, and stopped at the first cross-roads. A sign indicated the way to Paris. It also indicated the other direction, south. I knotted my scarf around my head to give myself time to think. A driver hooted behind me. I made a gesture with my hand that said, Go to hell and, taking my own advice, I went south. To have lunch in Paris didn't make any sense; I do that every day. I would go to Milly-la-Forêt, because it has a pretty name and because it would be an adventure, I would not have steak but something marvellous with raspberries, I would find a restaurant where they would put my table in the garden – now that's settled, you already have three Dubonnets under your belt, think about what you're doing or they'll have to tow you home. While I was at it, I started speeding.

I overtook a car just as I reached the turning for Milly-la-Forêt, which might explain why I found myself forced to stay on the main road . But I would have stayed on it anyway. So sweet the steering wheel in my hands, so sweet the sun on my face, so sweet the warm breeze that caressed me on the curves, and so long the curves, deep the slopes, silent and obedient and swift, to soar through the countryside, my great dream bird, my accomplice, my friend. I was beyond control, wild horses could not stop me now. I saw cars driving in the same direction as me, with kids pressing their noses to the window panes, already drinking in their holiday, beach balls in overstuffed boots that had been closed with rope, and boats with lowered masts being carried on trailers to the sea;

and on the faces of a couple who were abreast of me for a moment, an almost conspiratorial expression. I wanted to convince myself – and to convince others, no doubt – that at least until I left the main road I would stay with them, that we might stop at the same inn between Valence and Avignon that night. A mad girl.

When I slowed down to leave the main road, Mama Supe told me, "Please listen to me now, you'll only get yourself into trouble, take that car back." I swore on my life that I would go no further than the first restaurant that came along – or at least the first suitable one, and that I would return to Paris as soon as I had paid the bill. Mama Supe called it a drunkard's oath and said that it would be harder to put a stop to my foolishness later on. A sign told me that I had gone fifty kilometres. I felt a slight twinge of anxiety.

Only a few hours have passed since then, five or six maybe, but everything seems distorted and far away, like a dream upon awaking.

I stopped at a restaurant on the main road near Fontainebleau, a world of steel and laminated plastic, with huge plate-glass windows, one of which, almost opposite my table, framed the motionless Thunderbird. There were few people, only couples. My entrance had created a sensation, no doubt because of the car, and also perhaps because I had assumed an air of exaggerated assurance. The lights were very bright, so I could keep my dark glasses on.

I ordered leg of lamb with tomatoes à la provençale, a dandelion salad, and a half bottle of dry rosé, because there were no quarter bottles and because it would be less intoxicating than red wine – look who's talking, dear. I asked for a paper and they brought me the same *France-Soir* that I had left at Orly. I didn't read this one either. I looked at the crossword, thinking of Anita, who used to get annoyed with me because I finished first, and I thought that there must be about 2,000 francs in my bank account. I took out my chequebook to make sure. 2,300 francs, less one payment for the TV, and the 200 francs that I send to the orphanage every month. With what I had in my purse and in this morning's envelope, I calculated that I had over 3,000 francs at my disposal. Not enough to spend a year in Negresco, but for less than four days – I counted them on my fingers: Saturday, Sunday, Monday, Tuesday – I was rich, gloriously rich.

I was not very hungry; I left everything on my plate. But I had finished my half bottle of rosé, more than I drink in a whole week sometimes. A couple who were leaving stopped at my table – a man of about fifty, bald at the temples, tanned and relaxed, and a young woman in beige. The man asked me if I was happy with my Thunderbird. I looked up, pressing my index finger to the place in the middle of my glasses where they leave a mark on my nose. I answered that if I wasn't happy with it I would be sure to get in touch with him. His smile disappeared and he said, "Excuse me". I was annoyed with myself for snapping at him and I called him back. His smile returned.

I don't know what I said to them about the car, but they sat down across the table from me. I was finishing some raspberries with sugar. They had already had coffee, but they had another cup so they could buy me one. They said that they had watched me as they ate and that they were sure they knew me, or at least that they had seen me somewhere. The young woman asked if I was an actress I said, Heavens no, that I was in advertising, that I ran an agency. Perhaps she had seen me being interviewed or something on television? I answered that it was quite possible. She turned to the man and said, "You see, I was right." Was I going south or coming back? I said that I was going to visit friends in Cap d'Antibes, and also to take care of some business in Nice over the weekend. They said that I was lucky, they were on their way home. The road was fine until Montélimar but there they had waited over two hours, blocked by a line of cars going the other way that stretched for several kilometres. I should also avoid Lyon, it was death. The best thing to do was to take Route six and go through some town whose name ended in Demi-Lune, to get back to seven. I said, "Of course, that's what I usually do." He was an army doctor, a colonel. I said that my father had been one too, but in the German army, a weakness of my mother's during the Occupation, you know, shaved heads and all that. They found me very amusing, they went away charmed, leaving me an address scrawled on a piece of notebook paper. I burned it in an ashtray, after lighting a cigarette.

Mama Supe claimed that I was drunk, that it looked like rain, and that I had better go and hide in the bathroom before I burst into tears. But I did not cry. I decided that I would bring the car back on Tuesday evening, or even Wednesday morning. I would have it washed in a garage when I got back. Anita is not the type to look at the mileage. Nobody would ever know.

Outside I lit another cigarette and walked along the road for a moment. The sun cast a dark shadow in front of me, and when I got back into the Thunderbird the seats were broiling hot. I went to Fontainebleau. I found a parking place by the kerb. I put on my right shoe and got out. I bought a dress that looked pretty to me in the shop window and was even prettier when I tried it on – white muslin with a diaphanous skirt. In the same shop I also got a bright yellow bikini, a bra, two pairs of panties, a pair of turquoise trousers, a white sleeveless turtleneck sweater, two huge Turkish towels, and two face flannels, and that was it. While they were making an alteration to the dress, I crossed the street and bought a pair of sandals with gold straps to go with the trousers. Not for anything in the world would I have gone back to my apartment in rue de Grenelle to collect this kind of stuff, not so much because of the two hours I would waste getting there and back but for fear that I would have a chance to think it over, for fear I would no longer have the courage to leave.

Carrying my acquisitions in large paper bags, I went into a leather shop, picked out a black leather suitcase, and put everything in it. Above all I did not want to add up the cheques I was signing. I have a whole system of signals in my head anyway from the habit of economy, and if I had spent enough of my fortune to jeopardize this weekend, it would certainly have warned me.

I put the suitcase in the boot of the car, but immediately regretted not feeling it near me. I got it out again and put it on the back seat. It was four by the clock on the dashboard. Opening one of Anita's road maps, I estimated that by driving until dark I could sleep somewhere near Chalon-sur-Saône or maybe Mâcon. Looking further down the map, I read names that suddenly made my heart race: Orange, Salon-de-Provence, Marseille, Saint-Raphaël. I knotted my scarf around my head, took off my right shoe, and was on my way.

As I left Fontainebleau I remembered what the army doctor had told me; and I asked a woman who was tending a flower stall how to get to Route six. I bought a bunch of violets which I put against the windscreen. A little further on I saw some policemen on motorbikes chatting at a crossroads and suddenly I thought, Suppose Caravaille came back during the weekend? Suppose, for some reason or other, he came back this evening? In spite of myself, I slowed down.

When he did not find the car, he would think there had been an accident. He would undoubtedly call my apartment (did he even have my number?), but I would not be there, so he would go to the police. I imagined my description being transmitted everywhere, policemen stationed on the main roads. And then – no, it was ridiculous. Other people are just the opposite to me – when they say they are going to do a thing, they do it. Caravaille would not be back before Wednesday. He had his wife and daughter with him, he wouldn't spoil these few days of relaxation for them. He would tell the little girl to breathe-in the fresh air, he would take her for a boat trip on the lake. And anyway, what could he do in Paris if he came back? Everything was closed until Wednesday. Life was not normal; I was a car thief only for the length of a holiday waltz, why was I trying to scare myself and make myself think it was serious? I accelerated. The sky was cloudless and a deep, almost violet, blue. The wheat fields were sprinkled with warm light, a dusting of sun. Suppressed but persistent, the anxiety that I had already felt on leaving the main road lodged in me in the dimmest and most silent part of my mind, and sometimes at the least thing, for no reason, it would stir suddenly like a drowsy animal, or like another self turning over in its sleep.

I drove through the valley of the Yonne. I remember stopping at a coffee bar in Joigny to buy cigarettes and go to the toilet. Behind the counter there were photographs of lorry accidents and a red, white and blue notice announcing the weekend's festivities. Some lorry drivers were talking over their beers. They stopped talking while I was there, and, as I was paying for the fruit juice I had drunk, one of them told the boss that it was on him. I didn't want him to pay for it, but he said in a southern accent that that was all he needed, for me to refuse, and I took back my money. I was starting the car when he came out with another driver. Before going over to his lorry, he stopped beside me. He was a dark fellow about my age with

43

a nonchalant air and a toothpaste smile. Running his eyes from the end of the bonnet to my neckline he said, still in his accent, "You must go fast with an engine like that." I nodded in agreement. He said that was a shame, that in that case we'd never meet again. When I drove away he opened the door of his lorry and climbed into the front seat. He waved and shouted, "If we meet again, I'll give it back to you!" He was holding something that I was already too far away to see. When I looked at my windscreen I understood. Somehow he had managed to swipe my bunch of violets. After Auxerre I took a main road that is still under construction and I drove faster than I had ever dreamed of doing in my life. I got back onto Route six south of Avallon. The sun was lower, but it was still hot – yet I was cold. My head buzzed hollowly. I think it was the excitement, the fear I had felt when I pressed my bare foot harder and harder on the accelerator. I think this was also what made me exaggerate an incident of no importance that happened immediately afterwards. I mustn't mention it if they interrogate me. That would confuse everything. They would wonder whether I was in my right mind; they would no longer believe what I said.

It was a village, the first I came to after the main road. It did seem familiar to me, that's true. But any village with grey houses, a steeple rising to the blue sky, hills on the horizon and suddenly, there before me, the summer sun flooding a long street so that it hurt my eyes and I had to stop – any village of this kind would have given me this impression of *déjà vu*; a long time ago, a very long time, much too long to be able to pick out a detail, a name, for the memory.

A skinny old woman in a black apron with a wrinkled face was sitting on a folding chair in front of a café, whose door was nothing but a dark hole. I was driving very slowly, blinded, when all at once something made me turn my head and I saw this woman motioning to me, calling me. I pulled over to the kerb. She walked with difficulty, and came towards me very slowly. I got out of the car. Her voice was very loud, but hoarse and asthmatic; I could hardly understand her. She told me that I had left my coat at her café that morning. I remember that she was holding some peapods in one hand, and that she had had a basket on her lap when she was sitting down. I told her that she was mistaken, that I had not left my coat at her café, for the good reason that I had never been there. She insisted. She had served me coffee and rolls, she had realized that I was upset about something and had not been surprised when she found my coat on a chair. I told her that it was a mistake, thank you anyway, and hurriedly got back into the car.

She frightened me. Her eyes searched my face almost maliciously. She followed me. She clung to the door with a wrinkled brown hand, a hand whose knuckles protruded from the skin. She repeated that I had had a cup of coffee and some rolls while they were mending my car.

I could not find the ignition. In spite of myself, I found myself making excuses: that morning I had been in Paris miles away from here, she was simply confusing two similar cars. With her ugly, old woman's smile she said a terrible thing – at least it seemed terrible at the time:

"The car was being mended; I didn't even see it. But I saw you."

I don't know what came over me. I wrenched her hand off the door, screaming at her to leave me alone, that I did not know her, that she had never seen me, that she must not tell anyone she had seen me, ever, ever. I realized then that there were other villagers within earshot. They were looking at us. I drove away.

And that's it. This happened a quarter of an hour ago or less. I drove straight ahead. I tried to think about something

45

reassuring: Mama Supe; my bedroom; the sea. I couldn't do it. I saw a petrol station on the left side of the main road. At Orly I had checked the petrol gauge, which had been full. It was now half empty, but I could still do quite a few kilometres. I decided to stop anyway.

The man who came to help me was joking with two customers. He did not wear a cap or a uniform. I walked over to a building with white walls. I had taken off my scarf. I remember the crunch of my steps on the gravel, and above all, the sun, which was already shining through the trees on the hills in a thousand splinters of light. Inside, all was warm darkness and silence. I tidied my hair and turned on the tap. Then the other me that was my anxiety awoke screaming, screaming. Someone grabbed me from behind, so suddenly that I hardly had time to struggle, and coldly but desperately – yes, I know that throughout that interminable moment I understood what they wanted, and begged, pleaded with them not to do it – someone crushed my hand.

The Car

Manuel could have told them exactly what it was: a brand new Thunderbird, fully automatic, 300 horsepower, V–8 engine, maximum speed 180, tank capacity 100 litres. He had been working on cars since the age of fourteen – he was now in his late thirties – and was almost as interested in what has four wheels as he was in what has two legs and wears skirts. His only reading matter was *L'Argus de l'Automobile* and cosmetics brochures that he sometimes found at the chemist's counter.

In America he would have been delighted to show off his knowledge. There they listened to you, even when you did not speak their language well, when it took you forever to think of a word. Manuel, who was Basque, had spent his youth working in America. The longest period had been in Toledo, Ohio. He still had a brother over there, the oldest, his favourite. What he missed most about America was his brother, and also a girl with red hair with whom he had taken a boat trip on the Maumee River on an outing organized by the Basque colony. Nothing had happened. Another day she had come to his room and he had tried to put his hand inside her skirt but she had not let him.

He had had several mistresses while working in Toledo, but most of them were shopsoiled items or married women; he remembered them without nostalgia. He told himself that he had been too full of life then, too impatient, and that if he had made a little effort he could have had Maureen too. He called her Maureen when he remembered the picnic on the river, because it was like Maumee and had an Irish sound, but he could no longer remember her name. She may not have been Irish. Sometimes, when he was depressed, he was no longer really sure that she had had red hair. He had named his wife's daughter – she was two years old when he became her papa – Maureen too, but everyone had got into the habit of calling her Momo or Riri, even the schoolteacher, and there was nothing he could do about it. In life you can always try to keep something for yourself but they will always manage to take it away from you.

Manuel did not like to be thought of as long-winded, especially not by customers, and he knew from experience that, unless it was a French car, when someone asked you what kind of a car that was, they were only trying to find out how much it was worth. Technically speaking, they were convinced in advance that it was not worth a thing – except, of course, the connoisseurs, but they didn't ask questions; on the contrary, they were the ones who talked your ear off. So in the case of the Thunderbird with the sand-coloured seats, he answered merely, "It must run into five figures. Easily."

He had filled the tank and was cleaning the windscreen. Standing nearby were Charles Baulu, a wine grower from the village, and a land agent from Saulieu, a tall thin man with a Renault, who stopped in three times a week but whose name Manuel did not know. It was at that moment that they heard the screams. Like the others, Manuel had stood there for a moment without reacting, but he could not have said that he was really surprised. At least not as surprised as he would have been if it had been any other woman.

As soon as he had seen her, something had warned him that

she was not quite normal. Maybe it was her dark glasses or her silence (she had spoken only a few necessary words, or else, that way she had of leaning her head rather listlessly to the side as she walked. She had a very beautiful, very special walk, as if each forward movement of her long legs started with an arching of the back. Manuel had been reminded of a wounded animal without being able to decide whether it was an antelope or a big cat, but anyway it was an animal that had escaped from a nocturnal world: you sensed the presence of dark thoughts, night thoughts, under her blonde hair.

The three men surrounded her now as she walked towards Manuel's office. As they left the toilets they had tried to support her, but she had drawn away at once. She was not crying any more. She was holding her swollen hand against her. It had a big bluish groove just above the joining of the fingers. She had recovered her walk and her smooth, perfectly immobile profile, the nose short and straight, the lips closed. Even in her soiled white suit, with her hair slightly dishevelled, she still looked to Manuel like what she probably was, a supple animal for some rich guy.

There was something else that bothered Manuel even more than the vague feeling of self-pity that he had because a woman was beyond his means of seduction, or his means full stop. In the doorway to his office, standing beside her mother, the child was watching them approach. Manuel wished she were not there. She was seven years old and, although he was conscious every moment of his life that she was not really his daughter, she was the person he cared about most. She returned his love, and she even admired him, because the fathers of her classmates came to him with something like humility when their engines no longer worked, and because he knew how to put everything to rights with his bare hands. He hated her to see him in an embarrassing situation.

He helped the lady with the Thunderbird to a seat behind the big window in his office. Nobody spoke. It was too late to send away the child, who would not have forgiven him. He went into the kitchen and took a bottle of cognac from a cupboard and a clean glass from the sink. His wife, Miette, had followed him.

"What happened?"

"Nothing. I don't know."

He took a drink out of the bottle before going back. On principle Miette told him that he drank too much and he replied in Basque that this way he would die sooner and she would be young enough to marry again. Her first marriage had been to some Spaniard from the retreating army whom he did not want to hear about, but not out of jealousy. He did not love his wife, at least he did not love her any more. Sometimes he imagined that she had been unfaithful to her Spaniard and that anyone could have knocked her up. Anyone at all.

He put the half-full glass on the steel desk in his office. Everyone looked at it in silence. The lady with the Thunderbird merely shook her head, she did not take it. Manuel was annoyed to have to speak first because of the little girl, and because he knew that his accent would surprise them at a moment like this, that he would be ridiculous. He made a large gesture of irritation to distract their attention.

"You say you were attacked, but no one was around. Everyone who was, is here. Personally, madame, I don't know why you say you were attacked."

She looked at him through her dark glasses, he could not see her eyes. Baulu and the land agent remained silent. They must be thinking that she was an epileptic, or something of that kind, and be feeling uncomfortable. But Manuel knew it was something else. One night, the year after his return to

France, he had had his wallet stolen in a petrol station near Toulouse. He had the sense of being in a similar situation now, he could not have said why.

"Someone came in," the lady stated. "You must have seen him, since you were out front."

Her voice was as slow as her walk, but flat, without a trace of emotion.

"If somebody had gone in we certainly would have seen him," said Manuel. "The fact is, nobody did go in, madame, nobody."

She looked towards Baulu and the land agent. Baulu shrugged his shoulders.

"You don't mean one of us do you?" asked Manuel.

"I don't know. I don't know you."

All three of them stood, speechless, with stupid expressions, looking at her. Manuel's sensation of reliving a bad night in Toulouse became more vivid. At the same time he felt reassured because he had not left the other two the whole time she had been in the toilet – five or six minutes? – and because he guessed from a different kind of silence that they did not trust her either. It was the land agent who spoke. He said to Manuel, "Perhaps your wife should take the little girl away?"

Manuel told his wife in Basque that Riri should not stay here, and that if she herself did not want to get a beating she would not forget, she had better scram too. She answered in Basque that since he had violated her, the widow of an admirable man, without even taking off her mourning dress, she was not surprised to learn that he had done the same to another woman. Nevertheless, she left with the little girl, who turned around and looked at the lady and Manuel, trying to understand who was being blamed for what.

"None of us three went into that place," Baulu said to the lady. "Don't say things that aren't so."

He was a heavy man with a heavy voice. When they played manille in the village it was he who yelled the loudest. Manuel thought that he put it well: Don't say things that aren't so.

"Are you missing any money?" asked Baulu.

The lady shook her head without hesitation, very firmly. Manuel understood less and less what she was driving at.

"What, then? Why would someone have attacked you?"

"I did not use that word."

"Well, that's what you meant!" retorted Baulu.

He had taken a step towards the lady. Manuel suddenly realized that she was straining against the back of the chair with all her might, that she was afraid. And then two tears appeared slowly below her glasses and slid slowly and steadily down her cheeks. She did not look more than twenty-five. Manuel felt a curious mixture of embarrassment and excitement. He wanted to come closer, too, but he did not dare.

"First of all, take off those glasses!" said Baulu. "I don't like talking to people when I can't see their eyes."

Manuel could have sworn she would not do it, and so could the land agent, probably, and maybe even Baulu, who was exaggerating his anger to impress everyone, but she obeyed. Her reaction was almost immediate as if she were afraid they would force her to do it. As far as Manuel was concerned, it was as if she had taken off her clothes. Her eyes were large, dark and utterly vulnerable. You could see that she was holding back her tears, and it was true, for some damn reason, that this way she seemed more beautiful and more naked.

The other two men must have had the same impression, for there was another long silence. Then, without a word, she raised her swollen hand and showed it to them. Manuel took a step towards her then – she could not see him very clearly – and waved Baulu aside.

"What?" he said. "Oh, no! You're not saying that that happened here! You already had it this morning!"

Even as he spoke he was thinking, That doesn't make sense. He had thought he understood at last the meaning of this comedy – there was something fishy in it, but he was becoming aware of an absurdity that ruined the whole mechanism. If, for example, she had wanted to make it look as if she had been hurt at his place and to extort a little money from him instead of informing the police – it would never have worked, even though he had been in prison once – then why the hell had she already appeared that morning with the same wound?

"That's not true!"

She tried to get up, shaking her head vigorously. Baulu had to help Manuel restrain her. Beneath the neckline of her jacket they saw that all she had on was a white lace bra, and that the place where her breasts began was as golden as the rest of her skin. Then she subsided and they stepped back. She repeated, as she put her glasses back on, that it was not true.

"What? What isn't true?"

"There was nothing the matter with my hand this morning. And if there had been you wouldn't have seen it, because I was in Paris."

She had recovered her flat voice, her disdainful air.

Manuel saw that it was not so much disdain as an effort to keep from crying again, to preserve the appearance of a lady. She was studying her motionless left hand and that curious groove near the joining of her fingers.

"You were not in Paris, madame," said Manuel calmly. "You can't convince anyone of that. I don't know what you want, but nobody around here will believe that I am a liar."

She looked up, but not at him; she was looking out of the window. Following her gaze, they saw Miette filling the tank of a van.

Manuel said, "I fixed the rear lights of your Thunderbird this morning. The wires were disconnected."

"That's not true."

"I don't say things that aren't true."

She had come at dawn, he had heard her hoot as he was having a spiked coffee in the kitchen. When he had gone out she had been the same as she was now, calm and tense at the same time, ready to cry over nothing, but ready to defend herself if necessary. Through her dark glasses she had watched him stuff the tail of his pyjama top into his belt. He had said, "Excuse me. How much do you want?" because he had thought that she wanted petrol. She had answered only that her lights did not work and that she would come back for the car in half an hour. She had picked up a summer coat from a seat, a white summer coat. She had left.

"You're mistaking me for someone else," said the lady. "I was in Paris."

"With that car?" said Manuel. "I'm mistaking you for someone else who was you."

"You can confuse two cars."

"When I've worked on one of them, never! Not even with its twin sister. You're the one who is mistaking Manuel for someone else, madame. I could even tell you that I changed the screws on the mounts when I put the wires back and that if you look at them you can see they are Manuel's screws."

Suddenly he moved towards the door, but Baulu caught him by the arm and held him back. "You must have something in writing on that repair job, eh?"

"I don't have time for bookkeeping, you know," said Manuel. Then, since he wanted to be completely sincere, "Well, what do you want, I wasn't going to write down two thousand francs so Ferrante could have his share!"

Ferrante was the tax collector. He lived in the village and

he had an apéritif with them in the evening. If he had been there Manuel would have said the same thing.

"But I gave her a paper."

"A receipt?"

"If you want to call it that. A piece of paper, you know, a page out of my notebook, stamped and everything."

She looked at Baulu and Manuel in turn. She was cradling her swollen hand in her right arm. She may have been in pain. It was hard to know what she was thinking or feeling behind her glasses.

"Anyway," said Manuel, "I have witnesses."

"If she wants to make trouble for you," said the land agent, "the word of your wife or your daughter is not worth a thing."

"Leave my daughter out of this! If you think I'm going to mix her up in this, you can go to hell! I mean the Pacauds."

The Pacauds ran one of the cafés in the village. The mother and daughter-in-law got up early to serve the men who were working on the Auxerre main road. This is where Manuel had sent the lady in the white suit when she had asked him where she could find something open. It was strange; a woman driving alone at night, a woman who came out of the night in dark glasses (he had not understood then that she was short-sighted and wanted to conceal the fact). It was so strange, as it was, that he had not noticed the bandage that encircled her left hand until the last minute. A white bandage in the early-morning light.

"I am in pain," said the lady. "Let me leave. I want to see a doctor."

"Just a minute," said Manuel. "Excuse me, but you went to the Pacauds' place, they will verify that. I am going to call them."

"Is it a café?" asked the lady.

"That's right."

"They are mistaken too."

There was a silence. She looked at them without moving. If they could have seen her eyes they would have said she looked stubborn. Now Manuel understood too that she was mad, that she did not really mean him any harm, she was simply mad. He said, with a gentleness that surprised even himself, "You had a bandage on your hand this morning, I assure you."

"I didn't have one just now when I got here."

"You didn't?" With his eyes Manuel questioned the other two, who shrugged their shoulders. "We didn't notice it, that's true. So what? Because you had one this morning, I tell you!"

"It wasn't me."

"Then why did you come back,"

"I don't know. I didn't come back. I don't know."

Two more tears slid down her cheeks. "Let me leave. I want to see a doctor."

"I'll drive you to a doctor," said Manuel.

"Don't bother."

"I want to hear what you tell him," said Manuel. "You don't mean to make trouble for me, do you?"

She shook her head irritably, and as she was getting up this time they stepped back.

"You say that I am mistaken, that the Pacauds are mistaken, that everyone is mistaken," said Manuel. "I don't understand what you're after."

"Leave her alone," said Baulu.

When they left the office – first she, then the land agent, then Baulu and Manuel – there were several cars parked in front of the pumps. Miette, who had never been very fast, was going from one to the other, unable to keep up with the work. The little girl was playing on a pile of sand beside the main road with some other youngsters. She came towards Manuel with her arms dangling and her face dirty when she saw that he was getting into his old Frégate and that the lady from Paris was getting in with him.

"Go back and play," said Manuel. "I am going to the village. I'll be right back."

But she stood there silently beside the car door while he warmed up the engine. She did not take her eyes off the lady sitting next to him. When he swept around the pumps, Baulu and the land agent were relating the incident to some other customers. In the rear-view mirror he saw that everyone was watching him drive away.

The sun had disappeared behind the hills, but it would soon reappear, as if for a second twilight, at the other side of the village. Because he found the silence between them uncomfortable, Manuel told the lady that this was probably why they called the village Deux-Soirs-lès-Avallon. It was obvious that she was not listening to him.

He took her to Dr Garat, whose office was opposite the church. He was a very tall, old man, strong as an ox, who had worn the same rough wool suit for years. Manuel knew him well because he was a good hunter, a socialist like himself, and because he sometimes borrowed the Frégate to make his calls when his own car – a pre-'48 jalopy – was suffering from what he called its "heart murmur". In fact, despite several overhauls, it no longer had a heart, or anything else for that matter, and could not have made it to the scrap yard under its own steam.

Dr Garat examined the lady's hand, made her move her fingers, and said that he would take an x-ray, but that apparently the joints were not dislocated. The blow had bruised the muscles of the palm. He asked her how it had happened. Manuel stayed in the background because the doctor's office impressed him as much as the church opposite, and because nobody asked him to come over. After a brief hesitation the

57

lady replied only that it was an accident. Dr Garat glanced at her right hand which, however, was intact.

"Are you left handed?"

"Yes."

"You won't be able to use your hand for two weeks. I can give you an exemption note to show your employer."

"That won't be necessary."

He showed her into a white-walled room in which there were an examining table, apothecary jars and a big medicine chest. Manuel followed them as far as the door. A long white silhouette against the white of the walls, the lady half removed the jacket of her suit to free her left arm but Manuel caught a glimpse of the bronzed and satiny skin of her slim upper body, enough to suggest full, firm breasts, unexpectedly heavy for her slender body, under the lace of the bra. After that he no longer dared to look or leave, or even swallow his saliva; he felt stupid and strangely depressed.

Dr Garat took an x-ray, disappeared to develop it, and reappeared. He confirmed the fact that there was no fracture. He gave her an injection to deaden the pain, wrapped the swollen hand in a tight bandage, which held everything in position, and rolled a strip of gauze first between the fingers, then all around, very tightly, up to the wrist. The operation took a quarter of an hour during which nobody uttered a word. If she was in pain she did not show it. She watched her hand being dressed, or the opposite wall, and several times she pushed her glasses back with the index finger of her right hand. She did not seem any more unbalanced than the next person, in fact less so, and Manuel told himself that he might as well give up trying to work her out.

She had difficulty getting her bandaged hand through the sleeve of her jacket. While the doctor was putting his things away, Manuel came to her aid and ripped out a few stitches to loosen her sleeve. He smelled her perfume, which was sweet and light like her hair, with something warmer that was the smell of her skin.

They returned to Garat's office. While the doctor was writing out a prescription she rummaged in her bag, took out a comb, and tidied her hair with her right hand. She took out some money, too, but Manuel said that he would settle it with the doctor.

She shrugged her shoulders – without ill will, he realized, only from fatigue – and put the money back into her bag along with the prescription. Then she asked the doctor, "When did this happen to me?"

Dr Garat looked at her uncomprehendingly. Then he turned his eyes towards Manuel.

"She wants to know when she was hurt."

Garat was more confused than ever. He stared at the young woman sitting in front of him as if he had not really seen her yet.

"You don't know?"

She did not answer, either by word or gesture.

"Good heavens, I assume you came to see me at once, didn't you?"

"This gentleman claims that I already had it this morning," she said, raising her bandaged hand.

"It's possible, but after all, you yourself must know."

"It's possible?"

"Why not?"

She got up and thanked him. As she was walking out of the front door, Garat held Manuel back by the arm and looked at him questioningly. Manuel raised his hands in a helpless gesture.

He got behind the wheel again. As he drove her back, he wondered what she was going to do. He told himself that she could go home by train, that she could send someone for the car. Night was falling. Manuel could not get the sight of her swelling breasts out of his head.

"You won't be able to drive with your bandage."

"Yes, I will."

She turned only her eyes and he knew what she was going to say before she said it.

"I was driving this morning when you saw me, wasn't I? And my hand was like this, wasn't it? So what has changed?"

They did not speak again until they got to the petrol station. Miette had turned on the lights. Standing in the doorway to the office, she watched them get out of the Frégate.

The lady walked over to her Thunderbird, which someone, probably Baulu, had parked out of the way of the pumps. She threw her handbag onto the front seat and got behind the wheel. Manuel saw his little girl run out from behind the house and stop short to look at them. He walked over to the car, the engine of which was already running.

"I haven't paid for the petrol," said the lady.

He no longer remembered exactly how much she owed him, so he named a round figure. She gave him a fifty-franc note. He did not want her to leave like this, especially not in front of the child, but he could not think of anything to say. She knotted her scarf around her head and turned on her lights. She shivered. Without looking at him, she said, "It wasn't me this morning."

Her voice was low, tense, almost pleading. At the same time, she looked the way she had at dawn. But what difference did it make now?

"I don't know any more. Maybe I made a mistake. Anybody can make a mistake," he replied.

She must have sensed that he did not believe a word of what

he was saying. Behind him, in Basque, Miette yelled that three people had called for emergency repairs.

"What is she saying?"

"Nothing. Will you be able to manage with your bandage?" She nodded.

Manuel extended his hand over the car door, saying very quickly and softly, "Be nice, shake hands. It's for my little girl who's watching."

She turned her head towards the little girl, who was standing, motionless, a few feet away under the lights in her red-checked apron, with her dirty knees. She understood so quickly that his heart jumped, but what really moved him was not that, or even when she placed her right hand in his; it was – sudden, unexpected, unknown until then – her smile. She smiled at him. She shivered at the same time. Manuel longed to say something magnificent to thank her, something nice to blot out the rest, but all that he could think of was, "Her name is Maureen".

She drove away, off the forecourt and out towards Saulieu. He took a few steps towards the road to watch the two blinding red lights disappear. Maureen came and stood beside him, and he put his arms around her and said, "Do you see those lights? Do you see them? Well, they were broken, you see, and it was your papa, Manuel, who fixed them!"

Her hand did not hurt, nothing hurt, everything inside her was numb. She was cold, very cold, in the open car, and this contributed to her numbness. She stared ahead of her at the brightest zone of her headlights, just before that dusty fringe where they blended into the darkness. When other cars came towards her it took her right hand half a second to get hold of the other side of the wheel; half a second during which nothing held the wheel but the weight of her stiff bandage.

She drove carefully, but with stubborn regularity. The needle of the speedometer had to remain close to forty miles an hour, had at least to touch the big metal 4. As long as it stayed there, nothing or nobody was yet betrayed. The wheel did not move a millimetre, Paris was getting further and further away, she was too cold to think, that was good.

She knew all about betrayal, oh, yes. You say you love someone or believe in something, and then, in less time than it takes to feel the needle leave the 4, less time than it takes to feel tired, to breathe, to tell yourself, I could not care for this person, or love this thing all the way, a door closes, you run into the street, and after that you can take refuge in the warmth of tears and even try for months to erase it all from your memory: you have betrayed, you have betrayed, you have betrayed.

Saulieu: splotches of light and splotches of darkness, the road turning down a slope, the top of a basilica. After turning into one street and then another, she stopped less than a yard short of the grey wall of this basilica. She turned off the ignition and collapsed, her head against the wheel, her eyes dry, the sobs in her chest that she did not even try to control but that would not come out, giving her a ridiculous hiccup. Your mouth on your bandage. Your hair in front of your eyes, on the other side of those damned owl-spectacles. Now it's you, it's completely you, you have nothing but your right hand and this worn-out heart, but go on, don't ask questions, go on.

She allowed herself to stay like this for a few minutes – three or four, perhaps less – then she braced herself firmly against the back of the seat, telling herself that the world was big, life was long, that she was hungry and thirsty and wanted a cigarette. The night was clear and fine ahead of her. On the map, which she could pick up with her good hand, there were still names like Salon-de-Provence, Marseille, and Saint-Raphaël.

My poor girl you are what they call a manic-depressive. Right, I am a manic-depressive. A manic-depressive who is cold.

She pushed the button that operated the roof. As if by magic, it rose into the sky of Saulieu, blotting out the stars and enclosing her, Dany Longo, in a world that resembled the tents of her childhood, the ones she used to make in the orphanage dormitory with her sheets. She lit a cigarette. It tasted good and stung her throat, like the first ones she had smoked, at the age of fifteen, under those tents. You passed them around, one puff apiece, then you coughed your head off, and the girls who wanted to be in with the sister on duty went "Shhhh! Shhhh!" in the dormitory. Then the light would go on, and the sister on duty would arrive in a rough cotton nightshirt with some rag around her head to hide her close-cropped hair and administer blows at random. You had to pull your knees up to your chin and ward them off with your elbows. It was she who got hurt.

People went by, their footsteps ringing on the pavement. A clock struck loudly half past what? Past nine by the clock on the dashboard. Dany turned on a light – everything lit up in this car, you couldn't press a button without being dazzled – and rummaged in the glove compartment, looking quickly through the papers she had seen a few hours earlier. She did not find a garage receipt from Deux-Soirs-lès-Avallon. She was not expecting to find one.

Next, she emptied her handbag onto the seat beside her. Nothing there either. She asked herself a little nervously why she was going to so much trouble. She knew perfectly well that she had never in her life set foot in the garage belonging to the little man with the Basque accent, so what was she doing? She put everything back in her bag. How many American cars had been on the main roads between Paris and Marseille today? Dozens, maybe over a hundred. How many women might be wearing white in July? And of these, how many, Good Lord! would be wearing sunglasses? The incident would have been completely ridiculous except for her crushed hand.

Well, the little Basque man had lied, that was all there was to it. The wound, at least, was real, the bandage was right in front of her eyes, and there was only one explanation, or only one that she could see. One of the two customers, or even the man himself, had followed her into the toilets to take her money or for some other reason that she couldn't quite believe – that look in the doctor's office when she had taken off one sleeve of her jacket, that look that had been both disgusting and pathetic, was she making that up too? She must have struggled, he had realized that he was hurting her hand and had become afraid. Afterwards, to clear his friends or himself, he had made up some story in the office. The drink on the desk. The big red-faced man who talked so loud. They had seen that she was frightened and taken advantage of it. And without realizing that the car did not belong to her, all three must have guessed something was keeping her from calling the police as she should have done.

That was it, that must be it. She had the feeling she was cheating a little, because she could not forget the wrinkled face and spiteful eyes of an old woman in a long street flooded with sunlight, but that, too, had been a coincidence, a mis-understanding. Kneeling on the front seat, she opened the black suitcase in the back and took out the white sweater she had bought in Fontainebleau. It was very soft, with a new smell that reassured her. She turned out the light in the car, slipped it on under her jacket, turned the light back on again, and adjusted the turtleneck, looking at herself in the rear-view mirror. Each of these movements, which took time because she was clumsy with her right hand, made the old woman, the petrol station, and the whole ugly end to the afternoon, seem further away. She was Dany Longo, blonde and beautiful, on her way to Monte Carlo, wearing a suit that she would have to wash but that would dry in two hours, and she was famished.

As she left Saulieu a sign informed her that Chalon was eighty-five kilometres away. She was not going very fast and the road was winding and hilly; it would take her over an hour and a half to get there. But the lights of the cars ahead of her helped her on the turns, and she was not going to make any more stops. It was just as she was promising herself not to stop again that she was forced, with her heart sinking, to do just that.

First, on her left, at the crossroads of a main road that went to Dijon, there was the massive, heavy, outline of two motorcyclists who had stopped under the trees. She was not even sure she had seen uniforms as she went by. But what if they were policemen on motorbikes and what if they were following her? In the rear-view mirror she saw one of the two, still over two hundred yards behind, swing onto the road at top speed and rush after her with a roar. He was getting bigger in the mirror, she could make out his helmet and goggles. Sitting on the machine he looked like an implacable robot, he was not human. She told herself, It's impossible, it's not me he's after, he's going to pass me and keep right on going. He passed her with the noise of an engine gunned to the limit, drove on for a way, then slowed to a stop, looking at her and raising his hand. She pulled up by the side of the road twenty yards behind. He parked his motorbike, pulled off his gloves, and walked towards her in the glare of the headlights with a step that was exaggeratedly calm, as if to complete the shattering of her nerves. So it was all over before it had begun. The disappearance of the Thunderbird had been discovered, no doubt they had her name and description, everything. Meanwhile she, who had never spoken to a policeman except to ask for information in Paris, had a curious impression of *déjà vu*, as if she had already imagined this scene in all its detail, or as if she were living it for the second time.

When he reached her, the policeman glanced at the cars that were passing on the road, crossing the night with a loud rush of air. Then he sighed, raised his goggles over his helmet, leaned his elbows heavily on the car door and said, "Well, Mademoiselle Longo, going for a drive?"

He had a conscience and his name was Toussaint Nardi. He also had a wife, three children, a flair for marksmanship, a reverence for Napoleon, a private room with hot water and a garbage disposal unit at the barracks, a post-office savings account, and unlimited patience for learning from books what they had not had time to teach him at school, and he hoped to finish his days quietly as a police officer in some little town in the sun.

He had a reputation for being a man who didn't like to be crossed, but a good guy – for a policeman. In fifteen years of service he had never had an opportunity to demonstrate his skill on anything but training targets or carnival pigeons, and for this he considered himself lucky. Nor had he ever raised his hand against anyone either in uniform or as a civilian, not counting a few beatings he had given his eldest son who, at thirteen, had a Beatles haircut, bunked maths, and would become a hoodlum if his father didn't do something about it. Finally, his only concern, besides keeping out of trouble was to take proper care of his motorbike. First from discipline, and then because his life depended on it, and he couldn't see himself dying before his time.

When he saw the white Thunderbird with the black top go by at the crossroads of Route six and Route seventy-seven A, he was talking motorbikes with his colleague Rappart. Rappart was his favourite because he was on the same floor at the barracks and because he was having trouble with his son too. On day duty you didn't do much talking. On night duty there were three subjects of conversation tolerated besides motor-bikes: what a bastard the chief was; the faults of the respective wives; and the promiscuity of other women.

Nardi recognized the Thunderbird as soon as he saw it. It was not going very fast and he could read the number on the licence plate: 3210 RX 75. A number that was easy to remember because it sounded like the countdown on a rocket launching. For the past two hours he had had a vague premo-nition that he would see it go by. There are things that can't be explained. All he said to Rappart was, "Go and check the traffic on eighty, and I'll meet you here." He was sitting astride his machine so all he had to do was start it, release the engine with a big kick. He gave a delivery van right of way, bounced onto the road, and leaned to the right to make his turn as he picked up speed. In three seconds he had the back lights of the Thunderbird in his face, enormous lights of a dazzling red; lights that would give a Mini-driver a complex for life.

He could not see who was driving, but the bandage that she wore on her left hand caught his eye as he passed and he knew it was she. As he stopped her he could not remember her name, although he had read it along with her date of birth and everything, and he had a very good memory for names. It came to him as he was walking towards her: Longo.

She was different from this morning, he wondered what it was. First of all, she did not seem to recognize him. Then he realized that this morning she did not have that turtle-neck sweater on. The sweater, which was white like her suit, made her face seem rounder and more tanned by contrast. But there was the same curious emotional disturbance, the same difficulty in getting a word out, and he had the same impression of being in the presence of someone who was guilty.

Guilty of what? He had stopped her at dawn, just outside Saulieu on the road to Avallon, because her back lights were not working. It was the end of his duty and he had yelled at enough idiots that night for crossing the yellow lines, passing on hills, and endangering the lives of others to be fed up and to have said only, "Your lights aren't working, get them mended, goodbye, and don't come back." Even a woman, even a disturbed woman, wouldn't have got that panicky just because a tired policeman told her to have her lights mended.

It wasn't until afterwards, when he found her behaviour much too strange and asked her to show her papers, that he noticed the bandage on her left hand. And while he was looking at her driving licence – she had received it in the north at the age of eighteen and her residence at the time was a religious orphanage – he had noticed, although she remained perfectly silent and still, that her nervousness was growing, was approaching an extreme that could be dangerous to him.

Yet it was unexplainable, he could not have explained it in spite of all that damned psychology he had crammed into his head for his examinations, but he had had a very clear sensation of danger. It was almost as if, having reached the point of hysteria she might open her glove compartment, take out a gun, and send him to join all the other policemen killed in the line of duty. Besides, he should not have been alone; he had made a deal with Rappart, who wanted to go home early and get some sleep, because his little niece was being baptized the next day. He was not even guiltless in this business.

The papers seemed to be in order, though. He had asked where she was going: Paris. Her profession: secretary in an advertising agency. Where she was coming from: she had spent the night in a hotel in Chalon. What hotel: the Renaissance. She answered without actual hesitation, but in an unnatural, barely audible voice. It was in the half light between night and day, he could not see her clearly. He wanted to ask her to take off her glasses, but you can't ask people to do that, especially not a woman, without sounding like the heavy on a TV serial. Nardi had a horror of making a fool of himself.

The car was in the name of the advertising agency where she worked. She had given him the telephone number of her employer, he could confirm the fact that they often let her use it. There had been no report of a stolen Thunderbird on the roads, and if he pushed her to the limit without grounds, he might get into trouble. He had let her go. Afterwards he had regretted it. He should have made sure she was not armed. But why did he have this ridiculous idea that she might be? That was what bothered him the most.

Now, he didn't know any more. This was the same frightened, disturbing girl, but something had happened since this morning, something that had erased the quality he had sensed in her, the quality of aggression – no, it wasn't exactly that, of desperation – no, it wasn't that either. There was no way to describe the fact that at dawn she had been on the verge of an extreme point and that this extreme point had been crossed. He was certain that if a gun had ever been in the car, it wasn't there any more.

Actually, after his sleep, Nardi had felt a little ridiculous when he remembered the young woman in the Thunderbird. The reason he had not taken Rappart with him when he saw her for the second time was his fear of being even more ridiculous. He was glad now that he had not brought him along.

"Well, Mademoiselle Longo, we seem to be night owls, you and I. Don't you agree?"

She did not agree. She did not even recognize him.

"I see that your back lights are mended." Pause. "Was it a short circuit?" Pause. "Anyway, they're working." A century. "Was it in Paris that you had them mended?"

A tanned face hidden by glasses and lit by the glow from the dashboard, a plump little mouth that trembled a little, as if its owner were about to burst into tears, a blonde lock that had escaped the turquoise scarf. No answer. Guilty of what?

"Hey, I'm talking to you! Was it in Paris that you had your lights fixed?"

"No."

"Where?"

"I don't know. Near Avallon."

Hurrah, it talks. Her voice, as far as he could remember, seemed even less flat, more energetic. She had recovered a little of her calm.

"But you went to Paris?"

"Yes, I think so."

"You're not sure?"

"Yes, I am."

He ran his finger over his lips. He forced himself to study her carefully this time, although he was always a little embarrassed to look at women this way, even street walkers.

"Is anything the matter?"

She shook her head slightly, that was all.

"Would it bother you if I asked you to take off your glasses for a moment?"

She obeyed. She explained hurriedly, as if there were any need: "I am short-sighted."

Her eyes were so bad that when she took off her glasses she did not even try to see him. She did not seem to try to make any adjustment. Instead of shrinking like those of Rappart's little girl, who was also short-sighted as the result of a bad case of measles and whose attempts to see without glasses were pitiful, her eyes instantly grew larger. Empty and vulnerable, they changed her face.

"And you can drive in the pitch-dark with those eyes?" He had softened his voice, but he was annoyed at himself for sounding like a typical policeman. Fortunately she put her glasses back on very quickly, and made a slight movement of the chin for yes. Then there was that bandage.

"That's not very smart, Mademoiselle Longo, especially with a hurt hand." No answer. "And if I understand correctly, you've been at the wheel all day?" No answer. "Just there and back makes what, 600 kilometres?" No answer. "Must you drive? Where are you going now?"

"To the Midi."

"Where in the Midi?"

"Monte Carlo."

He whistled. "You're not going to do that without stopping?"

She shook her head very firmly. It was the first more or less definite reaction he had seen in her.

"I am going to stop at a hotel a little further on."

"In Chalon?"

"Yes, in Chalon."

"At the Renaissance?"

She looked at him blankly again.

"You told me you had spent the night at the Renaissance. Wasn't that true?"

"Yes, it was."

"Are they holding your room?"

"No, I don't think so."

"You don't think so?"

She shook her head and turned away to avoid his gaze. She sat there immobile with her bandage on the wheel, not with that arrogant patience of certain drivers who are thinking, Go

71

on, you fascinate me; when you have finished your little game then maybe I can leave, but simply because she seemed disoriented, lost, because words and ideas had stopped coming, because she had given up, just as she had when she took off her glasses. If he had asked her to come to the police station she would not have resisted, she probably would not even have tried to find out why.

He turned on his torch and shone the beam into the inside of the car.

"May I look in the glove compartment?"

She opened it. There was nothing inside but papers. She put her right hand on top of them to show that that was all.

"Your handbag?"

She opened that too.

"Is there anything in the back?"

"No. My suitcase."

He looked in her suitcase, which was black leather and contained only clothing, bath towels, a toothbrush. He was leaning through the open door and over the front seat. She had moved aside to make room for him without being asked. He was torn between the feeling that he was making a fool of himself and being a nuisance into the bargain, and the feeling that he was in the presence of something strange, something serious which he should have understood.

He closed the car door again, sighing, "You seem to have problems, Mademoiselle Longo."

"I'm tired, that's all."

Behind Nardi, cars roared by, flashes of harsh light shifted the shadows on the young woman's face so that it was never the same.

"Do you know what we're going to do? You're going to promise me you'll stop in Chalon. I'll call the Renaissance and reserve a room for you."

This way he could confirm the fact that she had been there the night before, that she had not lied. He did not see what else he could do.

She acquiesced with a nod. He told her to go slowly, that there was a lot of traffic on the roads this weekend.

He stepped back and touched his index finger to his cap, and all the time he was thinking, "Don't let her leave, before you know it this will turn out to be a monumental blunder."

She did not say goodbye. He had stationed himself on the road with his legs apart, slowing down the cars that were going in the same direction. He followed her with his eyes as he walked back to his motorbike. He told himself that after all it was true that you're not your sister's keeper, that he had done everything he could. If she was determined to end up with her picture in the paper, there would surely be a policeman more stubborn than he a little further down on six or seven to keep her from doing it. After fifteen years of service, he may have believed in only one quality in his colleagues, but he believed in it as in the Gospel: there were plenty of them and each was more stubborn than the last.

She was living, fully awake, in a dream. Neither a good dream nor a bad dream; an ordinary dream, the kind she sometimes had and forgot afterwards. But this time she was not going to wake up in her room. She was already awake. She was living in someone else's dream.

Does such a thing exist? To take a step indistinguishable from all the other steps you have taken in your life and, without realizing it, to cross a frontier of reality; to remain yourself, alive and wide awake, but in the nocturnal dream of, let's say, the girl next to you in the dormitory? And to keep on going in the certainty that you'll never leave it again, that you are the prisoner of a world modelled on the real one but

73

totally absurd, a world which is monstrous because it may vanish at any moment into your friend's brain, and you along with it?

As in dreams, in which motives change as you go along; she no longer knew why she was on a road driving through the night. You walk into a room where – click – a little picture shows a fishing port, but Mama Supe is there, you have come to confess to her that you have betrayed Anita and you can't find the words to explain it because it is obscene, and you hit Mama Supe again and again, but she has already turned into another old woman whom you came to see about your white coat. What was clearest was that she was supposed to get to a hotel she had already been to, before they could tell a policeman that she had never been there. Or the other way around. They say that when you're mad it is other people who seem to be mad. Well, that must be it. She was mad.

After Arnay-le-Duc a long row of lorries was inching along. She had to drive behind them along an endless coast. When she was able to pass them – one, then two then all the rest – a huge wave of relief flooded over her. It was not so much being able to pass the lorries and to find the black road, the empty night, in front of her again but, belatedly, not being arrested for stealing the car. They weren't looking for the Thunderbird: saved. She felt as if she had just that moment left the policeman on the motorbike. She had already done twenty kilometres in a confused state of mind in which she had lost track of time.

She had to stop this foolishness and take the car back to Paris right away. There was no longer any point in seeing the sea. She would go another time, by train. Or she would take what was left of her savings and make a down payment on a Citroën; the rest payable in instalments over eighteen months. She should have done it a long time ago. She would not go to

Monte Carlo but to some unpretentious little hole. Not to a big imaginary hotel with a swimming pool, soft music, and air-conditioned meetings, but to a very real family-type pension with a view of the vegetable garden, the forbidden fruit being an intellectual discussion about the plays of Anouilh at siesta hour with a lady butcher who knows her stuff or else, at best, with a long-sighted boy who knocks over sofas, the two of them would make a pair that would bring tears to the eyes of the local match-maker; "It's sweet but it's sad, if they have children they will have to sell their souls to the optician." Oh, she could make fun of it, look down on it, but it was her world, she did not deserve any other. She was only an idiot with delusions of grandeur. When you can't look at your own shadow without falling on your face, you stay in your corner.

Chagny: Burgundian roofs, enormous lorries lined up in front of a lorry-drivers' restaurant, seventeen kilometres to Chalon.

God, how had she managed to scare herself with such drivel? Take Caravaille, for instance. Did she really believe that, magically returned from Switzerland, he would rush to the police so the world would know that he had reform-school material among his personnel? Worse still, did she believe that he would have the nerve to make an issue of the thing in the face of Anita's huge merriment? Because this would be Anita's only reaction; she would imagine only too vividly her nervous little owl taking off to lead her own life at thirty kilometres an hour.

She had to get back. All she risked on her return was Caravaille saying, "Good to see you again, Dany, you look great, but you know, if everyone at the agency borrowed a car from me, I'd have to keep a fleet," and kicking her out. Not even that: she would have to explain or pay the price. He would ask politely for her resignation. All she would have to do would be to accept the offer that another agency made her every year, she would even get a pay rise out of it. Yes, you would, idiot.

The policeman knew her name. He, too, claimed to have seen her in the same place that morning. Well, there must be an explanation. If she had acted like a normal human being with him and the garage man, she would already know what it was. Now that she was rational, she was beginning to see. It was still not very clear, not absolutely all right, but if it was what she suspected, there was nothing about it that could scare a rabbit. She had a guilty conscience, that was all.

If people came close to her, if they raised their voices a little when they spoke to her, she lost her nerve. If they asked her to take off her glasses, she took them off. She had put herself into such a state of terror that if it had been her clothes the policeman had asked her to take off, she might have obeyed. Oh yes, she would have cried and pleaded. That's all she was good for.

And yet she knew how to stand up for herself, to defend herself, with violence even; she had proved it to herself more than once. As young as thirteen for instance, with Sister Mary of Pity, who had little of the virtue after which she had been named, especially when it came to other people's cheeks; she had slapped her right back one day with all her might. Even Anita who thought of her as an insect, had her to thank for the soundest beating of her life and for being thrown out of her room, bag and baggage. Afterwards of course, she had cried for days, but it was not for hitting Anita, it was for another reason, which was that never again would she be quite the same. And anyway if she had cried, she was the only one who knew about it. She was also the only one who knew that in less than an hour, and for no apparent reason, she could go from the most tranquil state of mind to the most paralyzing depression. Once in depression, she still knew from experience that she should be confident she would soon rise from her ashes like the phoenix. Other people, she was sure, must regard her as a quiet girl who was embarrassed about wearing glasses but who had character.

As she approached Chalon her hand began to hurt again. It must have been an unconscious attempt to close her fingers around the wheel, or the injection wearing off. It was not really pain yet, but she could feel her hand under the bandage. She had forgotten it.

In the light of her headlights huge billboards sang the praises of brands that were familiar to her. One of these was a mineral water that was on the account she worked on at the agency. It was not pleasant to find it in her path. She told herself that she would take a bath and go to bed. She would take the car back as soon as she had had some rest. If she did have character, now was the time to show it. She still had a chance to have the last word on those who claimed to know her: the hotel where the policeman was sending her, the Renaissance. A portentous name, because there the phoenix would be born again.

She was already certain that they would say they had seen her the night before. She was even certain that they would know her name. They would have to, since the policeman had phoned. But this time, instead of going to pieces, she would remember that she risked nothing for borrowing the car, and she would take the offensive. The Renaissance. Bring on the Renaissance! She felt a cold, delicious anger invade her. How had the policeman known her name? She had probably given it at the doctor's office or maybe even at the petrol station. Even though she was not talkative – or thought she wasn't – she leaked information wherever she went. Her mistake had been to connect the hurting of her hand with the rest, whereas the accident simply had not been a part of the – the word came to her, it was obvious – the joke. Someone was playing a joke on her, making fun of her.

Where had it started? At Deux-Soirs-lès-Avallon? With the old woman? No, it was before that, certainly. Before, she had met only a couple in a restaurant, shopkeepers, a lorry driver with a nice smile who had swiped a bouquet of violets and who . . . Oh, Dany, Dany, why don't you use your head for a change? The lorry driver, of course! If it was the last thing she did, she would find Toothpaste Smile again and give him what was coming to him.

At Chalon they had started to decorate the streets with red, white and blue paper flags and strings of little lights. She drove straight through the town to the quays of the Saône. Opposite, she saw islands, and on the biggest, a group of buildings that must be a hospital. She found a place to park beside the river, stopped the engine, and turned off her lights.

It was strange, this sensation she had of seeing and living all this for the second time. A boat in the black water. The lights of a café across the street. Even the Thunderbird, motionless and warm among the other cars lined up there on a summer's night in Chalon reinforced this impression that she knew what was about to happen. It must be the fatigue, the rawness of her nerves from the whole day, everything.

The next moment, taking off her scarf and shaking out her hair, she crossed the street, rediscovering the pleasure of walking. As she entered the brightly lit café, Barrière was singing about his life over the noise of the pinball machines, and customers were trying to talk about theirs through the din. She had to raise her voice too to ask the lady at the till how to get to the Hotel La Renaissance.

"Rue de la Banque, just keep on straight and then turn left, but I warn you, it's expensive!"

She ordered fruit juice but changed her mind. She needed a pick-me-up. She had a very strong cognac that burned her to the eyelids. Her glass was conical with pink pigs of all sizes painted on it. She felt like a little pink pig herself. The lady at the till must have understood what was going on in her head, for she gave a light, pleasant laugh and said, "Don't worry, go on, you're fine as you are."

Dany did not dare ask for a second cognac as she wanted to do. She took a bag of pretzels from the counter and munched one as she looked for a Bécaud record on the jukebox. She played "*Seul sur son étoile*", and the cashier told her that that song had a strange effect on her too – here! – and she patted her heart.

When Dany went out into the night of Chalon the air was fresh on her face, and she walked for a moment. Standing by the river, she thought that she did not want to go to the Renaissance now. She wanted to throw the bag of pretzels that was in her right hand into the water – and she did. She wanted to eat spaghetti, she wanted to feel good, she wanted to be in Cannes or somewhere in the diaphanous dress that she had bought in Fontainebleau, or naked in the arms of a nice boy who would reassure her, who would be naked too, and whom she would kiss passionately. A boy like the first one, the one who had ruined the others for her, whom she had met at the age of twenty (from twenty to twenty-two to be precise). But he had had what they called a settled life, a wife whom he was still madly in love with, a kid she had seen pictures of – God, how tired she was! What time must it be?

She walked back to the Thunderbird. There were some of those plants that they call "angels" beside the quay. She used to blow on them when she was a child, and the white and weightless flowers would fly away. She picked one, but some people going by looked at her and she did not dare blow on it. She wished she would find an angel in her path, an angel of the masculine sex, without wings, but pretty and calm and amusing, the kind of angel Mama Supe did not trust, but who would hold her in his arms all night. And do you know what? The next day she would forget this bad dream, they would go to the Midi together with the Bird of Thunder. Stop it, you goose.

She had never had much luck with prayers, but when she opened the door of the Thunderbird, she almost screamed. Angel or not, there he was in the car, a total stranger, rather tall, rather dark, rather disreputable-looking, comfortably settled on the seat beside the wheel with a filter cigarette in his mouth – from the packet she had left on the dashboard – his legs up, the soles of his moccasins against the windscreen, listening to the radio, probably the same age as she; in light coloured trousers, a white shirt and a crew-neck sweater. He looked her up and down with big black eyes and said in a flat but not unpleasant voice, as if slightly annoyed, "You took your time! Let's hit the road!"

Philippe Filanteris had at least one of the cardinal virtues. He knew that the world would cease to exist at the moment of his death, and that, consequently, other people were of absolutely no importance, even if he racked his brain to find a reason why they should be; that they were there to furnish him with what he needed, and that it was really ridiculous to rack his brain for anything anyway, since the mental effort might put a strain on the heart and shorten the time – sixty or seventy years – that he hoped to live.

As of yesterday he was twenty-six. He had been raised by the Jesuits. The death of his mother a few years ago was the only event in his life that had really caused him pain, and it still did. He had work as a copy boy for an Alsatian newspaper. In his pocket were a boat ticket for Cairo via Alexandria, a radio contract, and no money to speak of. In his opinion women, who are inferior by birth and do not usually require great mental effort of one, were the most desirable companions for a boy like him, who had to eat twice a day, make love occasionally, and get to Marseille before the fourteenth of the month.

Yesterday, on his birthday, he had been in Bar-le-Duc. He had been brought there in a Citroën by a teacher from near Metz, a great admirer of Liz Taylor and Mallarmé, who was going to visit her parents in Saint-Dizier in the Haute Marne. It was afternoon. It rained, then the sun came out, then it rained again. They had made a detour and parked behind an abandoned sawmill and then it had happened; it had never happened to her before, it was awkward and rather sordid on the back seat, an ugly memory. But she had been happy. She had hummed all the way to Bar-le-Duc, and had wanted him to leave his hand between her legs as she drove. She was twenty-two or twenty-three, she said that she was engaged but that she was going to break it off without hurting anyone, that it was the happiest day of her life, things like that.

In Bar-le-Duc she had left him in a brasserie after giving him thirty francs for dinner. She was supposed to have met him there around midnight after seeing her parents at Saint-Dizier. He had eaten sauerkraut and read *France-Soir*, and then jumped onto a bus with his suitcase. He had stopped for coffee outside the town in rather a nice hotel with a big wood-burning fire in the dining room and waitresses in black dresses and white aprons. After hearing them mention going to Moulins that night, he had made the acquaintance of a shapely fortyish brunette with very white skin and her brother-in-law, a notary in Longuyon. They were finishing dinner. He had said the first thing that had come into his head, that he was planning to devote himself to delinquent youth, that he had just got a job in Saint-Etienne.

As far as he could judge, the woman was nobody's fool. She smoked a cigarette after her strawberries and cream, visibly preoccupied. He had concentrated on the brother-in-law, who was stout, red-faced, and wore a loud summer shirt. He had told him that he had not realized that notaries were so modern. On the stroke of eleven they had all piled into a rather decrepit black Renault, and they were off.

By one o'clock in the morning he knew their life stories: the family property that they had been foolish enough to sell, the grandfather who made an ill-natured invalid, the lady's husband and the other brother in Moulins whom they were going to see. The notary had stopped to take a nap and Philippe and she had got out of the car and stood by the side of the road smoking vile English cigarettes. Stretching herself on tiptoe, she said that in the country when the weather was fine and everything was asleep, she felt young. They started down a dirt path that must have led to a farm. She stopped to identify some flowers in the darkness. He could tell from her voice, which trembled a little, that she had a lump in her throat, that she was out of control and full of ideas.

He screwed her under a clump of trees, after an insane amount of time had been spent finding a place that suited him, kneeling because she did not want to get her skirt dirty; wondering every time she began to come if she was going to have an attack and, limp as she was, end up rigid in his arms. She kept gasping out improbable and slightly disgusting comments – that it was the first time she had done anything like this, that he must not think ill of her, that she was all his – and once the desire he had had for her gleaming

82

white buttocks had passed, he was actually a little disgusted. Afterwards, as she straighened her clothes, she had asked him if he loved her. As if it hadn't been obvious.

In the car the brother-in-law was still asleep. They had woken him up. Since Thérèse – that was her name – wanted Philippe to sit next to her in the back, he must have had some idea of what had gone on, but he said nothing. Later, as they came into Beaune, she had fallen asleep. Philippe had made a sound as he opened her handbag and the good man, slowing down, had announced in a weak voice, "You are younger and stronger than me but please don't. I would defend myself, and one of us would get hurt." Philippe had closed the bag again and got out of the car. Thérèse had not woken up.

He still had a little over ten francs, his suitcase, and a great need to sleep. He had walked through the deserted town, following the sound of the trains to find the station. He had slept in the waiting room, uncomfortably. At about eight o'clock he had shaved in the gents, had coffee, and bought a packet of cigarettes. Then he had decided that in his case economy should be encouraged, and he had returned the cigarettes.

At the end of the afternoon he had taken a bus to Chalon-sur-Saône. He was broke, but it would really be bad luck if he did not get a lift on Route six. But it had been bad luck and even worse. He had hung around the whole afternoon in avenue de Paris and rue de la Citadelle without finding anyone, not even the price of a drink. He had no taste for professional robbery with violence. As long as he still had a little time left – he gave himself until midnight – he preferred to avoid lorry drivers and all other male victims. You start out by playing the honest medical student for the sake of a wallet, and you end up in a courtroom. Besides, though it may be simple and even advisable to rough a woman up a little, with

83

a man you really have to beat him up, if he is out of your class, literally smash him in the balls. Skulls are fragile and so is the rest. It's not worth smashing a skull just to get a wallet.

If it had been morning and any other day besides Saturday, he would have gone into a housing project and found some tired, misunderstood and politically minded housewife whose husband was at work and whose kids were at school, and he would have interviewed her for *Le Progrès de Lyon* right into the conjugal bed. Afterwards she would have explained that she had lost her purse at the corner shop. Or else he could have gone to the corner shop himself and hustled a salesgirl, but on Saturday afternoons they were overworked, they had their heads full of mistakes in arithmetic and the stupidity of customers, he didn't have a chance.

By five o'clock, after talking to some Belgian tourists who, unfortunately, were on their way home, he told himself that this time he had had it, that he would end up bumping off a father of four, the whole bit. Before catching his boat in Marseille on the morning of the fourteenth he intended to go to Cassis. He knew a man from Metz who kept a garage there and who could fix his engine, as it were. Today was the eleventh. At the rate he was going he wouldn't get to Marseille before the end of the month.

He had an idea, not inspired, but at least it was better than nothing: the kids coming out of school. He combed the streets and was beginning to drag his feet before he realized that summer holiday had already begun, and the schools were deserted. But he did find a vocational training class for young ladies, with waiting mothers. What annoyed him most was his suitcase. He looked like a bum.

When the chicks flew the coop, the sun was shining in his eyes over a factory roof and he had trouble choosing the one he was looking for. She was a tall blonde with a heavy body, a spectacular laugh and voice, and some books tied with a leather strap under her arm. On principle he decided that she was sixteen, because he would have felt vaguely ashamed if she were younger than that. Forward, march. She was surrounded by friends whom she left at street corners after long confabs. He learned first that her name was Grandchamp and then that it was Dominique. She had noticed that he was following them. Every so often he caught her gaze, which was blue-eyed and stupid, and fell onto his suitcase.

At last she was alone, near a stadium in rue Garibaldi. He caught her by the arm, called her Dominique, and said that he was a human being, that she must listen to him. Then, as she was terrified, he let go of her, and went and sat down on a little wall that ran around a football field. It took thirty seconds for her to come over to him. Without looking at her he said that he had always loved her, that he hated her at the same time, that he had just got into a fight and lost his job because someone had laughed at him over her, and that before he left he had to tell her how he had felt ever since he had first seen her, even if she laughed at him too – whatever came into his head. He looked at her then. She was standing there flustered and blushing, but she was no longer afraid, and as he patted the wall beside him to indicate that she should sit down, he wondered how much money she had on her or could get, and how much time he would have to waste getting it.

She had two ten-franc notes and a five-franc piece a kind of good-luck piece – in the pocket of her blazer. She gave them to him three hours later in the hall of her apartment building, which was depressing and smelled of cabbage soup. She wept softly, called him Georges – the name he had given her – and kissed him with lips that were tense, clumsy, and tear-stained. It had felt to him something like a massacre. He was annoyed that it should have been a massacre that took so much ammunition. He promised never to leave, to wait for her the next afternoon in front of some monument or other that he pretended to know. When she walked up the stairs and turned to him once more with the look of a poor idiot who believes in happiness, he said to himself that, for Christ's sake, nobody had ever given him any handouts either, that his shit of a father had played his mother for a fool all her life, and she was still his mother, wasn't she? To hell with it.

He bought himself a hamburger in a snack bar on a quay, looking out of the window at the night. He stayed for a long time because it would cost more to go anywhere else and because he knew from experience that after dark you have to know how to wait, to sit still and stick it out, that if you move, you miss your chance. He saw the white Thunderbird on the quay at about eleven, as he was eating another hamburger and drinking another quarter-bottle of wine. Inside he saw only a green or blue scarf, but at the back, the Paris number plate. He told himself that it was about time.

When he went outside, the young woman was getting out of the car. She was tall and dressed in white. She took off her scarf and her golden hair shone under the lamp beside the river. She wore a bandage on her left hand. She crossed the street and went into a café a little further on. He liked her walk, which was ladylike and loping at the same time.

Before going to look in the café, Philippe crossed the street and walked around the car to see if there was anyone else in it; it was empty. He opened the door next to the steering wheel. The inside smelled of the lady's perfume. He found a packet of filtered Gitanes on the dashboard, took one, lit it with the lighter, and checked the glove compartment. The suitcase in the back contained two pairs of nylon lace panties, a light-coloured dress, a pair of trousers, a bikini, and a nightdress that also smelled of the lady's perfume; all the other things smelled new. He put his own suitcase in the car just in case.

In the café, which he was content to watch from where he sat, she chose a record on the jukebox. She was eating a pretzel. He noticed that her dark glasses reflected the light strangely. Short-sighted. Twenty-five years old. Awkward with her right hand. Married, or involved with some guy who could afford to give her a Thunderbird for Christmas. When she bent over the jukebox he saw that the cloth of her skirt revealed the outline of round, firm buttocks and long thighs, but also that she had dirt on her in several places. Her hairdo was conservative, she had a small mouth and a small nose. As she talked to the red-hot mama who was minding the till, he also saw that she had troubles, or a trouble, for she had a sad smile. The men – in fact, all the customers – stared at her surreptitiously, but she was not aware of it. She was listening to a Bécaud song, which he could hear through the glass. It told her that she was alone on her star. Recently rejected! That kind was hard to find.

She wasn't rich, or at least she hadn't been rich for very long. He couldn't have said how he knew. Maybe because a rich girl wouldn't be stopping alone in Chalon at eleven o'clock at night – but why not? Or because of her suitcase, which contained very little besides a toothbrush. All he knew was that if she was what he thought, his luck had changed.

He sat down in the car and waited for her. He turned on *Europe I* and lit another cigarette. He saw her walk out of the café, cross the street, and stop by the river in the distance. As she came back, her strange and beautiful walk told him that she was a steady, sensible person, but also – something that encouraged him – that once that white suit was off she would love to be touched. He did not give her the ghost of a chance.

She started a little when she opened the car door and heard him reproach her for being late, but she gave no other indication of surprise. She sat down at the wheel, pulled her skirt down to cover her knees, and declared, as she looked in her bag for her keys, "Don't tell me you've seen me before. I'm sick of hearing it."

She had the most precise way of speaking that he had ever heard. She seemed to pronounce every letter of every word. For lack of anything better, he said, "Okay, you'll tell me about it on the way. Do you know what time it is?"

What bothered him most were her glasses. Two big black ovals which might be concealing anything. Her crisp voice: "Get out of my car."

"It's not your car."

"Really?"

"Really. I saw the papers in the glove compartment."

She shrugged her shoulders and said, "Be nice, will you? Get out now."

"I'm going to Cannes."

"Good for you. But get out. Do you know what I'll do if you don't get out?"

"You'll drive me to Cannes."

She did not laugh. She tapped him smartly on the legs because he had put the soles of his shoes against the windscreen. He took his legs down. She looked at him for a moment and then said, "I can't drive you to Cannes."

"You're breaking my heart."

"Exactly what do you want?"

"To see how this damn thing goes, for Christ's sake!"

She nodded her head as if to say okay and turned the ignition. He knew that it was not okay at all. He was not surprised to see her make a skillful turn and drive back towards the centre of the town. He told himself that she was perfectly capable of taking him to a police station without saying a word, but no, he decided, that wasn't her style.

She turned left into a street, stopping to look at the sign. She craned her neck, which was very slender, and a car coming from the other direction had to stop too. The driver swore through the window. Neither she nor Philippe answered, and they parked a little further on in front of a neon sign that said "Hotel La Renaissance". Naturally, a simple but conceited idea came into his head, but he dismissed it.

"Shall I stay in the car or come in with you?"

"Oh, do whatever you like."

He got out and joined her on the pavement. He was a head taller than she was. He told her stupidly that if she continued to use the familiar *tu* with him, he would use it with her too.

"Go ahead. I'll wake up all of Mâcon."

"We're not in Mâcon yet, this is Chalon-sur-Saône."

"Precisely: they'll hear me from here."

She looked up at him, indifferent, sure of herself, with the air of a girl who has been around, but at the same time he had the almost physical certainty that he would have her in his arms this very night, that he would get to know her eyes, that they would be together in broad daylight the next day. She did not push the glass door. She must have been thinking the same thing as he, because suddenly, without taking her eyes off him but in a different voice, as if she were tired, she said, "I won't put up a fight, come on."

And then she went in.

Inside there was a scene that he had some trouble making sense of. First the young woman questioned an elegant gentleman sitting behind the manager's counter, and then his wife, who came and joined them. A room had been reserved for her by telephone. Her name was Longo. She asked whether she had spent the previous night at the hotel. The people were embarrassed or confused; they looked at each other stupidly.

"But after all, mademoiselle, you must know that yourself!"

They had not seen her. It was the night watchman who had checked her in, but tonight being Saturday, he was off. The young woman replied, "Really? How easy it is."

"Wasn't it you who came last night?"

"That's what I'm asking you."

Philippe stood beside her, toying unconsciously with an ashtray he had picked up from the counter, pushing it around a spherical pen holder. The gesture might have annoyed her, for without looking at him she placed her right hand on his arm and left it there. Its gentle pressure was almost sisterly. Her fingers were very long and delicate, the fingernails short and unpolished. Secretary, thought Philippe. She was saying that if she really had spent the night here, there must be a card, a name on the register.

"We have your card, we told the policeman when he called. Let's see, you arrived very late, it would be with today's . . ."

The proprietress, who was beginning to lose patience, was rummaging through some papers on a shelf under the counter. She placed a little white card in front of the young woman, who glanced at it only once without picking it up.

"That's not my writing."

The man broke in at once. "Why should it be your writing when it was the night watchman who filled it out? It seems that you told him that you were left-handed, and you had a bandage on your left hand. You still do. Isn't it true that you are left-handed?"

"Yes, it is."

He picked up the card himself and read it in a voice that trembled a little.

"Longo. Danielle Marie Virginie. Age twenty-six. Profession advertising. Coming from Avignon. Residence Paris. Nationality French. Isn't that you?"

Now it was her turn to seem confused. "Coming from Avignon?"

"That's what you told the watchman."

"That's ridiculous."

The man held up his hands without answering. It wasn't his fault if she said things that didn't make sense. Philippe took in his own hand the warm one that was scratching at the sleeve of his sweater. "You've never been here before?" he asked her gently.

"I certainly haven't! Their story is perfect!"

"We can find the night watchman if you like."

She looked at him for a few seconds. Then she shrugged her shoulders, said it wasn't worth it, and walked away. She opened the glass door without saying goodbye.

"You're not taking the room?" the proprietress demanded in a shrill voice.

"Oh, yes," she said. "Just as I did yesterday. I'll sleep somewhere else, but I'll be here. I do it to make myself interesting."

In the car she lit a cigarette and exhaled the smoke wearily, preoccupied. Philippe decided that it was best not to say anything. After two good minutes she started the engine, drove through several streets, and took him back to the quay where he had found her.

"I'm not going to drive tonight. I can't take you to Cannes. I've wasted your time and I'm sorry, but that's the way it goes."

She leaned over briskly and opened his door. He did not try to take her by the shoulders, let alone to kiss her; he would have gained nothing but a slap on both cheeks, and when you're not in a position to return the compliment, getting slapped on both cheeks doesn't do much for you. Instead he said that he wasn't going to Cannes, that he had lied.

"That's not very nice."

"I have to be in Marseille on the fourteenth, to catch a boat for Guinea." (Another lie.)

"Send me a post card. Now, please get out."

"I have a work permit for Guinea. Jetplanes. I took a course when I was in the service. I can tell you a lot of things about jetplanes. You'll learn something, you know."

"What's your name?"

"Georges."

"And what are you, a gypsy or a Spaniard?"

"Half-gypsy, half-Breton. I come from Metz. I can tell you a lot of things about Metz."

"I'm allergic to travelogues. Is it true, the story about jetplanes?"

He raised his right hand, went through the motion of spitting on the ground, and said, "They need technicians."

"I thought they only hired Chinese."

He elongated his eyes with his two index fingers. "I'm a little Chinese, too."

"I assure you, I'm going to stop to sleep. For a long time."

"I can wait for you in the car."

"That wouldn't do."

"I can sleep with you, of course."

"That's impossible, I move around, I kick. But there are plenty of cars going down! Do you want some advice?"

"I'm over twenty-one."

She shook her head, sighed, and started the Thunderbird. Philippe told her that tomorrow, if she liked, he could drive. It must be awkward with her hurt hand. She replied that between now and tomorrow she would certainly find a way of getting rid of him.

Outside the town she parked in the garden of a hotel with God knew how many stars. It was full of cars with Paris or foreign number plates. She got out, but he stayed where he was.

"Don't you have money to pay for a room?"

"No."

"Have you eaten?"

"I was in the middle of dinner. You took away my appetite."

She took a few tentative steps towards the lighted porch. Through the huge open windows one could see a few late diners at a table. She stopped and walked back to the Thunderbird. "Well, are you coming?"

He joined her; she was tall, tired, blonde, and beautiful. She asked for and got, a room with bath for herself and a room for him on the next floor up. In the lift he said, "I could do with a bath myself."

"What did you say? Tomorrow morning I'll lend you mine. I'll even scrub your back if you like. Now are you satisfied?"

He followed her into a big room with drawn curtains. A man in a blue apron was at their heels carrying their luggage. When she saw Philippe's suitcase, she was stunned.

"That's not mine. Did you find it in the car?"

"It's mine!" said Philippe.

"Well, you were pretty sure of yourself, weren't you?"

She gave the man a tip – it took some time because of her hand – and asked him to order a cold supper for two in the dining room. She would be down in fifteen minutes. Once he had gone, she gave Philippe's suitcase a little kick and pointed to the open door.

He left her alone. It was past midnight, but downstairs you could hear the loud laugh of a night owl. The room they had given him was smaller and much less prepossessing than hers, and it looked onto the garden. He considered the

Thunderbird down in the dark, opened his suitcase, washed his face and brushed his teeth. He decided that he would be overdoing it if he changed his clothes. After forcing himself to read the rules of the hotel posted on the door to kill time, he left.

When he walked into her room without knocking she was standing, barefoot, in white panties and bra, carefully laying her damp suit over two chairs near the window. She wore glasses with colourless lenses and steel rims that showed more of her face – which he much preferred – and her body was as he had imagined, lithe and luscious. She asked him whether he saw a cut-glass vase near the door to the bathroom. He said that he did.

"If you don't get out this minute, I'll break it over your head."

He went down to wait for Miss Four-eyes in the dining room. She joined him wearing the turquoise trousers he had seen in the suitcase, which revealed her figure shamelessly, and she had put her barbaric sunglasses back on.

He wasn't hungry. He watched her opposite him, bare-armed, digging her spoon into a chilled melon. He cut her meat into little pieces. She talked in a slow voice, a little sadly. She ran an advertising agency. She was going to meet some friends in Monte Carlo. She told him a jumbled story full of people who recognized her everywhere as someone they had seen the day before, and he noticed that she was not using the familiar *tu* any more.

When he more or less understood her adventure, he burst out laughing. It was a good move. He realized at once that she was grateful to him.

"It strikes you as funny, too, doesn't it?"

"Sure. Someone was having fun with you. Where did you meet your lorry driver with the violets?"

"Just before getting on to the main road to Auxerre."

"He must use Route six all the time and know people all over the place. He rang them all up. It was a practical joke."

"But what about the policeman? Do you think a policeman would take part in such nonsense?"

"Probably a friend or relation of the garage owner. Anyway, why not? Do you think it takes much brains to be a policeman?"

She was looking at her bandage. She had the same expression on her face as when he had watched her through the window of the café in Chalon. The other diners had left. Philippe said that sometimes a joke misfired, that she may have struggled violently when they tried to scare her at the petrol station, that she could have hurt herself. Or she might have fainted and fallen onto her left hand.

"I've never fainted in my life."

"There's always a first time."

She nodded. He saw that she only wanted to be reassured. It was almost one o'clock. If they kept on talking about this ridiculous business he would never get her into bed. He told her that it was all over, that her tormentors would be only too pleased if they knew that she was still thinking about it. "What does your smile look like?"

She showed him, visibly making an effort to forget her afternoon, but was she forgetting her hand, which must be hurting her? This pain could be a serious handicap to him. Her teeth were small, even, and very white, with a tiny space between the middle two.

He asked carefully, "And your eyes, could I see them too?"

She nodded, but her smile vanished. He reached over the table and took off her glasses, and she submitted without moving, without trying to adjust her vision, which was dim and reflected only the lights. Then, because he had to break

95

the silence, he said with a constriction in his throat, "How do I look now?"

She could have answered, fuzzy, distorted, like a Picasso, or like a free-loader, anything at all to defend herself. Instead she replied, "Please kiss me."

He motioned for her to lean forward. She obeyed. He kissed her very gently. Her lips were warm and still. He put her glasses back on. She looked at the tablecloth. He asked, still with that surprising constriction in his throat, how many vases there were to break in her room. She smiled very briefly, as if she were laughing at herself, and promised him in a different, softer voice, that she would be good. Then she looked up suddenly and he saw that she wanted to say something but couldn't. All she said was that he was her favourite Chinese-gypsy-Breton from Metz.

In the room, where a low lamp cast a big star on the ceiling, she let him undress her holding onto his neck with her right hand while she had her sweater on, and he kissed and caressed her for a long time on the bed before he had the patience to take it off, and for a long time too before turning down the sheet, and for a long time too before taking off his own clothes, without leaving her, supporting her first with one arm and then with the other, her blonde hair sweeping his cheek, and then she murmured softly against his shoulders, he felt her pleading breath against his skin and her heart beating and her eyelashes closing over her pleasure.

Later she kissed his naked back, which was long and beautiful. He was sleeping with his head on his right arm. She turned out the light without disturbing him and went to sleep herself. She felt as if she woke up every hour, all night, but it might have been simply that she kept her lips on the boy's shoulder in her sleep, that she knew that he was there. Then it was day, and a blue light came into the room through the curtains, and it was he who was looking at her, she knew it before she opened her eyes. Mouth to mouth, warm against her, he murmured, Dany, Dany, how are you? She laughed, a real laugh. And then he went back to sleep. He was aware of a desire to brag, but his eyes closed, his head was already in the clouds.

Very carefully she managed to slip out of his arms. She put on her colourless glasses and ran her bath slowly with the door closed. She did not recognize her face in the mirror. Except for the shadows under her eyes, it did not show any signs of strain, and yesterday's sun had even given her some colour. On her way to the bathroom she had picked up the clothes that were lying on the carpet. She hung up the trousers, shirt, and grey sweater of – what was his name again? Georges. She felt the presence of a wallet in one pocket, and she had the odious idea to look in it, but she dismissed it easily.

Just because you have acted like a tramp doesn't mean you have to lower yourself to the level of the unfortunate wife. Actually there was only one thing she wanted to know.

She wrapped herself in a towel, went back into the room, bent over him, and woke him up enough to ask if it was really true that he was disappearing forever on the fourteenth. He said no, that he had only been teasing her, good night. She made him swear that he didn't have a boat to catch. He raised his right hand a few inches from the pillow; said, I swear, you're already trying to get rid of me, and went back to sleep.

She took her bath and ordered coffee, talking softly into the telephone. She went to the door to take the tray from the chambermaid, and gave her the now dry suit to iron. She drank two cups of tasteless liquid, contemplating the familiar stranger lying in her bed. Then she couldn't stand it any more. She locked herself into the bathroom and went through the wallet. His name was not Georges, but Philippe Filanteris, he was born in Paris, and he was exactly six days younger than she was. She was happy to learn that they were born under the same sign of the zodiac – at least their horoscopes would not contradict each other – but she could not help feeling panicky when she saw that he actually had booked a passage on a boat. He was leaving on the fourteenth (eleven o'clock, Quai de la Joliette), not for Guinea but for Cairo via Alexandria. It served her right, she shouldn't have looked.

She ran a bath for him and ordered a big breakfast, which he consumed with relish in the bathroom. She sat by him on the edge of the bath, wrapped in her towel, and now and then he planted a kiss on her thigh, relaxed, his hair glistening, with big black soulful eyes, unbelievable eyelashes, and long muscles that protruded beneath the skin. She rationalized as well as she could. He didn't have a soul, and if he hadn't met her it would have been someone else. So which did she prefer? She also told herself – God, it was already Sunday, the twelfth – that he might change his mind before his ship sailed, that even boys don't make love without feeling something: wishful thinking.

He picked up the phone and asked for the suitcase he had left in the other room. He took out a light summer suit, a little rumpled, and put on a black tie. He said that he did not want to wear any other colour because of his mother, who was dead. Then he helped her dress. He asked her to keep her colourless glasses on, and she pretended that it was impossible, that she could only see short distances in them. He answered that he would drive. She kept them on. When she was ready, he held her in his arms for a long time by the door, lifting the skirt of her suit to caress her thighs, kissing her with lips that tasted of coffee, saying that he could hardly wait until their next room.

It had rained during the night and the top and body of Bird of Thunder were spangled with big shining drops. They drove through Tournus, where the sun awaited them, then Mâcon, where the bells were ringing for high mass. She told him that if he liked she would not go to meet her friends in Monte Carlo, but would stay with him until his boat left. He repeated that he had no boat to catch.

After Villefranche, with the top down, he turned off into a road that avoided Lyon. It wound between banks of rock, they passed almost nothing but heavy lorries. He obviously knew the road. He must have been over it several times. As they came to Tassin-la-Demi-Lune she thought of the couple she had met in the restaurant by the road before Fontainebleau, and that suddenly reminded her of the adventure of the day before. Although nothing could have been more unreal, she felt anxiety stir in her again. She moved closer to him and put her head on his shoulder for a moment, and it passed.

He talked little and asked a lot of questions. She dodged the embarrassing ones as well as she could – whose car was it, who was waiting for her in Monte Carlo? She gave a vague description of her "advertising business" – it was the agency minus Caravaille. She concentrated on memories of the orphanage, and he laughed every time she mentioned Mama Supe. He found the old woman amusing, he would have liked her. Of course it was hardly imaginable that the nun would have reciprocated; one never knew, Dany said. But deep inside her, Mama Supe was saying, "If I were alive he would not be so pretty to look at, believe me, and it would not be to punish him for your lapses, but for the way he is going to hurt you. And first of all tell him not to go so fast, you'll both be killed in a state of sin, and in a car that doesn't belong to you."

After Givors they crossed the Rhône and found the National Route seven, which followed the river through some little towns in their Sunday best: Saint-Rambert d'Albon, Saint-Vallier, Tain-l'Hermitage. They stopped for lunch a few kilometres from Valence.

The sun was hotter, the accents more southern, Dany was holding, with all her strength in face and gesture, onto something irrepressible which must be happiness. They had their table in a garden, as had been her wish yesterday; she even found spaghetti on the menu. He told her about places she admitted not knowing, where they could make love that night, swim and make love again the next day, for as long as she liked. She chose Saintes-Maries-de-la-Mer, with raspberries, because that seemed right for a gypsy, even a false one who was not very Catholic.

He left her alone for a few minutes to ring "a friend". When he came back she sensed that he was preoccupied. After that his smile was not the same. As she paid the bill she saw that he had not called Metz or Paris; it had been much more expensive. Because she was so clumsy with her right hand she could not conceal the fact that she was taking her money out of a pay envelope; but he did not ask questions, he may not even have noticed. She was annoyed with herself for not having foreseen this, instead of using what little brain she had to go through a wallet.

They drove through Valence, which was a sunny town with tall plane trees. They came to another and more luminous town, which was soon more familiar than the others she had known. Down below the road, the Rhône was drying up between tongues of sand, and beyond Montélimar the earth, the rock, and the trees seemed parched by the sun.

Her left hand was no longer painful, but it made keeping her arm on the boy's shoulder uncomfortable. He drove fast, with an attentive profile that she would always remember. She lit his cigarettes for him, sometimes taking them back for a few seconds so she could smoke the one he was smoking. She liked the places where he was forced to slow down, because he would turn his head and kiss her, or lay a reassuring hand between her legs.

Orange: the long, straight road under the plane trees after they had avoided Avignon; a bridge with several lanes over the Durance. He had unbuttoned his shirt to the waist. He talked about cars (Ferrari), horses (Gélinotte, Sea Bird), films (*Lola Montez, Jules et Jim*), but never about himself. She continued to call him Georges. They stopped in a brasserie in Salon and had a drink at the bar while the tank was being filled. His hair was sticking to his forehead as it had when they had made love, and so was hers. They laughed at the same time without saying anything because they were thinking the same thing.

They drove another ten or twenty kilometres, but he went more slowly and kissed her more often, and his hand under her skirt became more insistent. She told herself that she was in for it. Nothing like this had ever happened to her in a car and her heart raced a little.

It was not exactly what he had had in mind. He took a short cut that led to Miramas, but stopped the Thunderbird by the side of the road and asked her to get out. They walked through a pine forest amid a deafening chorus of grasshoppers, and when they reached the top of a hill they saw Lake Berre, motionless as a huge spot of sunlight in the distance.

Dany's mind was a jumble. She was hot. She was ashamed. She was afraid. She did not know what she was afraid of, but when they left Bird of Thunder an image had come into her mind as in an over-exposed film, an image that she did not recognize. It was her room, or maybe the one she had been given at Caravaille's house. Anyway, Anita was in it, not the Anita of today, but the Anita she had deserted one night a long time ago, so long that she should be allowed to forget, the Anita who had lost her soul at dawn, whom she saw cry for the first time, and whom she had beaten and thrown out – Why didn't those grasshoppers shut up?

He made her sit beside him on a big rock covered with dry moss. He opened the jacket of her suit, as she had expected him to do, as she was even prepared for him to do, so she wouldn't act like an outraged idiot, but after caressing her through her bra, he left her alone. He asked her a question, but in such a low voice that she could hardly hear. Actually she had understood perfectly, he did not repeat his question. What she did not understand was why he was asking it, for it did not correspond with his personality, or why suddenly she no longer recognized his closed face, his shifting eyes. He wanted to know how many men she had belonged to before him – that was the expression he had used.

She answered, only one. He shrugged his shoulders.

She said that the others did not count. He shrugged his shoulders. She said that there had been two others, but that it was true that they did not count.

"Then tell me about the first."

"I don't want to talk about it."

She tried to button her suit jacket with her right hand, but he would not let her.

"When was it?"

"A long time ago."

"Did you love him?"

"I still do."

She knew from the turn the conversation was taking that it was a mistake, but she couldn't help saying it, she couldn't deny everything.

"Was it he who chucked you?"

"Nobody chucked anybody."

"Well, why didn't you get married and have a lot of kids?"

"Bigamy is against the law."

"There is such a thing as divorce."

"No, as a matter of fact, there isn't."

She saw his expression, which was almost spiteful. She caught his arm instinctively with her bandaged hand, and said softly, "And there was another reason. He already had a child."

"How long did it last?"

"Two years."

"What is his name?"

"Please."

"What is his wife like?"

"Very nice. I never met her."

"How do you know she's nice?"

"I know."

"Have you seen him since?"

"Yes, yes, yes! Twice!" (She was losing her temper too, it was too stupid, and she couldn't get her jacket buttoned.) "Do you want the dates? The eleventh of September two years ago, and the seventeenth of August last year! All right?"

"And he still didn't chuck his wife! She wasn't a spare! She wasn't a piece you pick up in Chalon and drop two hours later! Right?"

It was too horrible to hurt her as much as he must have thought it did. What hurt her was that she did not understand why he was ruining everything this way, why he had deliberately started this senseless quarrel.

"Well, say it!"

"Say what?"

"That I'm a bastard!"

She declined. She took off her glasses because they were steamed up from the heat. She took a handkerchief out of her purse to wipe the lenses. Then she sat motionless with the glasses in her right hand, forcing herself not to think about anything. She felt his eyes on her, and then he said in an unrecognizable voice, "I'm sorry, Dany. I'm going to the car for cigarettes. It will give us time to calm down."

He bent over her and buttoned her suit jacket, and she felt a kiss on her mouth, a kiss as sweet as the one he had given her the night before, in the dining room of the hotel.

She had the same lips as then, warm and unmoving, and the same dark eyes. He left without turning around. He waited until he was in the trees before he started to run. From then on, the important thing was to move fast. She would not immediately be surprised not to see him come back. At first she would blame his lateness on the quarrel. He gave himself a quarter of an hour before she would notice that the car had disappeared. After that – he knew the area – it would take her a good thirty to forty minutes to reach a phone.

If he was mistaken, and the car really was hers, she would go directly to the police. He would have lost. It would take another ten minutes to alert the first policemen, but the first to be warned would be those on the motorway to the North and the roads leaving Marseille. They would have seen the Thunderbird go by, it was impossible not to notice it. They would catch him red-handed on the road to Cassis.

An hour, at best; it wasn't enough. He was gambling everything on the certainty that Dany Longo would not go to the police, not immediately. The story she had told him at dinner last night made no sense unless she was hiding something herself. When someone hurts your hand, you make a complaint. When a policeman tells you he saw you that morning and it's not true, you don't just accept it.

There were plenty of other peculiar things about Miss Four-eyes. The pay envelope in her handbag. And above all that impression she had given him consistently of being two people at once: one rather shrewd, lively, and confident, the other neurotic and masochistic. She talked in her sleep. All she said was a name – Mama Supe – and a short phrase that had really worried him, something that sounded like "kill me". She had said it only twice, very close to his mouth, and he was not sure that he had heard right. There was something schizo about that girl.

He got into the Thunderbird, a little out of breath, put the key in the ignition, and started the engine at once. She certainly couldn't have heard through the screen of trees and the din of the grasshoppers. He made a silent U-turn, driving into the ditch on each side of the road because of the length of the car's body. Thinking that Dany's suitcase did not contain anything of interest to him, but that it might be an annoying burden to her, an additional loss of time, he took it, opened it, and threw it out of the car. The clothes scattered in the grass beside the road. A grotesque turquoise shape – the trousers she had worn the night before – caught his eye disagreeably. Telling himself that he was mad or worse, he got out, picked them up, rolled them into a ball, and was about to put them back into the suitcase, when he stopped short: she was standing there, he had not heard her come. Then he saw that it was only her white muslin dress, caught on some brambles. He hurled the trousers into the woods, got behind the wheel, and drove off.

It was four thirty by the dashboard, about the time he had stolen a big new Citroën here last summer in the same way. It had taken him an hour and fifteen minutes to get safely to Cassis, to the garage of Big Paul, his friend from Metz. The Thunderbird was more powerful than a Citroën and he would not make the various wrong turns he had made the first time. He could improve his time by five to ten minutes. He told himself a quarter of an hour to cheer himself up, but he knew that it was wishful thinking.

As he turned onto the main road he congratulated himself on not meeting a single vehicle on the side road where he had left Dany. There was a secondary road to Miramas less than two kilometres to the south which was better kept, wider, and more frequently used. It might take Miss Four-eyes longer than he had anticipated to find a lift.

He had never heard anything about the woman in the Citroën. He did not know how she had reacted. That was all to the good, of course, but he was a little sorry, because he might have been able to improve his plan this time, especially since he was taking more risks. The woman in the Citroën was married to a doctor from Arles: she had probably given the car up for lost to avoid a scandal. Philippe had met her in Roanne, where she had come to visit somebody at the old people's home. She was shy, plump, left almost a virgin by her husband, and so overcome by her first adultery that on the way – at Tarare, to be precise – she had bought a deluxe edition of *Madame Bovary*, high-class pornography in a cellophane wrapper. And with her he had shown no mercy. Under the trees on the hill he had taken off all her clothes and abused her in such a way that, unless he was an idiot, her doctor husband could not have mistaken the signs of her misfortune. Then he had knocked her down with a punch in the stomach, thrown her dress over her, and left. He had thrown her underwear, shoes and handbag (from which he had taken nothing but money) into a dustbin in Marseille.

This time he did not feel the same anxiety he had felt then, although he had neglected to take the same precautions. He had not had the heart to undress Miss Four-eyes, still less to hit her. All afternoon, after calling Big Paul, he had been convinced that he ought to, but at the last moment he had not been able to do it. He despised all women as greedy, self-centred, stingy creatures. The only exceptions to this rule were those endowed with some simplicity; they disgusted him less. There had been three times when he had even liked Dany Longo. At the door to the hotel when she had told him, "I won't put up a fight, come on." Then, when she had left her hand on his arm at the desk, as if he were her brother in a hostile world. Above all, it was when he had taken off her glasses at the table. Her face had been as vulnerable as the heart of his own mother, who had died unmarried at forty, her only comfort, lying at the foot of her hospital bed, her shit of a bastard son who could not have comforted a mangy street dog.

He had to forget Dany (Marie Virginie) Longo, he had done her enough favours. He was leaving her handbag so she could get along, a fight so she would stop believing everything she heard, and an hour to get revenge. She had her chance.

He raced along the motorway, which slopes down all the way to Marseille, drove around the bypasses, sped along the Aubagne main road. If it had been a weekday, there was a shorter route to Cassis through the Gineste pass, but on a Sunday afternoon too many people from Marseille were using it. He did not want to risk being held up by a column of slow-moving cars, or by an accident.

The hairpin bends of the Bédoule road, on and on through the pine woods. He thought about the unknown man whom Dany Longo still loved. He thought about her, in the light of a lamp that cast a star shape on the ceiling, lying in his arms on the bed, her legs and belly bare, still wearing the white sweater that he had thrown into the brambles. What did it mean to still love someone?

That was enough of *that*.

Last summer Big Paul had given him a hundred notes for the new Citroën. At noon today on the telephone he had offered him three hundred for the Thunderbird, but he had made him swear in code language that it was not some car he had picked up by the side of the road and driven off, and that the girl, like the first one, would be reluctant to make a complaint. He was perfectly willing to increase the automobile supply to the states of Black Africa as long as there was no risk to himself. Philippe agreed. At Pas-de-Belle-Fille, when he turned towards Cassis, some policemen watched him go by without reacting. It was five twenty. He began to have reasonable hopes of catching his boat on the fourteenth with pocket money, a virgin-pure record, and a first-class cabin just like anyone else.

Less than a quarter of an hour later his hopes were shattered. The Thunderbird was parked in front of the sea by the port, under the vast silhouette of Cap Canaille. He was leaning on the car with both hands, struggling with all his might to keep from throwing up. His life had just become a nightmare and he was alone under the sun, torn between rage and fear. As for his record, it was going to be violated. A lavish deflowering, in a class by itself, a blood-bath.

She collected her scattered garments and put them carefully into her black suitcase. She did not take the deserted road by which they had come. She climbed the hill again and, tearing open the paper bag her new sandals had come in, she spread it on the flat rock where they had sat. On it she wrote in lipstick in large shaky capitals with her right hand, TONIGHT 10 PM IN FRONT OF 10 CANBIÈRE. The name of this street was all she knew about Marseille, along with the fact that the people are liars like everyone else. She secured her message with a big rock. She knew it was absolutely useless, but she could not overlook anything, not even the possibility of the boy coming back after she had gone.

On the other side of the hill, five or six minutes later, she found a road that she had seen from above, over the trees. There were plenty of cars on it. The first to come along was a bright red Renault or Simca, which stopped. Inside were a man, a woman and a baby. She sat on the back seat, with her suitcase on her lap, beside the baby who was sleeping in a canvas cradle.

They let her out in front of a roadside stall on the main road outside Marseille. She forced herself to smile when she thanked them. She drank a glass of mineral water at the bar, and then showed the waiter the bill from the restaurant near Valence where she had had lunch. She asked him to get the restaurant on the telephone.

There was no phone booth. She had to talk in front of the other customers, who lowered their voices and listened. It must have been the proprietress who answered. Yes, she remembered the lady in the white suit and the young man who was with her. Yes, she also remembered that he had made a phone call at the end of the meal. He had called Cassis in Bouches-du-Rhône, but she did not know what had become of the slip of paper she had written the number on. She was sorry.

When she had hung up, Dany asked for a phone book for Bouches-du-Rhône. There was no listing in Cassis under the name of Filanteris. And yet she was certain she had read *"Cassis-sur-Mer"* as she was guiltily going through his wallet that morning. She did not remember anything else, except that it was printed, not written by hand. She thought of looking through the whole phone book, but she decided that she would be wasting her time.

She asked the waiter if any of his customers were going to Marseille. A man in shirt-sleeves with a blond moustache gave her a lift in his Renault. On the way he listed all the bars he knew in Paris. He had spent three months there during his military service. He let her out on a big sunny square that opened onto a garden and some long avenues which he called the Rond-Point du Prado. The city looked warm and pleasant to live in, once one was past the stretches of dirty suburb. He told her that she could get a bus to Cassis here. When he had gone, she read the schedule on the stop sign and saw that she had half an hour to wait. She walked across the square, carrying her suitcase and handbag in her right hand, and got into a taxi. The driver was an enormous red-faced man in a cap. He said, Poor her, it would be expensive. He understood that she did not feel like talking and started the car.

It was through the hairpin bends of Mount Gineste – she read the name at the top of the pass – that she got her first look at the Mediterranean, as blue as it was on the post cards, shimmering, extending to a horizon scarcely less blue; more beautiful than she had ever imagined. She forced herself to look away. They arrived in the village of Cassis at six thirty, a little over two hours after the Judas kiss she had received on the hill overlooking Lake Berre. The barefooted, barelegged crowd lining both sides of the main street was thicker than the one in front of the Galeries Lafayette. The driver sighed and said that on weekdays it was bad enough but that on Sundays it was a disaster.

She made him stop at the port, in front of boats and masts with multicoloured flags. When she paid for the ride and was standing on the street with her suitcase at her feet, dazed by the sun and the voices around her, the driver made a sweeping gesture and declared in a drawling voice, "Don't worry sweetheart, everything will work out, it's bound to!"

Before he had finished speaking she had looked all around what must be the heart of Cassis, and already seen the familiar, overwhelming white shape of the Thunderbird. It was more than two hundred yards away among some other cars parked in front of the beach, but she would have picked it out among a thousand, if only by the quickened beating of her heart. Her throat was so tight that she could hardly breathe, but what she felt was delightful, it was a kind of gratitude towards everything: Cassis, the sea, the sun, the big taxi driver, and herself, she who hadn't shed a tear, who had come straight where she had to come.

She walked the distance that separated her from Bird of Thunder like someone in a dream. All fatigue had vanished, she was crossing a stretch of empty space. Philippe Filanteris had left the top down. It did not look as if he had abandoned the car because of an accident. She put her suitcase on the back seat and looked around. She was in front of a wide boardwalk that ran along the beach, next to the port. She looked at people playing in the waves. She heard shouts and laughter. An enormous rocky mass hung over Cassis, perpendicular to the sea.

The keys were not in the ignition. She opened the glove compartment and found them there, along with the car registration. She got behind the wheel and for several minutes she tried to work out what had gone through the head of the boy from Metz who needed money but had not touched her purse, who had taken the car only to abandon it fifty or sixty kilometres later. She gave up. There must be a reason for all this, but it no longer interested her. Maybe he was somewhere in the village in his linen suit and black tie, maybe he would come back, but that did not interest her either. And then, suddenly something inside of her gave, she felt a loosening sensation in her chest, and she saw herself as she was, sitting here far from home, defenceless, stupid, alone, with one hand in a rigid armature. She began to cry.

"Want to play cards?" said a voice.

She had on her dark glasses, so the little boy who stood on the other side of the car door seemed even more tanned than he was. He was four or five years old. He was blond with big black eyes, very pretty, barefoot, and was wearing navy-blue stretch bathing trunks with big white stripes and a red towelling polo shirt. He held a buttered roll in one hand and a pack of miniature playing cards in the other. She dried her eyes.

"What's your name?"

"Dany."

"Want to play cards?"

"What's *your* name?"

"Titou," he said.

"Where is your mama?"

He made a vague gesture with his roll. "There, on the beach. Let me get in your car."

She opened the door and moved over so he could sit at the wheel. He was a very poised, very serious little man who did not much like answering questions. She learned, however, that his father had a blue car – his had a roof – and that he had found a sea urchin in the water and had put it in a glass jar. He taught her his card game, which was extremely complicated: he gave each person three cards and the one with the most face cards won. They played a trial game and he won. "Get it?" he asked.

"I think so."

"What shall we bet?"

"Do we have to bet something?"

"It's not interesting unless you do."

"What are you betting?"

"Me?" he said. "Nothing. You have to bet something. How about your glasses?"

He gave Dany three cards; choosing them carefully: two sevens and an eight. He took three kings for himself. She said that that was too easy, that she would deal. She dealt. He won again. She took off her glasses and put them on him, holding them at the sides because they skipped off his nose. He said that you saw all funny, that it wasn't interesting. She gave him a fifty-centime piece instead.

"Now eat your roll."

He ate two bites, watching her attentively as he did. Then he said, "Who is the man in your car?"

In spite of herself, she looked at the back seat.

"There isn't any man."

"Yes, there is," he said. "Where you put the luggage. You know."

She laughed, her heart sinking.

"What man?"

"The one who's asleep."

"What are you talking about?"

He did not answer right away. He ate his roll, staring through the windscreen with a melancholy expression, his head resting against the back of the seat. Then he gave a little sigh.

"I think he's asleep," he said.

The Glasses

Mama Supe.

One night in Roubaix I looked at her wrinkled face through a glass of Alsatian wine. We were across from the station. You could hear the train whistles.

Kill me.

Zurich: it was the eighth of October. Four years ago on the eighth of October. More trains. More rooms. Everything so light.

What did they used to say when I was little? Light is my hair, dark my eyes, black my heart, cold the barrel of my gun. I don't know what I'm saying any more.

I have seen so many cypress trees since yesterday. Provence is a cemetery. Here I shall sleep delivered, far from the blare of parties.

The Hotel Bella Vita, outside Cassis. A drop of water on my forehead in an alley. The freight yard in Marseille. The heights of Villeneuve, all those battlements. God, how I have searched, only to find myself.

My glasses were steamed up when I opened the boot and too dark for me to see inside. The seven o'clock sun slanting onto the boardwalk hit the front of the car, carving out a large chunk of shade. An appalling smell rose towards me from that horror in the dark.

I went back to the little boy named Titou. I asked him to give me my handbag and I changed my glasses. I could stand up, my hands hardly trembled. I did not think of anything. My mind was as if paralyzed.

I opened the boot again. The man was wrapped in a rug, barefoot, his legs bent. His head protruded from the thick red pile, wedged sideways against the side of the boot. I saw his open eye, his glossy hair, white at the temples, his almost translucent skin, stretched tightly over prominent bones. He was forty and he was ageless. I tried unsuccessfully not to breathe, I was suffocating. Reaching out with my bandaged hand, I drew aside a section of the rug and uncovered him. He was wearing a garment that must be a dressing gown, of light blue or green silk, with a darker kimono collar, which hung open, revealing a pallid chest. There were two neat but gaping holes between his bare breasts, and the blood that had flowed from the two wounds formed a black crust that had spread upward as far as the throat.

I closed the lid of the boot, swaying, sinking onto it. I was conscious of wanting to get up again, of struggling in the sun, I even felt the car's burning surface under my right hand and against my cheek. And then I realized that the little boy Titou was beside me and that he was frightened. I tried to tell him to wait a minute, that it was nothing, but I couldn't.

He was crying. I heard his sobs, and loud laughter far away on the beach. Some girls in bikinis were chasing each other down the boardwalk. Nobody paid any attention to us.

"Don't cry. It's all over, see?"

His playing cards were scattered on the ground. He choked back his sobs, his arms around my legs, his head in my skirt. I leaned down and kissed his hair several times, reassuring him.

"You see, I'm fine. I lost my balance because of my shoe."

Now that the boot was closed he probably could not smell the odour that was still making me sick, but I made him go to the front of the Thunderbird anyway. He demanded his cards and the fifty-centime piece I had given him. I picked them up. When I came over to him he was drawing circles on one bumper of the car with his index finger. He told me they were sea urchins.

I drew him to me, sitting on the boardwalk so his face would be on a level with mine, and asked him how he had seen inside the boot. I spoke very low, very softly, in a distant voice; it was probably easier for him to hear the beating of my heart.

"You couldn't open it yourself, could you? Who opened it?"

"The other man," said Titou.

"What other man?"

"The other one."

"The one who was driving my car?"

"I don't know."

"Did you look inside with him?"

"No, I was over there."

He pointed to a yellow Dauphine parked beside the Thunderbird.

"Was it a long time ago?"

"I don't know."

"Did you go and see your mama afterwards?"

He thought it over. I wiped the tearstains off his cheek with my fingers.

"Yes. Two times."

"The man who opened the boot didn't see you looking, did he?"

"Yes. He told me to beat it."

I was a little surprised, because I was expecting an answer to the contrary. Then, suddenly, everything went cold in the sunlight. I was certain Philippe had not left Cassis, that he was spying on us.

"He saw you? Are you sure?"

"He told me to beat it."

"Listen to me. What did he look like, this man? Did he have a tie? Did he have black hair?"

"He had a black tie. And a suitcase."

"Where did he go?"

He thought again. Then he shrugged his shoulders, like an adult, and made a vague gesture indicating the port, the village, anywhere.

"Come on, you must go back to your mama."

"Will you be here tomorrow?"

"Okay."

I dusted off the front of my skirt and led him by the hand over the boardwalk. He pointed out his mother, the youngest of a group of women in bikinis lying on the beach. She was blonde and very tanned, and was laughing with her friends amidst magazines and bottles of suntan oil. She saw her little boy and raised herself onto one elbow to call him. I kissed Titou and helped him down some steps. When he joined his mother I walked away. My legs felt as stiff as those of a mannequin in a shop window.

I did not want to go back to the car, to be near that man with the wounds in his chest. I could see only one reasonable thing to do: go to the police station. Anyway, I had to get away from the beach I told myself. If Philippe knows that little Titou saw the inside of the boot he must be worried; he has stayed in the wings to watch him. He may be there, watching me. I will force him to come out.

At the same time I found this argument absurd. If he had disposed of a body by putting it in a car he believed to be mine, it was because he did not care what I might say about it afterwards. Why would he have attached more importance to the testimony of a five-year-old child?

I walked along the port mingling with an indifferent crowd, my heart stopping whenever someone jostled me, then through deserted alleys that the sun had abandoned several hours before, where I was cold. Washing was drying in the windows. A drop of water that fell on my forehead when I stopped to look behind me made me start violently and almost scream. I had to accept the evidence though, nobody was following me.

Later, I asked for directions and found the police station on a little square edged with plane trees. From a distance I could see two men in uniform smoking in the doorway. I thought I could still detect the stale, terrible smell of the dead stranger in the Thunderbird on myself. I did not have the courage to go over. What could I say to them? "I took my boss's car; a boy I know nothing about stole it from me, I found it here with a body in the boot, I can't explain anything, but I am innocent." Who would believe me?

I waited for night in a pizzeria opposite the police station, sitting by a second-storey window. I hoped to recover a little calm and to work out what could have happened in the two hours Philippe had had the car to himself. It must have been something sudden and unexpected, for no hint of such an event had been in his face when he had left me. I was sure of it. Well, almost sure. And then I was not sure at all.

I ordered a cognac which made me nauseous when I brought it to my lips and which I did not drink.

If I walked across the square on the other side of the window, they would not release me until they had made an investigation, and that might take days, even weeks. My mind filled with a whole series of images: they would take me to Marseille prison, they would make me take off my clothes, they would give me the grey smock of those awaiting trial, they would take fingerprints, they would put me in a dark cell. They would also search my past, from which they would unearth only one crime, which was no doubt peculiar to many women, but it would be enough to humiliate my friends and the man I love.

I would not go.

What I most wanted to believe, I think, was that nothing of what was happening to me was true. Or at least, that something would happen all of a sudden, and it would no longer be true.

I remembered the first part of my baccalauréat examination, the night of the oral in Roubaix. The results were posted very late. I looked at the lists several times, but my name was not there. I walked the streets for hours with a tragic face, but with my heart full of a ridiculous hope: they had made a mistake, they would make it up to me. It was after ten o'clock when I went back to Mama Supe in her brother's pharmacy. She let me cry as I needed to and then she said, "We're going to go back and look at those lists, my eyes are better than yours." Together, in the middle of the night, in the deserted schoolyard, we struck one match after another, pouring over the results, looking for my name, knowing that it must be there, which, in the end, it was, I even had an honorable mention.

It was that night, in a restaurant near Roubaix station, after a supper at which we drank Alsatian wine "to celebrate," that I promised Mama Supe that I would talk to her as to a living person after she was dead. I always have, except at the time of my trip to Zurich, four years ago, because I was ashamed and I would have hated myself even more if I had taken refuge in her memory.

As I sat by the window of the pizzeria I thought about

her, about Zurich, and also about the son of the man I love, and of course about little Titou, who was not much more than four, and everything got mixed up. I remembered Anita's little girl and even the little girl at the petrol station in Deux-Soirs-lès-Avallon – what had her father said her name was? It occurred to me that these children in my path, with their faces and their toys – the bald doll, the card game – were so many signs of a monstrous punishment.

The woman who had brought me the cognac came over to my table. It must have taken me several seconds to become aware of her presence. As if she were repeating it, she said in a patient voice that came not from a distance but from another universe, "Excuse me, but are you Mademoiselle Longo?"

"Yes."

"You're wanted on the telephone."

"Me?"

"You are Mademoiselle Longo, aren't you?"

Since nothing else made sense, I don't know why I was surprised. I got up and followed her. As I crossed the room I became aware of what had been my surroundings for the past hour: the customers – there were a lot of them – the red-checked tablecloths, the smell of warm pasta and sweet marjoram. The phone booth was on the ground floor near the pizza oven, and the air was thin and oppressively dry.

His voice was different, but it was Philippe all right. "How much longer are you going to sit there, Dany? I've had it, I give up. Do you hear me?"

"Yes."

"We can do something, Dany."

"Where are you?"

"Nearby."

"Did you see me come here?"

"Yes."

"Please tell me where you are, Philippe."

He did not answer. I heard his breathing at the end of the line. I understood that he was afraid too. At last he said in a hissing voice that made the phone vibrate, "How do you know my name?"

"I looked in your wallet this morning."

"Why?"

"To find out."

"And what did you find out?"

It was my turn not to answer.

"Listen, Dany. If you do exactly as I tell you, we can meet."

"And if not?"

"If not, I'll go straight to that station you see opposite you! Do you hear me?"

"I hear you. I don't understand."

Another silence.

"Philippe?"

"Stop calling me that."

"Where do you want me to meet you?"

"At the end of the port there's a road that leads to the bay of Port-Miou. If you don't know, ask someone. Two or three kilometres after you leave the village you'll come to a hotel, the Hotel Bella Vista. They have a room for you."

"For me?"

"I called them. I tried to get a room here, but there's nothing available. Take the car."

"I don't want to get into that car again."

"And I want you to get it out of there and I want you to be seen in it. When you get to the Hotel Bella Vista take off your suit and put on something else. I'll ring in twenty minutes to make sure you're there. After that, we'll meet."

"Where?"

"First go there. Be careful, Dany, don't try anything with me, you have much more to lose than I do."

"You think so?"

"I know so. And don't forget: get rid of that suit, change your clothes."

"I'll do no such thing."

"Suit yourself. I'll ring in twenty minutes. After that, you're on your own."

"But why can't we meet here now?"

"Do you want to see me? Well, it has to be on my terms, not yours."

"I still don't understand."

"Why should you?"

He hung up. So did I, with a hand that trembled.

It was dark when I got into the Thunderbird. Behind me, at one end of the immense square, some carnival tents were all lit up. Rifle shots could be heard through a Viennese waltz. Further off, an orchestra stand and some rows of Chinese lanterns were ready for tomorrow night.

I drove slowly through the port. The terraces of cafés overflowed into the street. Through a smell of the sea and of anise, a carefree crowd walked in front of the car, moving aside reluctantly. I asked for directions. The road rose steeply after I left the village. It passed some new buildings where people were dining on balconies. Further on, it overlooked a beach with white pebbles that lay deserted under the moon.

The Hotel Bella Vista lifted its vaguely Moorish towers at the edge of a promontory surrounded by pines and palm trees. It was crowded and brightly lit. I left the Thunderbird at the entrance to the garden. I gave my suitcase to a porter in gold braid, put down the top, and locked the doors and boot.

At the desk a young woman signed the register for me.

As I told her who I was and where I was from, I thought of the hotel in Chalon, and suddenly I remembered the Philippe I had met, handsome and disarming, and my spirits lifted a little. I'm a creep.

The room was small, with a bathroom tiled in flowered porcelain, new furniture, a fan that stirred up the hot air, and a window overlooking the sea. For a moment I watched some boys and girls leaping and shouting in an illuminated swimming pool down below. Then I undressed and took a shower, keeping my hair and my bandage out of the water.

The telephone rang as I was drying myself. They put the call through to my room. "Are you ready?" asked Philippe.

"Almost. What shall I wear? I don't have much."

"Anything except your suit."

"Why?"

"I've been seen enough in its company. I'll meet you in Marseille in an hour."

"Marseille? But that's absurd! Why not here?"

"I've also been seen enough around there. Anyway, I'm in Marseille now."

"I don't believe you."

"Whether you believe me or not, that's where I am. Do you know Marseille?"

"No."

"Shit. Let me think."

I let him think. On my body I saw a mark he had given me the night we had made love. I said gently, "Philippe, I left a message in the place where you left me, on the hill."

"A message?"

"In case you came back. I asked you to meet me at ten o'clock in front of Number Ten La Canebière."

"Do you know La Canebière?"

"No, but I can easily find it."

"Good. Let's make it ten thirty. Leave the car in a side street and come on foot. I'll wait for you."

"Don't hang up."

It was too late. I asked the desk where the call came from. Marseille. I dressed, after hesitating a moment between the trousers I had worn the night before and the white muslin dress. I chose the dress because he obviously did not want to be seen with me in something I had already worn during the trip. If I had not been in such a state, these professional precautions would have struck me as funny. I ran a comb through my hair. In the mirror I was so terribly myself, everything was so real, that I closed my eyes.

Marseille is the most sprawling and confusing city I have ever driven through. The streets, which are narrower than Paris streets, go off in all directions, and no matter which way you go, they lead nowhere. I stopped at the kerb several times to ask directions. I did not understand any of what I was told except that I was a poor girl. My poor child, poor mademoiselle, poor you, they said. I turned my back on La Canebière every time.

At last I found an enormous car park near a place called La Bourse. I locked the Thunderbird and walked straight ahead, and the first street I took ran into the big avenue I was looking for, at almost exactly the appointed place. Number ten was a travel agency at the end of La Canebière, in front of the old port. There was a big restaurant, the Cintra, next to it, a lot of people on the pavement, blue buses in the road, neon lights everywhere.

Philippe was not there, but I sensed that he was stationed somewhere watching me. I waited for a few minutes, pacing up and down, staring blankly at some optical instruments in a window. Then he touched my arm. He was still wearing his beige linen suit and his black tie. We looked at each other for a long moment without saying a word, face to face in the jostling crowd. The minute I saw his drawn face I was sure that he had never killed anyone, that this business amazed him as much as it did me.

He asked, "Where is the car?"

"Down there, in the back."

"Is he still in it?"

"Where do you think he is?"

"Who is he, Dany?"

"You tell me!"

"Don't shout. Come on."

He grabbed me by the elbow and dragged me towards the port. We walked across an illuminated square, moving from one safe place to another, dodging cars. He had taken my right hand in his own and kept it there. We walked for a very long time along a quay called the Quai de Rive-Neuve. In a flat voice, never looking at me, he explained that he had taken the Thunderbird to sell it, that he had not stopped once until he reached Cassis, that while making a final inspection before turning it over to a dealer there, he had opened the boot and found the dead man. Then he had panicked, he saw little Titou, he did not know what to do. He imagined that I had killed this man and that I would take advantage of the situation and let him take the blame. He was sure he would never see me again, my arrival had completed his confusion.

We sat down at the end of the quay in the dark, on a pile of boards eroded by the sea. He asked how I had caught up with him after he had abandoned me in front of Lake Berre.

"I called the restaurant where we had lunch that noon."

"You're a cool customer."

"Did you follow me in Cassis? Why didn't you speak to me right away?"

"I didn't know what was going on in your head. Whose car is this?"

"My employer's."

"Did he lend it to you?"

"No. He doesn't know I took it."

"Go on."

I saw a host of questions in his eyes. The same ones he must have seen in mine. He was still holding my right hand, but mistrust paralyzed us both. At last he asked, "You really don't know this man?"

"No."

"You didn't know he was in your boot?"

"You saw me open it in Cassis. Did I look as if I knew what was in it?"

"You could have been putting on an act."

"So could you! You're a pro, aren't you? You haven't stopped acting since last night."

"Somebody put him in there, and it wasn't me. Think a minute, Dany. He was dead before I met you, you know."

"How do you know?"

"I have eyes! He's been dead for at least forty-eight hours."

"You could have put him in the boot long after you killed him."

"When, for example?"

"In Chalon, last night."

"And you think I'd travel around for a whole day with a stiff on my hands? Even in Chalon? Forget the movies, come down to earth! Besides, it breaks my heart to have to threaten you, but I have plenty of witnesses for yesterday and the day before. Sure I was dragging a suitcase, but if you're going to try to prove that I could have hidden him in it, lots of luck!"

He got up and walked off a little way.

I said very quickly, "Please, Philippe, don't leave me."

126

"I'm not leaving you."

He stood with his back turned for a while, beside a battered boat, looking at the black water of the old port streaked with unmoving lights. The sounds of the city seemed very far away. At last he asked, "What's he like, your boss? A little homicidal around the edges?"

I shrugged my shoulders without answering.

He turned around, restless and tense with irritation, and shouted, "For Christ's sake, I don't know anything about it! But maybe this stiff was already in the car when you took it!"

"No, the boot was empty when I took it. I know because I looked."

"I see. And did you open it on the way?"

"Yes, I think so." "When was the last time?"

I thought back along Route seven and Route six: Fontainebleau. I remembered opening the boot to put in the suitcase I had just bought. Then I had changed my mind.

"At Fontainebleau it was empty."

"That's a long way from here. Where did you stop after that?"

"In Joigny, at a café. That's where I met that lorry driver, the one who took my violets. But it was daylight and the car was right by the door; nobody could have put that man in it then."

"And you're sure you didn't open the boot again until Cassis?"

"I'd remember it."

"Where did you stop after Joigny?"

"At a petrol station near Avallon. There I left the car for a long time. Somebody even moved it while I was at the doctor's."

He looked at my bandage. I could see that he was remembering what I had told him: my crushed hand, those people who recognized me from seeing me going the other

127

way, although I claimed to have been in Paris. All he said was, "Your story is hard to swallow, you know."

I couldn't think of anything else to say to justify myself. I didn't even want to. Noticing that I was cold in my white dress, he took off his jacket and put it around my shoulders. Putting his face close to mine he murmured, "You're not lying, are you, Dany?"

"I swear it."

"Even if it was you who fired those shots, I'll help you. Do you understand?"

"Shots? What shots? Was he killed with a gun?"

In spite of myself, I raised my voice and it broke, shrill and ridiculous. I did not know why, but tears came into my eyes, perhaps because I was confused.

"I assume so, since it's in there with him."

"What's in there?"

"The gun, for Christ's sake! Large as life! In your boot! The gun! Do you recognize me, at least?"

He had taken my face in his hands and was shaking it from side to side as if to wake me up.

"Stop! I didn't see any gun!"

"What did you see? Did you see a rug? Did you see a man? Well, there's a gun too!"

He let go of me, turned on his heel and walked off with his hands in his pockets, his shoulders hunched in his white shirt. I got up and followed him. He made me cross the street, saying that he was out of cigarettes, hungry, and broke. We went into a crowded coffee bar whose walls were covered with fishnets and seashells. I bought a pack of Gitanes and some matches. He drank a half-bottle of wine at the counter and ate a sandwich. He did not talk or look at me.

I asked, "How did you get to Marseille?"

"Forget it."

"Where is your suitcase?"

"Forget it."

When we left, he put his arm around my shoulders and pulled me towards him. I did not want to pull away. We walked side by side along a pavement stacked with empty crates that reeked of seaweed. We crossed the big square in front of the old port. In a mirror in the front window of a restaurant I caught a glimpse of our faces going by, my white dress, his jacket over my shoulders, the two of us looking like lovers in the neon glare a thousand kilometres from my life. I don't think I'm lying when I say that this seemed more unreal than all the rest.

On La Canebière, people looked at us. I asked him where we were going.

"To the car. We have to find out who that guy is. We have to look again."

"Oh, please, I can't do it."

"I can."

In the car park where I had left it among hundreds of other cars, we stood in front of the Thunderbird for few minutes. I had taken the keys out of my bag but he wasn't taking them. A troop of teenagers went by, talking and gesticulating, then a lone woman in a rumpled dress muttering to herself, her head bowed over her own troubles. Philippe told me to drive. We had to find a quieter place to open the boot.

We drove along the Quai de Rive-Neuve, going back over the road we had followed on foot. As I turned into a street that climbed through the city, he suddenly said, "We may have a chance to get out of this, Dany. If somebody planted this guy on you during the trip, nobody knows it except the son of a bitch who put him there. There's no connection between him and you. So we do the same. We dump him anywhere and forget about it. It's none of our business."

I turned into one street after another, still going uphill. Then he made me take a road with a stone boundary wall on the outside: the Chemin du Roucas-Blanc. Here there were no more cars or people, but it was so steep and so narrow that I had to stop to make a turn. My bandaged hand was clumsy and painful; he helped me turn the steering wheel. Further on, through a gap between two crumbling walls, I saw the city far below, glittering beside the sea.

He laid a hand on my knee as a signal to stop. We were in front of number seventy-eight – I remember, because it was my locker number at the orphanage. A dark yard, giving onto a new building. We waited for a few seconds, listening, then coasted into the yard. My headlights revealed a row of garages with varnished doors, some foliage, a staircase. A car was parked outside. I parked behind it, turned off the ignition, and turned off the lights. The yard was quiet but small and I wondered anxiously how much time it would take to turn around if for some reason we had to leave in a hurry.

I gave Philippe back his jacket and we got out. Overhead a few windows were lit; through a drawn curtain you could see the blue gleam of a television. I opened the boot and turned away quickly without looking. But the smell hit me in the face, appalling, and it was through a fog of dizziness that I heard Philippe ask me for a handkerchief. He was gasping with revulsion. It made him look emaciated, aged, unfamiliar. I shall never forget the horror in his eyes when they met mine.

I heard him close to me, moving the dead man. I stared desperately at the entrance to the yard, but it was not for fear someone would come. I wasn't even thinking about that.

Philippe murmured, "Look, Dany."

He showed me the gun, a long one with a black barrel.

"There are initials on the butt."

"Initials?"

"M. K."

He made me look and run my fingers over two letters engraved in the wood. I did not know anyone with those initials. Neither did he. He said, "It's a Winchester rifle. Three bullets have been fired."

"Do you know about those things?"

"A little."

He wiped the gun with my handkerchief and put it back in the rug in which the dead man was wrapped. I saw his face: his mouth was open in the white light of the boot. Philippe was going through the pockets of his dressing gown. From his silence I sensed that he had just discovered something, that he was holding his breath. Suddenly he straightened up. He tried to speak, but nothing came out. He was paralyzed with incredulity. I had time to see a piece of paper in his left hand. Then he shouted. I don't know what he shouted, probably that I was out of my mind, that he had got mixed up in a madwoman's dream, because I know now that that was the meaning of his expression. I think I also saw in this expression that he was going to hit me. I think I raised my arm to protect myself.

Just then a pain in the pit of my stomach knocked the wind out of me and doubled me up. Before I hit the ground he grabbed me by the waist and dragged me to the car door. I was aware of suffocating on the front seat of the car and of hearing him close the boot and walk away. After that everything went black.

Much later everything was peaceful, I was alone, I had managed to sit up beside the wheel, I was breathing the night air through my mouth, I was all right, I was crying. My glasses had fallen onto the floor of the car. When I put them back on I saw that it was one o'clock in the morning by the dashboard. As I smoothed my dress over my legs, I found in its folds the piece of paper Philippe had taken out of one of the dead man's pockets.

I turned on the light.

It was a telephone message on the letterhead of Orly Airport. It was addressed to a certain Maurice Kaub, a passenger on Air France flight 405. It had been received by a hostess with fine handwriting on 10 July at 6:55 P.M. It took me a moment to work out that that was Friday, two and a half days ago. The thought of everything I had done in those two days filled me with a kind of cold, dizzy terror.

The message read, *Don't leave me. If you do, I'll follow you to Villeneuve. In the state I'm in now I could do anything.*

It was signed *Dany.*

The Paris telephone number written in the box marked "origin of message" was mine.

The road turning and turning, the sea below, the moon above. That is all I remember. I don't know how I got back to the Hotel Bella Vista. I don't even know if I meant to. It was cold. I was cold. I think I was no longer fully aware that I was in the Midi. No, I was on the road to Chalon, I had just left a doctor who had taken care of my hand, a garage man, a policeman on a motorbike. Now I was going to meet Philippe on a quay of the Saône, but this time I wouldn't stop, no, I wouldn't stop, and everything would be different.

Then there was my white suit. I think that the idea of getting my white suit back was important at that moment. As I drove, I thought about that suit in a strange room, and the thought of it consoled me. It was something of my own, something that had belonged to me before that Friday, 10 July. In recovering it, I would recover myself.

In Cassis there were still lights on in the port, an open bar from which you could hear electric-guitar music, some boys

132

clowning in front of the car who forced me to stop. One of them leaned over the door and kissed me on the mouth with breath that smelled of alcohol and tobacco. Next came the beach with the white pebbles, and the Moorish towers of the hotel. A big round moon hovered beyond the leaves of the palm trees.

A night watchman in a white-and-gold uniform gave me my key. I seem to remember that he talked to me about horse racing, and that I answered in a normal voice. After I had bolted the door of my room I began to cry again. The tears flowed uncontrollably, I felt as if they weren't mine. I picked up the jacket of my white suit from the bed and held it against myself for a while. I recognized the perfume I have been wearing for years and the smell of my skin, but they did not console me.

I undressed and got into bed with my suit lying at my feet and the message from Orly in my right hand. I re-read it several times before turning out the light and later I turned my bedside light back on and read it again. I did not know this Maurice Kaub. I had never sent this message. On Friday 10 July, at six fifty-five I was at Villa Montmorency, beginning to type, I was with the Caravailles and their little girl. During this time someone had entered my apartment in rue de Grenelle and used my name and telephone number. That was evident.

The gun Philippe had found in the Thunderbird had the initials M. K. on the butt, the exact initials of Maurice Kaub. This link between the gun and the message proved that the corpse had not been placed in the car at random, as I had believed, but that somebody had deliberately chosen me, Dany Longo, as far back as Friday, to take on this nightmare. That, too, was evident.

I don't know whether I slept or not. At times, details of my trip since Orly crossed my mind with a clarity and suddenness that made me open my eyes. A little white card on the counter of the Hotel La Renaissance. The exasperated voice of the manager, "Longo, Danielle Marie Virginie, age twenty-six, profession advertising, isn't that you?" A sudden presence behind me in the toilet of a petrol station. The beam of the policeman's torch turning inside the car. He wants me to open my purse. The little girl's name is Maureen. They say that they have seen me, that they have talked to me, that I was driving in the opposite direction, towards Paris, this Saturday at dawn.

And then it really was dawn and my eyes were open. I watched the light gradually fill the room and thought, No, it wasn't a silly joke thought up by somebody I met on the road. Everything must be connected in this conspiracy that has been mounted against me. For God knew what abominable reason, someone had to make it look as if I was already between Mâcon and Avallon that Saturday morning. Just as they used my telephone, they used my appearance, my dark glasses, my identity. Those people who recognized me were not lying. They had "seen" me, but it was another woman, in another car, who . . .

I collapsed head first against a blinding wall.

I sat up in bed, I almost screamed. It was madness. *No conspiracy was possible – for anyone.* No matter what I told myself, nobody, unless he had a supernatural gift, could have decided in advance to connect me by a telephone message with a dead stranger whom they would put in the car *a day and a half later*, hundreds of kilometres from where I lived. Still less could anybody arrange in advance to have another woman imitate me somewhere along Route six, *twelve or fifteen hours before I got onto the road*. Nobody in the world could have known last Friday at six fifty-five, or last Saturday at dawn, that I would have the brainstorm of my life, that like an idiot I would keep my boss's car, and that that evening I would actually be on Route six on my way to the sea. Nobody. *I didn't even know it myself.*

I told myself, Wait, wait, think again, surely there's an explanation, there has to be. But there couldn't be. The most frightening part – yes, my mind was collapsing with fear – was this: *I didn't know I was going to leave myself.* So everything had begun outside me and outside other people. Nothing human could have sent that telegram or assumed my identity on the road. I had to believe that for a whole night and a whole day before I suddenly decided to keep the Thunderbird, I had already been chosen and was being controlled by some will outside the universe and the whole universe no longer made sense.

Chosen. Controlled. A presence behind me. My hand that hurts. My stomach that hurts where Philippe hit me. A punishment. My little baby killed inside me four years ago in Zurich. Some unknown force outside the universe, implacable and vigilant, following me, always there. Once again, that sense of living, wide awake, in somebody else's dream. And all I wish for now, with all my strength, is to sleep too – or else that whoever is dreaming will wake up, and everything will be silent and peaceful, that I will die, that I will forget.

Monday 13 July. This morning.

The flowers on the wallpaper of the room: blue with red centres. My dirty bandage. My wristwatch on my right wrist, its tick-tick close to my ear. My bare legs outside the sheets. The burning carpet beneath my feet where the sun hits it. Two blonde girls swimming side by side with long silent strokes in the pool under my window. The oven of the sky through the unmoving palms; the sea I had wanted to see. Everything so clear, yes.

I washed the underwear I had worn yesterday with a little sample cake of soap that I found on the basin. It smelled of, what was it? I don't remember. I don't remember what has really happened to me. There are certain things that come back to me suddenly with great precision, and others that are gone forever. Or perhaps the things I remember clearly are also in my mind. Madness, I know now, is these very precise things: blue flowers with red centres; a dirty bandage; the sun through the palm trees – hard details that don't go together, that lead to nothing but yourself.

I could easily have stayed in that room all day, and the next day, and the next, without moving. I would have kept on washing the same pair of panties and the same bra until there was no more soap, no more material, until there was nothing left, no more child, no more blood, no more lies to tell yourself.

Mama Supe talked to me now and then. It was she who ordered coffee – at least, she in me, watching over me, talking on the telephone through my mouth, which amounts to the same thing. It was she who told me, "Dany, Dany, do something, look what has become of you." I looked at my face in the mirror over the basin. I wondered what there was behind my own eyes, what secret, like a lost bird tearing its own wings, was turning and turning in the back of that head, in the depths of that heart.

And then I drank two cups of black coffee and took a cold shower and everything seemed better. It always does. All I have to do is wait, to submerge for a while. Then I hear Mama Supe's voice again, something inside me falls into a heavy sleep, and I am calm for a while, everything is better.

I got dressed – white suit, damp bandage, dark glasses – after I discovered, while looking in my handbag for a comb, that this time Philippe had not left me without taking my money. My pay envelope was empty, and so was my wallet.

I don't think I felt any bitterness. It was something natural, something I could easily explain. Besides, if Philippe had stayed with me I would have given him that money anyway. Since he was broke, he was welcome to it. Aside from that he could go to hell.

Since I did not have the slightest idea what I was going to do, short of going to the police and accepting all the blame or jumping into the sea, this theft helped me – it really did. I thought that before I did anything else, I must go to a branch of my bank and withdraw the money in my current account. Mama Supe said, "That's better than staying here and brooding. *Andiamo.*"

I went downstairs, asked at the desk where to find the bank, and told them I was keeping the room. In the garden where I had left it, the Thunderbird was broiling hot. I was sorry I hadn't parked it out of the sun, but when I sat down at the wheel I did not smell the odour I was dreading. I tried my best not to think about what, in this heat, could gradually happen to a body that had been dead for over two and a half days. I am familiar with this kind of effort. As far back as I can remember, I have always tried to banish some horrible image from my mind. My mother's sobs while they were shaving her head a few minutes before she lay smashed on the pavement two stories below. Or my father's screams as he lay trapped under a freight wagon that suddenly started to move again. I tell myself, Stop it, you idiot; but after all, what do you forget?

Sunlight. I parked the car on the shady side of the main street of Cassis, which opened onto the port. I had lowered the top so that the air would carry away the foul smell and bad dreams. I walked into a bank where everything was shiny and reassuring. They told me I could withdraw seven hundred and fifty francs from my Paris account, but since there could

137

not be too much of that left after the purchases I had made in Fontainebleau, I took only five hundred. Mama Supe told me, "Take all you can, nobody else can use it, get out of the country, disappear." I didn't listen to her.

While I was waiting for my money, I saw a big road map posted on one wall. I thought of the telegramme: "I'll follow you to Villeneuve." I looked to see if there was a Villeneuve in the vicinity of Routes six and seven between Paris and Marseille. I counted so many that at first I was discouraged: Villeneuve-Saint-Georges, Villeneuve-la-Guyard, Villeneuve-sur-Yonne, Villeneuve-l'Archevêque, Villeneuve-lès-Avignon, and more, and no doubt there were still other Villeneuves of lesser importance which weren't on the map.

I noticed, however, that Villeneuve-la-Guyard was just after Fontainebleau, where I had seen the boot empty for the last time, and that Villeneuve-sur-Yonne was near Joigny, where I had met the lorry driver who took my violets. But that probably didn't mean very much. Mama Supe said, "It doesn't mean anything at all if you go by that telephone message. It was addressed to a passenger on an aeroplane. You don't take an aeroplane to go to Villeneuve-la-Guyard, it's only a stone's throw from Paris, look and see."

I put the money they gave me in my bag. I asked if there was a travel agency in Cassis. There was one in the next building; all I had to do was walk out of one door and in through another. I saw a sign that my luck was returning; there were notices on both doors announcing that this Monday 13 July, everything closed at noon. God had let me withdraw my money and I still had over an hour left. Mama Supe said, "To do what?" I didn't know, really. Maybe just to move around, to perform a few last gestures of a living being, a free being before they caught me with that corpse in the car and locked me up and I stayed in the dark at last with my head in my arms, curled up as I must once have been, warm and safe in the belly of Renata Longo née Castellani, born in San Appolinare in the province of Frosinone.

I asked for an Air France timetable; which I consulted outside on the blazing hot pavement in a crowd of summer visitors going to the beach. The Air France Flight 405 mentioned in the message was a nonstop flight from Paris to Marseille by Caravelle, Fridays except holidays, which left Orly at 7:45 P.M. and arrived in Marseille-Marignane at 8:55 P.M. Immediately I thought, The Villeneuve you're looking for must be Villeneuve-lès-Avignon, it's the only one you saw that low on the map. At the same time there was something unpleasant I could not put my finger on that stirred in my memory, which I could not bring to the surface, which bothered me.

I looked for the Thunderbird, parked on the other side of the street. Suddenly that identity card on the counter of the Hotel La Renaissance in Chalon flashed into my mind. I realized it was that that was bothering me. Yes, that was it, they had told me at the Renaissance that when I had come there the first time, I was coming from Avignon. I had answered that that was ridiculous. "You see," said Mama Supe, "it's a conspiracy, it's all worked out ahead of time. If somebody discovers that body in your boot now, who is going to believe that you have nothing to do with it? Please run away, anywhere, and never come back." Once again I didn't listen to her.

I walked through the port. The night before, as I was asking the way to the Hotel Bella Vista, I had noticed a post office at the end of the quay. I also remembered that in the same place a few hours later, a boy who was a little high had kissed me on the mouth, and instinctively I wiped my mouth with my bandaged hand. I told Mama Supe, "Don't worry, I haven't begun to fight, give me time. I'm all alone, but I've always been all alone, so even if the whole world is in on it, they won't beat me." I did my best to pull myself together.

Inside the post office it was dark, especially after coming in out of the bright sun, and I had to change my glasses. I found a row of telephone books of the provinces attached to a slanting counter. I opened the one for Vaucluse. There *was* a Maurice Kaub in Villeneuve-lès-Avignon.

Deep down I must not really have believed it, for my heart began to pound. I can't explain. It was printed, cold, real, it was even more real than the message telephoned from my apartment, or the corpse in the car. Anyone at all – and not just for the past two days but for months – could open this big book and read this name and address. I can't explain.

It read, *Maurice Kaub, builder–contractor, Domaine Saint-Jean, Route de l'Abbaye.*

Once again I felt a memory, of God knew what, stir suddenly and try to come to the surface of my mind. Domaine Saint-Jean. Route de l'Abbaye. Builder–contractor. Villeneuve-lès-Avignon. I did not know what I was supposed to remember. The impression vanished, and I was no longer even sure I had had it.

I opened another directory, the one for Yonne. I found that there were several coffee bars in Joigny, but only one on Route six: *A l'ancien de la Route, T. Pozzon, Proprietor.* That must be the one where I had stopped, where I had met the lorry driver who took the violets. I made a mental note of the telephone number, 2–20, and walked out.

When I got back to the car the sun was high, the shade only half covered it, but I had no time to worry about that. Two policemen in khaki uniforms were standing in front of it.

I did not see them until the last moment, when I was almost upon them. I always look at the ground when I walk, for fear

I'll trip over an elephant or something that I haven't seen. Until the age of eighteen I wore glasses that were not nearly as good as the ones I have now. I was upside down more often than not, they used to call me "the suicide plane". One of my favourite nightmares, even today, is a big pram abandoned in the doorway to an apartment building. One time it took three people to pry us apart.

When I looked up and saw – I almost fainted from the shock – the two policemen in front of the Thunderbird, I wanted to turn tail and run. Mama Supe told me, "For heaven's sake, keep going, look away, pass them." In the end, I stopped.

"Is this your car?"

I said yes. At least I tried to say it; no sound came out of my mouth. They were both tall, and the younger one wore dark glasses, like me. He did the talking. He asked to see my papers. I walked around the Thunderbird to get them out of the glove compartment. Meanwhile they walked over to the boot without saying a word. Mama Supe said, "Don't just stand there like a lump, now is the time to run, go on, scram, do something." I walked over and handed the younger one the plastic folder containing the papers. He took them out and glanced at the car registration.

"Driving licence, please."

I took it out of my bag and gave it to him. He looked at it, then back at the registration.

"What does 'R.B.C.' mean?"

"R.B.C.?"

He showed me the card with a weary, slightly annoyed gesture. After "name" I read, as I had done in Orly, "R.B.C., Inc." I did not know what those initials meant I swallowed and said, "It's an advertising agency."

"Well?"

I improvised, "Robert B. Caravaille."

"Who is Caravaille?"

"The man who founded the agency. But it's mine now. That is, I'm the director, do you see?"

He shrugged and said, "I see that there is a 'No Parking' sign right in front of your car. How long have you been in Cassis?"

"I arrived last night."

"Next time pay attention. This street is narrow enough as it is, if everyone did this . . . " Etc., etc.

I began to breathe again. He returned the papers, took off his cap, mopped his brow with a handkerchief, and after looking sideways at his companion, said, "Just because you're a pretty girl and have a big car doesn't mean you can do whatever you want. It's true, you know."

As he spoke, the most terrifying thing in the world began to happen before my eyes: the older man, who was listening with an attentive half smile and who had not said a word, was playing unconsciously with the lock of the boot, was pressing his thumb on the big metal button. *And it was unlocked.* The night before, when I had returned from Marseille like a sleep-walker, I had not thought to bolt it. I had unlocked it for Philippe, and it was still unlocked.

I saw the policeman's thumb press, release, and press harder. I heard the opening click, and I brought my right hand hastily down on the lid of the boot. Too hastily, for the one in the dark glasses stopped talking, intrigued. He looked at the boot and then at me, and dark glasses or no, he saw that I had gone pale. He said, "Feeling all right?"

I nodded my head. Desperately I tried to think of something to say to divert his attention from the car, which he was looking at again, but nothing came to me. The other one was also looking at my right hand, which was glued to the door. I took it away.

After an interminable silence the young one said, at last walking away "Be good. From now on use a proper parking place."

He touched his finger to his cap, and they both walked off towards the port without turning around. I looked in my bag for the car keys with feverish hands. I locked the boot. Then I had to wait several minutes, sitting at the wheel staring into space, before I could start the car. I was trembling from head to foot. I'm a very sensitive creep.

In my room at the Hotel Bella Vista the fan droned in the dusty sunlight without providing me with a breath of air. I closed the blinds, undressed, and lay down on the remade bed with the telephone beside me.

I asked the switchboard for two numbers: 2–20 in Joigny, and the home of Bernard Thorr, a layout man from the agency who is fond of me and who had accompanied the boss to Geneva for the Milkaby account several times. He must know what hotel Caravaille usually stayed at. I would call Anita, confess that I had kept her car, and tell her I needed her testimony to get out of a jam. Anita would help me.

I got the bar in Joigny first, almost immediately, as it happened. I asked to speak to the proprietor. At first he did not remember me. White suit, blonde hair, dark glasses; American car, nothing clicked. He remembered the lorry driver when I mentioned the drink he had insisted on paying for, and his smile.

I said, "Do you know him?"

"A tall dark fellow with a Somua? You bet I do! That's Jean, Jean with the Somua. He stops by every week."

"Jean who? I don't understand."

"The Somua is his lorry. I don't know his name. He's from Marseille. They call him Toothpaste Smile."

That was funny, I called him the same thing myself. I laughed. I was happy. At last I had a contact, I felt as if all my troubles were going to vanish into thin air.

"You say he is from Marseille? Do you know if he is in Marseille? Do you know where I can find him?"

"Now you're asking too much. I know he was going down Saturday. But I have no idea where he is. Do you want me to give him a message when he stops in again?"

I said that that would be too late, that I had to find him right away. He said "Oh", and there was a rather long silence, I even thought he had hung up. But he hadn't. Suddenly he said, "Wait, I have an idea. Just a minute mademoiselle."

I now heard the sound of talking and the clatter of dishes at the other end. I tried to remember the room I had seen two days before: the long wooden counter, the pictures of accidents, the red, white and blue poster announcing the July 14 festivities. I pictured lorry drivers eating lunch, the circles their wineglasses made on the oilcloth covering the tables. All of a sudden, I was very hungry and thirsty. I had had nothing but two cups of coffee since the day before.

Then another voice said, "Hello? Who is this?"

"My name is Longo, Danielle Longo. I was telling the man who just spoke to me . . . "

"What do you want with Handsome?"

It was also a southern voice, thick and wheezy, the voice of a bad-tempered person interrupted in the middle of lunch. I started all over from the beginning, apologizing and using my best manners.

He said, "He's a colleague of mine, Handsome is. So I wanted to know who I'm talking to. If it's because you go for him, okay, but if it's for something else, well, I don't know, it'll be my neck, and I don't want any trouble. See my point of view? Put yourself in my place."

Blah blah blah. I thought my nerves were going to give. But I kept my humblest voice, when I could get a word in. I told him that actually he had been right, I wanted to see his friend again because we had made a date, I had stood him up, and now, naturally, I was sorry – in short, that was it, he had been right.

His delicacy would have melted stone; considering the price of the message unit it truly belonged to the realm of art. "Well, say no more. If it's pussy business, I have no objections. I wouldn't want to deprive a colleague of a piece of ass. But be sure and tell Handsome I helped you because something was eating you; he might think I talk too much."

Killing. In the end he told me that his friend's name was Jean Le Gueven and that he lived in a section of Marseille called Sainte-Marthe. He did not know his exact address, but I could get it by calling his shipper Garbaggio Brothers, boulevard des Dames, Colbert 0910. It would have taken me too long to write all this down with my right hand; I made him repeat it so I would remember. Before letting me hang up, he kept me another half century: "Tell him there are four tons to pick up in rue du Louvre, if he's coming up. Tell him The Sardine told you so. That's me. He'll understand. Four tons of stuff. Rue du Louvre. So long, good luck."

At the hotel switchboard they hadn't reached Paris yet. I asked for Colbert 0910 and ordered lunch in my room. I got Garbaggio Brothers right away.

"Le Gueven?" said a woman's voice. "Poor you, he's already left! Let me see, he must be loading. Call Colbert two two one eight, he might still be there. But you know, he's taking vegetables to Pont-Saint-Esprit tonight. So I'd be surprised."

"You mean he's going back to Paris? With his lorry?"

"What do you expect him to do? Take the train?"

"He's not staying for the fourteenth of July?"

"Well, madame, far be it from me to say it to someone with an accent like yours, but people eat in Paris too. Even on the fourteenth of July!"

I asked for Colbert 2218. Just as the call went through, there was a knock on my door. Before going to open it I waited to find out whether I could get Jean Le Gueven on the phone. I was told only, "Here he is," and there he was. I was expecting him to be miles away, at first I couldn't find my voice.

"Yes? Hello?" he said. "Hello!"

"Jean Le Gueven?"

"That's me."

"This is – we met on Saturday afternoon in Joigny – you know, the white car, the violets?"

"You're kidding!"

No, I'm not. Do you remember?"

He laughed. I recognized his laugh, and I could even picture his face very clearly. There was another knock at my door. He said, "The flowers are faded, you know. I'll have to buy you another bunch. Where are you?"

"In Cassis. But I'm not calling about that – or rather, I – just a minute, please. Can you wait a minute? You won't go away, will you?"

He laughed again and said he wouldn't. I jumped off the bed and went to the door. A man's voice on the other side said that it was my lunch. I was in my underwear. I had to run to the bathroom, wrap myself in a towel, and come back. I opened the door a crack, took the tray he brought, thanked him very much, and closed it again. When I picked up the phone again Toothpaste Smile was still there. I told him, "Excuse me, I am in a hotel room. Someone was knocking at my door. They brought me my lunch."

"What are you having?"

"What am I having?" I looked. "Fried fish. I think it's mullet."

"Is that all?"

"No. Some kind of casserole, salad, shrimp. I – I called Joigny because I had to talk to you."

"Lucky me. Why? Because of the violets?'

"No. Not exactly."

I didn't know how to say it. The silence became interminable. I asked, "After you left me the other afternoon, you didn't do anything against me, did you?"

"Against you?"

"Yes. I had trouble on the way. I thought it was a practical joke – well, that it was you. I thought you were playing a joke on me."

"No, it wasn't me." He said it calmly, his tone of voice no less friendly or cheerful. "What kind of trouble?"

"I can't talk about it on the telephone. I'd like to see you."

"To tell me your troubles?"

I didn't know what to say. After a few moments I heard him sigh. Then he said, "Your fish will be cold."

"I don't care."

"Listen, I've finished loading, I was just getting my invoices signed, I'm about to leave. Can't it wait two or three days, what you have to tell me? I have to be at Pont-Saint-Esprit tonight without fail."

"Please."

"How soon can you meet me in Marseille?"

"I don't know, half an hour, three quarters of an hour?"

"Good. Let's try. From here I'm going to the freight yard in Saint-Lazare. Ask a policeman, everybody knows where it is. I'll wait until one fifteen. After that, I can't."

"I'll be there."

"The freight yard in Saint-Lazare. Did I tell you the other day that you're pretty?"

"No. Well, yes, in a way."

"I hope your troubles aren't too serious. What's your name?"

"Longo, Dany Longo."

"Your name's pretty too."

After that I did everything at once: put on my suit, ate some lettuce, put on my shoes, and drank a glass of mineral water. Just as I was about to leave, the phone rang. It was my layout man from Paris. I had completely forgotten.

"Is that you, Bernard? It's Dany."

"Well, you've certainly had me worried! Where in the world are you?"

"In the Midi. I'll explain."

"Why did you hang up like that the other night?"

"The other night?"

"Yes, the other night. First you wake me up . . ."

"What other night?"

"Friday, for Christ's sake! Or Saturday, rather! It was three o'clock in the morning, you know!"

He was shouting. I told him I hadn't called. I had sat down on the bed again with my handbag on my lap. I was falling into hell again. While I was tracking down Toothpaste Smile just now, while I was talking to him and even while I was mentioning my troubles, it was as if nothing that had happened this weekend was real. I had forgotten the body in the car, the gun, the message from Orly, everything. I was listening to the calm, gentle voice of someone who wanted to know what I was having for lunch, I was in a world which murder and fear could not invade.

And yet they had invaded it. Even Bernard Thorr, whom I have known for years, who must be the friend I see most often, the one who knows me best, was suddenly an instrument of my nightmare. I did not understand him. He did not understand me. It took us several minutes of shouting even to hear what the other wanted to say. He said that I had called him late Friday or Saturday morning, that I must have been talking long distance or had a bad connection because he could not understand anything I was saying, that I seemed very upset, and that I had hung up suddenly. I said angrily that I had not called either at night or during the day, that I had not called at all. I asked; "Are you sure it was my voice?"

"What do you mean? Of course it was you! I couldn't hear you very well because there was a lot of shit on the line, but it couldn't have been anyone else."

"It wasn't me."

"Well, you must have been drunk, then! What's going on? Where are you?"

"It wasn't me, I tell you!"

"What little you did say, nobody else knows. Don't give me that . . ."

"What did I talk about?"

"Zurich! It was you, all right."

I began to cry. It was like the night before when I had come back to the room: the tears flowed from my eyes as if they had a will of their own, as if they weren't mine. It was Bernard Thorr who helped me four years ago, who got the information, who lent me the money for the operation and the clinic. And yet he was only a friend at the time, someone I never thought about when I wasn't with him. Apart from Anita, he's the only one who knows about my trip to Zurich. I had procrastinated, wasted almost four months lying to myself and to the man I love, out of bravado, out of stupidity, knowing very well that I would not have the courage to have this child. In the end it had been a nightmare. I imagine even the doctor who took care of me despised me.

"Dany? Dany? Do you hear me?"

I said I did.

"Are you crying?"

I said I was.

"Where are you, Dany?"

"I'll explain. I wanted to know what hotel Caravaille stays at when he goes to Geneva."

"You already asked me his phone number the other night. Haven't you reached him yet? And anyway, what . . . ?"

"It wasn't me, I tell you! Are you sure it was me?"

"But, good heavens, this is terrible, you must know that yourself!"

I kept getting the same answer. I must know myself whether I had a bandage on my hand when I didn't. I must know myself whether I had spent the night in a hotel I had never seen before. I must know myself whether I had called to ask the number of someone whose house I was in at the time. Everyone was telling the truth. It was I who was mad.

Those damn tears wouldn't stop.

"Bernard, what hotel does Caravaille stay at?"

"The Beau Rivage. Listen, Dany . . ."

"Do you have the phone number?"

He left the phone for a moment to get a notebook. He gave me the number. I opened my handbag and wrote it on a piece of paper with my right hand.

"Please, Dany, don't hang up this time."

"I have to see someone who might not wait. I have to hang up, Bernard."

"But what in the world was going on the other night?"

"What did they say on the telephone?"

"Who, you? Oh, things, things that didn't make sense, I don't remember. You talked about a hurt hand, about Villeneuve-lès-Avignon, and then, oh yes, you said, 'He's in the rug, you know, Bernard, he's in the rug, I've wiped out Zurich!' That was all, then you hung up. Oh yes, you also said that what happened in Zurich was my fault, that I should not have done something or other, things like that. Nonsense."

"If I said all that, you would have recognized my voice, wouldn't you?"

I was shouting again. They must have heard me at the other end of the hall. In the warm shade of the room my whole body was damp with sweat, and yet I was cold.

"Good heavens, do you think I recognize your voice right now?" said Bernard, shouting too. "You sound completely mad! At least tell me what . . ."

"Where will you be tonight?"

He said he would be at home. I promised to call him back. I hung up as he was asking me not to. I wiped my face and eyes in the bathroom. I did not want to think. I wanted to see that lorry driver. It was even more necessary for me to meet him than it had been before. Just now, on the telephone, I had realized that in this conspiracy planned so perfectly against me there was at least one fault, one mistake. There was no longer any question of an otherworldly will, of the supernatural, of the devil. The devil never makes mistakes.

The sea sprawls beneath the sun. The Gineste pass. How many times before have I followed this strip of asphalt through these arid hills? I have known it all my life.

I drove fast. At every turn I lurched to the side and caught myself desperately, and the pain in my left hand radiated through my whole body. At one point on a straight stretch of road I came to a side road that disappeared into a wasteland of rocks and dry grass, and I slowed down. A sign indicated that it led to a military camp, Carpianne. Mama Supe told me, "Turn here, you'll find a place to get rid of that horror in your boot." I hesitated. I didn't do it.

* * *

I told myself that all those people who thought they recognized me on Route six at dawn saw a woman in a suit wearing dark glasses who must have been blonde like me and about my height, but doubles don't exist, the imitation could not have been perfect. What caught the attention of these people so that they were blinded to everything else was the big car, of course, but also the fact that the false Dany Longo had a bandage on her left hand. That was the mistake. The bandage was a clever way of creating the illusion, but it was not deliberate, it was not planned ahead of time, since it had been necessary to take care of it *after the fact* in the bathroom of a petrol station. So the problem was not to make that woman look like me, but to make me look like her. That was why they had hurt my hand.

I would be able to go to the police and tell them everything, and there was a chance that they would believe me. The testimony of the Caravailles alone might have left the police sceptical, since they were friends who might be suspected of wanting to protect me; but I had another witness to confirm it. The last person who had taken a good look at me before the petrol station was Jean Le Gueven, in Joigny. He would remember that my hand had been intact. They would know that I was telling the truth.

I also thought, "You may not be the only object of this conspiracy you may not even be the real victim. Someone tried to imitate you, but there is one incomprehensible element which is connected with you only by chance: the Thunderbird. The Thunderbird belongs to Caravaille. After all, that is the most important thing: the body was placed in the Caravaille car."

Think, now. It was necessary to put an identical car on the road this Saturday at dawn. If it weren't identical, the garage man with the Basque accent would not have been fooled. If it did not carry the same number plate, the policeman on the road to Chalon would have noticed. Or else, there was only one Thunderbird. It was taken out of the Caravaille garage during the night and returned in the morning. In any case, it was the Caravailles whom someone was trying to implicate in this loathsome business.

But then why imitate me, instead of Anita, when I was the last person who would leave for the Midi with that car?

Madness.

I told myself that there must be another explanation. I couldn't trust anyone, least of all the Caravailles themselves. After all, to imitate me that well, to know how I dress, that I am left-handed, and my whole identity, and plenty of other details, the false Dany Longo would have to know me pretty well. Whom would I have told about Zurich?

Anita knows all that. She is slightly shorter than me, she is not exactly my type, but she is blonde too, and she knows me well. She would be able to imitate some of my gestures, I'm sure, and even my walk, which is very characteristic: fifteen or twenty years of fighting short-sightedness have completely distorted it. She would also be able to imitate my way of speaking, certain pet phrases I must have, and although it is difficult to mimic someone else's voice; on the telephone; under cover of noise on the line, she could at least have given the illusion that she was a Dany Longo who was hysterical, not herself. Finally, she knows Bernard Thorr, who was already with us in the first agency where I worked, and she knows about my relationship with him.

Until last year he was nothing more to me than a nice boy who had done me a big favour and with whom I went out once in a while, for dinner, a movie and a drink. And then one evening I got tired of putting on the Garbo act when he brought me home, as if my rejection meant that he would go home humiliated or a little sad. I got into his car, it was I who went home with him. I think there are other girls in his life, but he doesn't talk about them, or about the boys there might be in mine. He is still as nice as ever, and the only thing that has changed about our evenings is that after dinner, a movie and a drink, we sometimes prolong the friendly feeling by making love, and it is very pleasant.

One afternoon at the agency, as I was leaning over his desk watching him correct the layout of an advertisement, I unconsciously put my hand on his shoulders. He did something which is typical of him. Without stopping what he was doing he put his left hand on mine and left it there, gentle and affectionate, as if part of ourselves were somewhere else, far away. Suddenly I wanted him so much that I thought that the past was really over and that I was in love for good.

I remember telling this and a lot of other nonsense to Anita months ago – the Saturday before Christmas. I had met her in the toy department of the Galeries Lafayette. We were sitting at a table having coffee in a café near the Opera. She laughed. She made fun of me. "My poor innocent, I went to bed with Bernard before you did. In fact, you're giving me ideas. I'll have to call him one of these days." I was uncomfortable, but I laughed too. She added, "We could have a threesome, since you don't care for four." I saw her eyes, in spite of her laugh, that she was hurting herself on purpose, that for her, at least, the past would never be over, that she would always hold it against me. Then, lifting one hand as if to protect herself and using that arch tone that has always disgusted me, she said, "Are you going to hit me again?" I took my handbag and my purchases and I stood up. She grabbed me by the arm and said, her face contorted and pale under her makeup, "Please,

Dany, don't leave me like this, in front of all these people. You know I was only kidding, don't you?" I waited for her. Outside on the pavement, flashing her coquettish smile, she said in an ugly voice, enunciating distinctly, "Dirty little child-killer, all you know how to do is leave people, isn't it? All you know how to do is save yourself."

I turned and left. It wasn't until I was in the metro, when it was too late, that I realized that once again I had proved her right.

That night she called me. I think she was drunk, and God knows where she was. She said, "Dany, Dany, darling, it's water under the bridge. I know it wasn't your fault, let's not fight any more, don't think you're not my friend . . ." things like that. Of course, my room filled with sobs. I was as sickening as melting candy. She promised that we would see each other again very soon, that we would bury the hatchet forever, that she would buy me an enormous bottle of our perfume for Christmas – we wear the same kind, I started to use hers when I was twenty – and even that we would go and hear Bécaud at the Olympia and eat in a Japanese restaurant in Montparnasse, a memorable armistice that would have made 11 November 1918, and 22 June 1940, look pathetic.

The most pathetic thing of all was that for the next two weeks, except on Christmas Eve, when I knew she couldn't leave her little girl, I ran home and refused to leave the house for fear I would miss her call. I did not see her again until Friday 10 July, when her husband brought me to work at their house.

Yes, and why had he brought me to their house? To cut me off from the world for a whole night so that he could later state that I was not in Auteuil but on Route six, that was why. Everything increased my suspicions. I had been alone from nine o'clock in the evening until two o'clock in the morning, they had had ample time, the two of them, to do anything they liked. Anita had forgiven nothing, forgotten nothing, quite to the contrary. She was making me pay for a certain early morning in May by . . .

Madness.

By doing what? By murdering some man so she could pin it on me? By admitting to her husband, so he would help her get even, that once when we were twenty she had spent the night in my room and served as a miserable plaything to two drunken escorts, while I, who had not enough control over her to stop it, ran as far away as my legs could carry me?

There, it was starting again; the tears suddenly blurred my eyes uncontrollably, until I could no longer see the road. I told myself that I could cry my eyes out, but it was my fault, it was true. I had left her with them, desperate with alcohol and bravado – yes, I know it was bravado towards me. I could have got her out of there by force, calmed down the two overheated boys, roused the neighbours, anything, but all I did was run away, feeling, besides, that I was acting like a respectable girl, that I was a pure and radiant angel in a world of sinners. Dany Longo, patron saint of snivelling and the clean conscience, a panic-stricken Judas. And yet, was I not really responsible for her, since I called myself her friend? Oh, yes, I deserve to be punished and punished again, and again . . .

"Stop," said Mama Supe. "Stop."

I stopped by the side of the road outside Marseille. I waited until it was over. It was after one thirty according to the dashboard. Jean Le Gueven had given me up, and I might have to drive through the whole city before I got to the freight yard.

How could I imagine that Anita could have murdered anyone? How could I imagine her on the road, playing this sinister comedy? I must have lost my mind for good.

Even when I reasoned – as well as a moron like me can reason – it did not hang together. How could one accept the idea that the Caravailles, having a dead body on their hands and wanting to avert suspicion, would have put it in the boot *of their own car?* Besides, the woman who had played my part must really have been wounded in the left hand, since it had been necessary to wound me so I would look like her. But Anita was not. Above all, how could one accept the idea – I kept coming up against it – that she could have known exactly where to imitate me on Friday night, when I didn't know myself that I would be there the next day?

I might just as well accuse Bernard Thorr, or another lover of mine who went back to live in his country on the other side of the globe, or – why not? – the man I love. Any one of the three men in Dany Longo's life. Or Philippe, of course, who made a miserable fourth. Or the girl who lives next door to me ("She's getting rid of me because she wants my apartment"), or a copy girl at the agency ("She's almost as short-sighted as I am but she wants to be unique") or all of them put together ("They're fed up with Dany Longo, so they got together").

After all, why not?

There remained one last solution, the only one that hung together perfectly from beginning to end, but which there was no danger of my being willing even to contemplate. It took another afternoon and evening before I found myself trapped in it.

I was forty minutes late when I reached the freight yard having asked directions of all the pedestrians whom I had just missed running over at the crossings. The people of Marseille are very nice. First of all, they don't insult you any more than most people do if you try to run them over, but they also take the trouble to look at your number plate. When they see that you come from Paris they tell themselves that obviously they must not expect too much of you, they tap their foreheads with their index finger, but without ill will, simply because it's the thing to do. If at that moment you announce, "I'm lost, I don't understand anything about your rotten city, the traffic lights are out to get me, I'm looking for the freight yard in Saint-Lazare, does it even exist?" they take pity, they blame the good Mother for your misfortune, and a dozen of them crowd around to give you information. Turn right, then left, and when you get to the square with the Arc de Triomphe, watch out for the trams; they'll run you down, my cousin's wife's sister stopped one of them and now it is she who has stopped in the family plot, and since she's at the Canet cemetery she's too far to take flowers.

Contrary to all expectations, Toothpaste Smile had waited for me. He was standing by some diesel-fuel pumps, leaning against the back of a lorry that must be his in a little patch of shade, talking to someone who was squatting by one wheel. He was wearing a washed-out blue shirt open at the chest, a pair of trousers that must have been blue too, and a red-checked cap with a high crown and a long visor, very stylish and unexpected.

The freight yard looked like an ordinary petrol station except that it was a little bigger and was filled with heavy lorries. I made a right angle turn and stopped dead in the sun, beside Toothpaste Smile.

Without saying hello or anything, he said calmly, "Do you know what we're going to do? Little Paul's going to leave first with the lorry and you and I will catch up with him on the road. That way you'll let me drive that rocket of yours. And now, no kidding, we're late."

Little Paul was his driving companion, the man who was testing the pressure in the tyres. When he looked up to say

158

hello, how are you, I recognized him. They were together in Joigny.

I got out of the car. I hesitated for a moment, because I did not want to get too far away from that body in the boot, whose odour I thought I could smell when I stopped, but it was long enough to make Jean Le Gueven lose his smile. I walked over to him and stood looking up at him for a few seconds.

He put out his hand and touched my cheek, saying, "I can see that your troubles are big ones. Did you have time to get a bite?"

I told him I hadn't, shaking my head slightly. His hand moved towards my hair. He was much taller than me. He had a rather strange nose, like a boxer's, and dark, attentive eyes, and I supposed that he was everything I am not – strong and calm, pretty much in harmony with life – and also, simply from the touch of his hand, simply from his smile, which had returned, that he was a good man. It sounds silly, I don't know how to say it, but he was a man. With an incredible red-checked cap on his head.

He told Little Paul – his hand had dropped onto my shoulder – okay, see you later, that if we hadn't caught up with him by such and such a bridge, he should wait for us. He put his arm around me as if we were old friends, and we crossed the street and went into a café where some other lorry drivers were finishing their lunch.

Most of them knew Toothpaste Smile, and he shook hands and stopped to talk about haulage, price per tonne, overload, things I did not understand. He still had his arm around me, and I saw in the eyes of his friends when they looked at me – I nodded my head as if I understood their problems perfectly – that it was taken for granted I was with him. And I think this pleased me in a way. I am a pro-slavery creep: the best thing I can think of is to belong to someone.

We sat opposite one another by a window that looked onto the street. I could see one end of the Thunderbird behind his lorry, and could make sure nobody came near the boot. I didn't care any more. I felt good. I had such a longing to feel good, not to care, for the whole thing to be a dream. I made a comment on his cap – something to do with some French skiing stars I had seen on TV with similar headgear. He laughed, took off his cap, and put it on my head. I looked at my reflection in the glass to see how it suited me. I left it the way he had placed it, a little back, because for once I liked the way I looked.

Around us everybody seemed to be eating the same dish, *paupiettes*. He asked me whether I liked them and turned to a fat woman in black at the counter, raising his index finger to order a portion. Nobody will ever know how much better I felt at that moment, how everything became brighter.

And then he said it: "What's the matter with your hand?"

I wanted to talk. I wanted to talk before he did. I wanted to interrupt him. But it was already too late. He added sincerely, "Did you have that the other day?"

"That's the point! You saw me: Did I have it? Tell me. That is precisely what I wanted to ask you."

The tearful tone I used, and no doubt also the tension he saw in my face, confused him. He did his best, I think, to understand what I meant, he looked a long time at my dirty bandage on the table, but at last, it was inevitable, he replied, "My God, you must know that yourself?"

The other customers had left, a few at a time. Toothpaste Smile had ordered a quarter bottle of rosé for me and a cup of coffee for himself. From time to time he would say, "Eat a little, it's cold." I told him everything from the beginning. I told him that I worked for an advertising agency, that my boss had brought me home to work in his house, that the next day he had let me use his car, and that on an impulse I had kept it for the holiday. I told him about the people I had met: the couple in the restaurant on the main road, the salespeople in Fontainebleau, himself in Joigny, the old woman who claimed I had left my coat at her place, the garage man and his two friends when my hand had been hurt, the policeman on the road, the people who ran the Hotel La Renaissance. I told him all this in detail exactly as it had happened. I did not mention the body in the boot or – because it was not necessary and I was embarrassed to – Philippe Filanteris. I ended my account at Chalon-sur-Saône.

"And then what happened?"

"Nothing. I went to Cassis and took a room in a hotel."

"Eat something."

"I'm not hungry."

He sat looking at me for a while. I shoved the food around my plate without putting any in my mouth. He lit a cigarette – the third or fourth since I had started talking. It was almost three o'clock, but he did not once look at his watch. He was a good person, Toothpaste Smile.

He had told me a little earlier, I don't remember in what connection, that he was not an intellectual, that for him it was quite an achievement to know how to read and write, that he had not even graduated from high school, things like that. Even so, the next time he opened his mouth he put his finger on the weak spot in my story.

"There's one thing I don't understand. This whole thing is over now, isn't it? So why does it bother you so much?"

"I want to know that's all."

"But why? Maybe it's true that somebody was playing a joke on you – it wasn't me – but why go to all this trouble, move heaven and . . ."

"I'm not going to any trouble."

161

"Oh, I see. You called Joigny and came here just to see me. Well, that suits me fine." After a pause. "Tell me what's wrong, go ahead."

I shrugged my shoulders and said nothing. I wasn't eating. He warned me that if I kept on this way, some day I would go right down the drain, and he ordered me a cup of coffee. We did not speak until the fat woman in black brought it to us. He told her, "Listen, Yvonne, try to get Joigny 220 for me as fast as you can. And then give me the bill because Little Paul is going to start taking root – he left ahead of me."

She replied, Oh, misery, something unintelligible about walking being good for you, and went to the telephone. I asked Toothpaste Smile why he was calling Joigny.

"Just an idea. Your petrol station man and your policeman, that's just words, just hot air. Even that hotel form in Chalon doesn't prove anything, since it wasn't in your handwriting. They could have told you any old story. But the coat left with the old woman in Deux-Soir-lès-Avallon is something tangible, something that exists. That's where we should begin. We'll find out whether it's yours. And if it is, you're the one who's telling a story."

He paused for breath. He was talking quickly and precisely, I sensed that he was a little annoyed now. No doubt he was disappointed at the idea that I was hiding something from him.

I asked – and you should have heard the plaintive voice I used – "You mean you think there's a possibility that that woman on the road is really me? Do you think I'm lying to you?"

"I didn't say you were lying; I'm sure you aren't."

"Then you think I'm mad."

"I didn't say that either. But I have eyes, I've been watching you. How old are you? Twenty-four, twenty-five?"

"Twenty-six."

"Too young to have vices. Do you drink? No, you haven't even touched your wine. What is it, then? The other day when I saw you I didn't need a diploma to know that something was on your mind. It's gotten worse, that's all."

I didn't want to cry, I didn't. I closed my eyes, I couldn't see him any more, I pressed my eyelids hard, hard. I cried anyway.

He said in a worried voice, leaning over the table, "You see, you're all upset. What's going on? I wouldn't ask if I weren't interested. I want to help you. Tell me what's going on."

"I'm not that woman. I was in Paris. It wasn't me."

I opened my eyes again. Through my tears I saw him looking at me, worried, attentive, and then he said it, he had to say it, I took it the way I wanted to: "You are very nice, very pretty, I like you, but there are only two solutions. Either it was somebody else, or it was you. I don't know how it's even possible, but if you're going to so much trouble to convince yourself it was somebody else, it's because deep down you're not so sure it wasn't you."

Instinctively my left hand reached for his face. Fortunately he ducked and I missed him. Afterwards I went on crying with big sobs, my head in my arms on the table. I am a violent creep.

He got the owner of the coffee bar in Joigny on the phone. He explained who he was. He asked if The Sardine had left. He had. He asked if there were any other drivers coming towards Marseille. There wasn't anyone. He said; "Listen, Theo, look in your phone book and give me the number of a restaurant in Deux-soirs-lès-Avallon." And to me, holding the receiver to my ear: "What was the name of it?"

"At the petrol station they mentioned some people named Pacaud. The Pacauds."

The man in Joigny found the number for us. Toothpaste Smile told him he was a good man, goodbye. Then he called

Deux-Soirs-lès-Avallon. We had to wait twenty minutes for the call to go through. We drank another cup of coffee in silence.

A young woman was on the phone. Toothpaste Smile asked her if she still had a coat that somebody had left at her restaurant.

"The coat belonging to the blonde lady with the bandage on her hand? Of course I have it, who are you?"

"A friend of hers. She is with me."

"She passed by on Saturday afternoon and told my mother-in-law the coat wasn't hers. What am I supposed to think?"

"All right, all right. Tell us what it looks like."

"White, a silky material. It's a summer coat. Wait a minute."

She went to get it. Toothpaste Smile had put his arm around me again. Behind him, through the windows of the restaurant, I saw the Thunderbird motionless in the sun. A few minutes ago I had gone to the bathroom and splashed water on my face, combed my hair, and put on a little lipstick. I had given Toothpaste Smile back his checked cap, it was on the counter in front of us. The fat woman in black was walking back and forth in the empty room, clearing the tables, surreptitiously listening to everything we were saying.

"Hello? It's white and lined with a flowered print," said the young woman at the end of the line. "It has a little mandarin collar. There's a shop label inside: Franck Brothers. Rue de Passy."

With a weary nod I told Toothpaste Smile that this coat might really be mine. He squeezed my shoulder to give me courage. Into the phone he asked, "Is there anything in the pockets?"

"Oh, I didn't think to look."

"Well, look now."

A silence. This woman whom I could not see seemed very close. I could hear her breath and the sound of paper rattling.

"There's an Air France plane ticket. At least, what's left of it. It's like a notebook cover with the pages torn out. The name written on it is Longo, Miss Longo."

"A ticket from Paris?"

"Paris-Orly to Marseille-Marignane."

"Is there a date?"

"July 10 at eight thirty P.M."

"Are you sure?"

"I can read."

"Is that all?"

"No, there are some other papers, some money, and a kid's toy. It's a little pink elephant. You press it and it moves. A little elephant, that's what it is."

I slumped heavily against the counter. Toothpaste Smile supported me as well as he could. Meanwhile I motioned to him with my bandaged hand to go on, that he had to go on, that I was all right. He asked, "The other papers, what are they?"

"Say, isn't this enough for her to recognize her coat? What do you want?"

"Are you going to answer my question?"

"The other papers are all kinds of things, I don't know. A receipt from a garage."

"What garage?"

"Vincent Cotti, boulevard Raspail, Avignon. Seven hundred and twenty-three francs. It's also dated July tenth. The car that was repaired was an American make, I can't read the name, licence number 3210 RX 75."

At first Toothpaste Smile turned his head towards the window to look at the number of the Thunderbird, but you couldn't see it from where we were. He looked at me questioningly. I nodded to show that that was the number, and replaced the receiver. I did not want to hear any more. I managed to get to a chair to sit down. What happened after that is rather vague in my memory. I felt empty inside. Toothpaste Smile talked on the phone for several more minutes. It wasn't with the young woman any more but with a motorist, a German, I think, who had stopped for a drink at the woman's café with his family. Toothpaste Smile had trouble making himself understood.

Later he was standing in front of me, holding my face between his hands. My mind had wandered for a moment, that was all. I tried to smile. I saw that it cheered him up. I felt as if I had known him for a very long time. The fat woman in black, too, who stood behind him, not speaking.

He said, "I have an idea. Somebody could have got into your apartment while you weren't there and stolen that coat. Was it there?"

I shook my head. I couldn't remember. Toothpaste Smile was not an intellectual, but I at least had to stop kidding myself. My door in rue de Grenelle has two bolts and it is a very heavy, very solid door. Nobody could get into my apartment without breaking it down with an axe and waking up all the neighbours. That went for the coat, but also for the message to Maurice Kaub. I had to stop kidding myself.

What time must it be? What time is it now? I go from room to room in this house in which everything really began. I pace, I walk in circles. Sometimes I push back the curtain from a window and see points of light in the dark. Once I even try to count them. Sometimes – the longest time – I lie on a leather sofa in the light coming from the hall, holding my gun against my chest.

Mama Supe does not talk to me any more. I do not talk to myself any more. I only repeat that song from my childhood: "Light my hair, dark my eyes, black my heart, cold the barrel of my gun." Over and over again.

If somebody comes to get me I shall aim calmly in the half light, I shall aim for his head, no matter who it is. A single flame, everything so clear.

I shall try to kill him with one shot, to save bullets. The last one will be for me. They will find me at peace, my eyes open, looking at my real life, in my white suit stained with red, sweet, clean, and beautiful, as I have always wanted to be. I will have given myself only one weekend's reprieve to be somebody else, and then no more, I shall not have succeeded because you never do succeed. You never do succeed.

We drove very fast along a road that he knew by heart. He was worried, of course, and somewhat confused by that phone call to Deux-Soirs-lès-Avallon, but I also sensed in him the pleasure of handling a new car, a joy that was simple, childish, and annoying. He was wearing the red-checked cap again. He drove at top speed almost constantly, with the quick reflexes and decisions of a professional.

As we were going through a town – Salon, I think – he was forced to slow down, and he took the opportunity to get a cigarette out of his shirt pocket. He talked to me a little, not about the coat or my adventure, but about himself, his childhood, his work, probably to help me forget for a moment what I was going through. I learned that he was born of unknown parents, that he had been taken in by a welfare agency and then, at about ten, adopted by a peasant woman from near Nice whom he called "my own mother," and for whom he seemed to have a real veneration.

"She had a farm north of Puget-Théniers, you know the area? I was ridiculously happy. Christ, I was happy. When her husband died, I was eighteen. She sold everything and that's how I started. At first I had an old Renault, I was in mineral water in Vals. To make it pay you've got to travel, and it's still hard going, but you know, I may seem like a clown, but I'm a good worker. Now I have the Somua and a Berliet that does Germany with a pal from the orphanage, a guy who is like a brother to me, you could cut off both his hands, and you still wouldn't get him to say a word against me. His name is Baptistin Laventure. He's quite a guy. Didn't I tell you? We've decided to become millionaires, the two of us. He thinks it's a good idea."

He was hitting a hundred and sixty again. He stopped talking. Later I asked him, "Jean Le Gueven – is that Breton?"

"Actually, I was born in Aveyron. They found me on the steps of a church, like in *Les Deux Orphelines*. That was the name they gave me. They got it out of the newspaper or somewhere."

"And you never found your real mother?"

"No. I didn't even try. What difference does it make who had you or who left you? It's only talk."

"You don't hold it against her now?"

"Who, her? Well, to have left her kid, I suppose she must have had her problems, too. Besides, I'm here, aren't I? That's the main thing, she gave me that. Me, I'm glad just to be alive."

We did not talk again until we came to that big bridge over the Durance that I had crossed with Philippe the night before. The Somua was waiting for us, parked in the sun by the side of the road. Toothpaste Smile stopped behind it and we got out. Little Paul had fallen asleep on the seat. When he woke up at the sound of the door opening he told Toothpaste Smile that they would never get loaded at Pont-Saint-Esprit that evening, and that tomorrow everything would be closed.

"We'll make it," said Toothpaste Smile. "Forty k's by six, can do, and I'll grease their palms to make them stay a little late. Go on, go back to sleep."

He left me at the side of the road by the car, saying, "I talked to a tourist on the phone just now at the café in Deux-Soirs-lès-Avallon. He's bringing your coat down. He thought he would reach Pont-Saint-Esprit around nine or nine thirty, and I said I would meet him. When I've finished loading I could meet you here, in Avignon. How would that be?"

"But aren't you going on to Paris?"

"Sure I am. I'll fix it with Little Paul. I'll get a friend to meet him a little further up. But maybe you'd rather not hang around the neighbourhood until this evening?"

I shook my head and said I didn't mind. He told me to meet him in Avignon at ten thirty in a brasserie opposite the station. That way I wouldn't forget. I would see, everything would work out.

I watched him walk over to his lorry. On his back there was a big perspiration stain, a big spot of a blue darker than the rest of his shirt. I ran after him and caught his arm. I didn't know exactly what I wanted to say. I stood there in front of him like an idiot. Finally he nodded his head and put his hand on my cheek as he had done at the freight yard. Dark in the sunlight, he said, "Until ten thirty, okay? Know what you ought to do until then? First go to a doctor in Avignon and get a clean bandage. Then go to a movie, any movie, and if you get out too early, go to another one. Try not to think about anything until I get back."

"Why are you like this? I mean, you don't know me, I'm interfering with your work, but you're so nice to me – why?"

"You're nice too, you just don't know it. Besides, you have a terrific cap." He handed it to me.

I put it on.

When the lorry disappeared down the road in front of me, I raised the visor with the back of my bandaged hand. I promised myself I'd settle this whole thing one way or another before I saw him again, and afterwards, as God was my witness, I would help him become a millionaire, him and his Baptistin Laventure, if I had to work overtime the rest of my life.

Avignon.

Still the sun, burning my eyes. I saw notched ramparts and a long street lined with café terraces whose holiday flags formed an endless multicoloured tunnel. A double line of cars preceded me, driving in fits and starts. On the pavements I looked at people who wore their nationalities on their faces: Germans, English, Americans with brick-red arms and legs, the women in nylon dresses so transparent that they all looked naked; and as I drove from building to building I crossed alternating bands of friendly shade and harsh light – where was I, Mama Supe, where was I?

I found boulevard Raspail off this street to the left. I unleashed a chorus of hooting behind me as I waited to turn. I did not remember the name of the garage the young woman at Deux-Soirs-lès-Avallon had mentioned on the phone, only the name of the street, so I drove three hundred yards, alternately scrutinizing both sides of the street. I saw the sign I was looking for over a canary yellow awning: "Vincent Cotti, licensed Ford dealer, all foreign makes." There was a hotel next door, the Hotel Angleterre, and in front of it were a couple having difficulty getting some suitcases out of a sports car and a dog with drooping ears who had paused from his stroll to watch them.

I parked in front of the garage. Under the awning a man was removing a wheel. He turned his head and saw the Thunderbird. As I was getting out he got to his feet and said with a strong Provençal accent, "What? Still not working? I don't believe it!"

I walked towards him with my purse in my right hand and my cap on my head, in a suit which I knew was rumpled and sticking to me with perspiration, trying not to feel like a mess. He was a short man in overalls zipped all the way up the front, with eyes that were faded almost yellow and big bushy blond eyebrows.

I asked him, "Do you know this car?"

"Do I know it! We kept it for two weeks; took the whole engine apart. There aren't many I know as well, believe me. What's wrong now?"

"Nothing, everything's fine."

"Doesn't it run?"

"Oh, yes. I – do you know him, the owner of the car?"

"The gentleman from Villeneuve? Not really. Why?"

"He would like a copy of the receipt you gave him. Is that possible?"

"Oh, fine. He wants a copy. Why? Did he lose the other one? You know, it's things like this that ruin business. You're never finished."

He led me through the garage, where several mechanics were working, to a glassed-in cage occupied by two women in yellow blouses. The four of us looked in a ledger. They were all very friendly, very open. One of the two women, a brunette of about thirty with large white breasts under her yawning blouse, realized "from my accent" that I was a Parisian and told me that she had spent five years in Paris in the quartier de la Nation, but that she "wasn't happy" there because the people are uncivilized, nobody talks to anybody. I saw with my own eyes that a certain Maurice Kaub had left the Thunderbird in this garage at the end of June because of some trouble with the automatic transmission. He called for it on the evening of 10 July, paying 723 francs in cash. The woman who had spoken to me was the first to act suspicious when I asked to see the person who had talked to Kaub. She said with dark eyes and full lips, "What do you want with Roger?

You wanted a receipt, didn't you? You have it, don't you? Well? And who are you, anyway?"

Nevertheless, they went to get him. He was a rather tall, muscular young man whose face was stained with grease. He wiped it with a dirty rag. Yes, he remembered very well the M. Kaub who had come to pick up his Thunderbird on Friday evening. It had been about nine thirty, maybe ten o'clock. He had called from Paris that morning to be sure that the car would be ready and that there would be someone at the garage.

"If I understood him right, he was coming to spend the weekend here. He told me he had a house in Villeneuve. Just what did you want to know?"

I could not think of anything to answer. The four of them were all over me in that tiny room where suddenly I couldn't breathe. The dark-haired woman studied me from head to foot. I said, "Nothing, thank you, thank you very much," and rushed out. Their eyes followed me as I walked through the garage. I was so embarrassed, so eager to escape their stares, that I did not see the abandoned tyre under the porch, and I executed Dany Longo's special flying number complete with loop the loop and four-point landing. The dog with the droopy ears in front of the Hotel Angleterre bayed like a lost soul calling for help.

In Villeneuve there were grey arcades, narrow streets with big paving stones, courtyards with people hanging washing out to dry, and, on a big square festooned with lanterns in preparation for that evening's dance, a wedding procession. I parked the car when it had passed. The bride was tall, dark-haired, and bareheaded, and held a red rose in her right hand. The bottom of her white dress was covered with dirt. Everybody seemed to have had plenty to drink. When I walked through the procession to get to a bar I saw in front of me, two men took my arms to lead me to the wedding dance.

I said thank you, thank you very much, and made my escape. The customers in the bar had come outside and were standing on the threshold encouraging the groom. I found myself in an empty room looking across at a blonde woman, lost in her own memories, who was minding the till. She told me how to get to Domaine Saint-Jean, route de l'Abbaye. I drank a glass of fruit juice, bought a pack of Gitanes, and lit one. It seemed a thousand years since I had smoked.

She asked me, "Are you a friend of M. Maurice?"

"No. Or rather, yes."

"I see he lent you his car."

"Do you know him?"

"M. Maurice? Just to say hello to. Sometimes he hunts with my husband. Is he here right now?"

I did not know what to answer. For the first time I wondered whether the unknown man in the boot of the Thunderbird was Maurice Kaub or someone else. I moved my head in a way that could mean anything at all. I paid my bill, said Thank you very much, and left. She called me back to tell me that I had left my change, my cap, my Gitanes, and the keys to the car on the bar.

Domaine Saint-Jean: a wrought-iron gate, a long pink asphalt drive, and a low, rambling house with a tiled roof, which I saw through vines and cypress trees. There were other estates on the same road, perched high above Villeneuve like the towers of a fortress, but I did not see anyone until I was standing in front of the gate, and a voice in the six o'clock sunlight forced me to turn around.

"There's nobody home, mademoiselle. I looked three times."

A blonde girl of about twenty was leaning over a stone wall on the other side of the road. She had a rather pretty triangular face and very bright eyes.

173

"Is it Monsieur Maurice you're looking for?"

"Yes, Maurice Kaub."

"He isn't home" – running her index finger over the bridge of a little turned-up nose – "but you can go in, you know, everything is open."

When I came over to her, she finished her speech, stood up suddenly on the wall in her dress, which was pink with a full skirt that revealed long, golden thighs, held out her arms, and said, "Will you help me down?"

I did the best I could, holding her by one leg and the waist. She landed on her feet, which were bare, and I managed to stay on mine. She was a little shorter than me with long sun-bleached hair like a girl in a Swedish movie. She was neither Swedish nor from Avignon, but was born in Cachan (Seine) and had gone to school in Aix-en-Provence. Her name was Catherine (Kiki) Aupieu ("Don't say anything, I've already heard all the jokes you can make about my name, they drive me mad"). She said this very fast, along with a lot of other things (that her father was in construction like M. Maurice, that she was "still a virgin, but strangely nymphomaniacal, so of course, psychologically speaking, she was something of a mess"), not letting me get a word in, walking towards the Thunderbird. She heaved a few sighs, telling me that she had had a ride in this car a few weeks before, in June, with M. Maurice. He had let her drive as far as Forcalquier one night, and sure enough on the way back she had felt all funny, rather devilish, but he had been a real gentleman, M. Maurice, he had not taken advantage of the opportunity to simplify her psychology. Did I hold it against her?

"Why?"

"You're his girlfriend, aren't you?"

"Do you recognize me?"

I was very close to her again, I saw her cheeks flush slightly. She said, "I've seen pictures of you. I think you're very, very beautiful. It's true, to tell the truth, I was sure you would come. If I tell you something, you won't laugh? You're even more beautiful without clothes."

She was mad. I was talking to a mad person.

"Then you recognize me?"

"Oh, I must have seen you arrive sometimes. Surely. I really like your cap."

It took me a few minutes to think clearly, to decide how to handle this. Meanwhile I got into the car and told her to open the gate. She obeyed. When she came back I asked her what she was doing here. She was spending the holidays with her aunt in a house behind the hill that you couldn't see from the road. I asked her why she was so sure there was nobody home at Maurice Kaub's house. She hesitated – that gesture of running the index finger over the bridge of her short nose was a mannerism – and said, "After all, you can't be jealous. You know how M. Maurice is, don't you?"

Saturday afternoon she had driven another woman who was coming from Paris to his house, a redhead who was on TV, the one who ran the lady's program Marité What's-her-name. All the doors were open at Kaub's house but nobody was home. The star had gone away and come back a little later with the same success. After that she had left for good, dejected; on awful spike heels, carrying her fancy leather suitcase.

"Isn't there a servant or someone?"

"I didn't see anyone when I came back this morning."

"You came back?"

"Yes, I was worried. M. Maurice came home on Friday night, I'm sure, I heard him. And there's something else that worries me, but it's probably silly."

"What?"

"Well, somebody fired a rifle in his house on Friday night. I was in the olive grove out at the back. Three shots. I know he's always using his guns, but it was after ten o'clock; it worried me."

"Why didn't you go and see?"

"Well, I wasn't alone at the time. To tell you the truth, my aunt is older than Methuselah and when I want to have fun with somebody I have to do it outside. You don't look as if you get what I mean. Do you really not understand, or are you just playing dense?"

"No, I understand, I understand very well. Who were you with?"

"A boy. So, what's wrong with your hand? Don't answer like Bécaud or I'll kill myself."

"It's nothing, I assure you. Has anyone come since Saturday?"

"You know, I'm not the doorkeeper around here. I have a very demanding personal life myself." A triangular face, very blue eyes, a pink dress tight over little pointed breasts – she had a vivacity that pleased me but made me sad, I don't know why.

I told her, "Well, thanks, goodbye."

"You can call me Kiki, you know."

"Goodbye, Kiki."

As I drove up the pink asphalt drive I saw her in the rear-view mirror, barefoot, blonde, running her index finger over her nose again, then climbing up the wall again.

The rest, the end of the voyage towards myself, took place three or four hours ago, I don't remember. I walked into Maurice Kaub's house which was open, empty, silent, and familiar, yes, so familiar that as soon as I was through the door I knew who I was. I have not left. I am waiting in the dark with my gun in my arms, lying on a leather sofa which is cool against my bare legs – and when the leather gets warm under my skin I move, I seek the cold.

When I came in, the inside of this house was strangely similar to what I remembered – or imagined – of the Caravaille house. The lamps, the rug with unicorns in the hall, this room I am in now: I knew them. Then on one wall I saw a light box, and when I pressed a button a fishing port appeared, then another and another: colour transparencies. I knew it was Agfacolour, because I've been in this rat race too long not to recognize the quality of a red.

The door to the next room was open. In it, as I expected, was an enormous bed covered with white fur, and on the wall opposite, mounted in a wooden frame, a black-and-white photograph of a girl who was completely naked, a very fine photograph showing the grain of the skin. This girl was not sitting across an armchair, but standing with her back to the camera, with the top of her body and her face turned towards the lens. It was not Anita Caravaille, or anyone else whom I could saddle with the burden of my own life. It was me.

I waited until I had stopped trembling. I took the time – a very long time – to change my glasses with fingers that wouldn't move, with a soft, sickening lump heaving in my chest. I made sure it was my neck, my shoulders, and my legs, that it could not have been a collage. Here again, I know too much about the business to make a mistake. Besides, there was a sense of monstrous clarity, you know very well when it is yourself.

I think I spent over an hour sitting on that bed in front of that picture, my mind a blank, for later, when it got dark, I must have turned on a light.

Then I did a silly thing, which I am ashamed of: I unhooked my skirt and went into a bathroom – it was not black-tiled as

I thought it would be, but red and orange and very large, with a mirror – to make sure it really was my body. A silly thing in the silence of that empty house; me with my skirt at my feet, my panties down, suddenly meeting my own glance, a strange, lifeless, bespectacled glance, a glance emptier than this house, and yet myself, really myself.

I put my clothes back on and went back into the room with the black leather armchairs. On the way I looked at the photograph again. As far as I could still be sure of anything, it had been taken at my apartment in rue de Grenelle. I was halfway between the bed and the cupboard, I was looking around with a smile that clearly expressed either affection or love, I don't know which.

I turned on more lights, opened some drawers, inspected the floor above. Up there I found a kind of photographer's studio. In a drawer I found two more big pictures of myself, slightly underexposed, among dozens showing naked girls whom I did not know. In these two I was not dressed, but only half naked. In one, my breasts were bare and I was sitting on the edge of the bath with a blank expression, taking off my stockings. In the other, a front view, I was looking down slightly, wearing a blouse I threw out at least two years ago, and naked from the waist down. I tore these two pictures to pieces, holding them against me because I couldn't use my left hand. I couldn't help it. I even think it did me good.

After that, I searched other rooms and found myself everywhere. I found underwear, an old turtleneck sweater, a pair of black trousers, two dresses that belonged to me. And, by an unmade bed whose sheets were still impregnated with my perfume, an earring that I recognized, some notes in my handwriting, and a man's leather belt, very wide, which meant nothing to me.

I collected all my things – God knows where I left them when I went downstairs – and came back to the room where I am now. On the wall opposite the light box there was a gun rack with several guns in it. Then on the floor, in the middle of the navy-blue carpet, I noted a big rectangle distinctly less faded than the rest, as if there had been a rug in this spot that had been removed. On a chair a man's suit, also navy blue, had been carefully laid out, the trousers across the seat, the jacket on the back. In one of the jacket pockets I found Maurice Kaub's wallet. The picture on his driving licence proved that this was indeed the man with the prominent cheekbones and sleek hair who was decomposing in the boot of the Thunderbird. I had no other memory of him, and the contents of the wallet, which I examined carefully, did not remind me of anything either.

I had seen a telephone in the hall. In my handbag I found the scrap of paper on which I had written the number of the Caravailles' hotel in Geneva. I gave the number to the operator, who told me to expect an hour's wait. I left the house, got into the car, and drove it behind the house, near a kind of barn containing a tractor, pitchforks, and a big winepress. It was dark. I was very cold. I could not stop trembling. But I liked the cold, and something angry and obstinate in me, a kind of mysterious energy, kept me going and gave me great confidence in what I did. Through the mental confusion I was in, I also had the impression that I was thinking quickly and well; it was very strange.

I opened the boot, paying no attention to the smell that might be inside or to the pain that shot up through my left arm. I took hold of the man in the rug with both hands and pulled with all my might, rested, and pulled until he fell out of the car. Then I dragged him into the barn. I left him in the back against a wall. I covered him first with the rug, then with everything I could find: boards, wicker baskets, tools. As I left I closed the double door, which creaked. I remember that creaking noise, and also that I had the gun with the black barrel in my right hand, that I did not want to let go of it even long enough to close the door, that I did not want to let go of it again for anything in the world.

Later, when the Thunderbird was parked in front of the house again and everything had been quiet and dark outside for a long time, the phone rang. I was leaning against the wall right next to it with my eyes closed and the gun in my left arm, waiting for my last chance not to give way to madness. All I had to do was put out my hand and pick up the receiver.

A woman's voice said, "I have Geneva. Go ahead."

I thanked her. I could still talk. Another voice said that it was the Hotel Beau Rivage. I asked if Mrs Caravaille was there. She was. A third voice – surprised, lively, friendly – Anita's voice. At this moment my tears began to flow again, and I was seized by the most desperate hope – or need for hope – that I have ever felt in my life.

I talked to Anita as I would have done before I ever came into this house, and even as I would have done years ago, when we were twenty, before that night in May when I did not even try to help her as she was slipping into a kind of madness, before that dawn in May when I found her in my apartment, sobbing before my eyes for the first time, sober, full of self-hatred, that dawn when I refused to take the slightest responsibility for what she had been through – "But why did you leave me," she kept saying, like a litany, "why did you leave me?" – when I did not even have the courage to listen to her, when I hit her with all my might to make her shut up and threw her out.

I told Anita, who did not understand a word I was saying and made me repeat the same things three times, that I had kept her Thunderbird since I had come to work at Villa Montmorency. She did not own a Thunderbird. She did not even know what it was, she could not understand the word over the phone. All she did understand was my sobs. "My God, Dany, where are you, what's going on?" She had not seen me since the week before Christmas, when we had had that fight in the café in Place de l'Opéra. She had never lived at Villa Montmorency – "My God, Dany, is this a joke? Tell me it's a joke! You know very well where I live!" She lived on avenue Mozart, M-O-Z-A-R-T, and anyway, if Michel Caravaille had brought me to their house to do some typing, she would have seen me, she would know about it – "Please, Dany, tell me what's going on."

I believe that, through my tears, through the sobs that prevented me from answering, I laughed. Yes, I laughed, if you could call it that. Now she was upset. She kept repeating "Hello! Hello!" and I heard her hurried breathing at the other end of the line.

"Where are you, Dany? My God, please at least tell me where you are!"

"In Villeneuve-lès-Avignon. Listen Anita. I'll explain everything, don't worry – I think it will pass, I . . ."

"Where did you say you were?"

"In Villeneuve-lès-Avignon, in the Vaucluse. In a house."

"My God, how – what house; Dany? Who are you with? How did you know I was in Geneva?"

"I must have heard it at the office. I don't remember. I must have heard it."

"Is there someone with you? Let me speak to them."

"No, there isn't anyone."

"But my God, you can't stay alone in the state you're in! I don't understand, Dany, I don't understand."

Now I heard her crying too. I tried to reassure her, to tell her that I felt better already from hearing her voice. She said that Michel Caravaille was due back any minute, that he would know what to do, that they would call me back. She would take a plane, she would come to where I was. I had to promise that I would not go away, that I would wait for them to call me back. I had no intention of waiting for anyone but I promised I would, and when I hung up I thought with real relief that in her anxiety she had not asked for the phone number of the house and that she would not know where to find me.

The door to the hall, a rectangle of light. Me in the dark. Time has expanded like a worn-out spring. I know that time can expand, I know it very well. When I had that blackout in the petrol station in Deux-Soirs-lès-Avallon, how long did it last? Ten seconds? A minute? That minute was long enough for reality to get lost in.

Yes, it was then, when I came to kneeling on the tile floor, that the lie began. I was born for lies. It was inevitable that one day I would get trapped in the most abominable one of all.

The truth? I, Dany Longo, followed a lover who was leaving me. I threatened him in a telephone message. I caught a plane three quarters of an hour after he did. I found him here in this house after he had picked up his car that had been left in a garage for repairs. During the quarrel that followed I took down one of the guns from the rack in this room. I fired three bullets, two of which hit this man in the middle of the chest. Then, terrified, I had only one thought: to take the body away from here, to hide it, to get rid of it. I dragged it to the car boot wrapped in a rug. I drove all night in a kind of trance along the main roads to Paris. I tried to get a few hours' sleep in a hotel in Chalon-sur-Saône. I was stopped by a policeman because one of my lights wasn't working. I left my coat in a café near the Auxerre road. It must have been from this café that I called Bernard Thorr. Then I must have changed my mind because I did not know how to get rid of the body and because anyway when it was discovered it would not be hard to trace it to me. I turned back, half mad from fatigue and fear. My left hand had already been hurt, probably during the quarrel with my victim. I went back to the petrol station where I had been that morning, for no reason, perhaps like a robot who follows the same path over and over again, who can't stop. There, in front of a basin tap that was running, something inside me snapped, and I fainted. That was the beginning of the lie.

When I opened my eyes again – ten seconds, one minute later? – I remembered only the alibis I had invented during the night. I must have willed so forcefully, so desperately, that the reality not be true that it stopped being true for me. I clung to an insane story made up out of whole fabric, in which imaginary details were mingled with real ones: the light box, the white fur bed, that picture of a naked woman really existed. I was filling the void into which I had pushed Maurice Kaub and everything related to him with a nightmare logic. Once again, in the face of an event that my mind would not accept, I was choosing flight, but since there was no other choice, it was a flight into myself.

Yes, I know it, all this is in character.

Who was Maurice Kaub? Why do I still have no memory of him, if now I accept the idea that all this happened? In one of the pictures of myself that I tore upstairs I was wearing a blouse that I haven't had for two years. So Maurice Kaub knew me longer even than that. That I had already been in this house several times before was obvious from the clothes left around and what the blonde girl who lives across the road said. And if I allowed that man to take such pictures of me, I must have been intimate with him in a way that you can't just erase from your mind or your life. I don't understand.

But what is there to understand? I know that madness exists. I know that mad people don't know they are mad. All I know is what I've picked up from skimming women's magazines or one psychology lecture, which I've long since forgotten. I am incapable of understanding by what mental aberration I reached this state, but my interpretation of the facts can no longer be very far from the truth.

Who was Maurice Kaub?

I must get up, turn on the lights, and search this house more carefully.

The window: I open the curtains. The sense of being suddenly more vulnerable: I left the gun on the sofa. It's absurd, who could come at this hour? Outside it is night, a clear night dotted with peaceful lights. Besides, who is looking for me? I am the only one who is doing that. Zurich. All that white. That's it. I wanted to die too. I told the doctor, "Kill me, please kill me." He didn't do it. You can't live for years with the certainty of your guilt without eventually giving in to it, and going mad. That must be it.

When Mama Supe died I was told too late, I wasn't able to get there in time for the funeral, and one of the sisters said, "There were other girls to tell, you're not unique." That day I ceased to be unique for someone, and I've never been unique for anyone since. And yet I could have been unique for a little boy. I don't know why – the doctors didn't say anything – but I've always been sure that the child I would have had was a boy. I have a portrait of him in my heart, as if he were still growing. He is now three years and five months old. He would have been born in March. He has his father's black eyes, mouth, and laugh, and my blond hair, and a space between the two middle teeth in the top row, like me. I know how he walks, how he talks, and I can't stop, I can't stop killing him.

I can't be alone any more.

I have to get out, away from this house. My suit is dirty. I'll go and get my coat from Jean Le Gueven. The coat will cover up the dirt. I'll keep the car. I'll head straight for the Italian or Spanish border, I'll get out of the country, I'll use the rest of my money to get further away. Put water on your face. Mama Supe was right, I should have taken all the money I could at the bank, I should have run away then and there. Mama Supe is always right. I would already be out of this by now. What time is it? My watch has stopped. Comb your hair.

Outside, when I turn on the lights in the Thunderbird, it is after ten thirty by the clock on the dashboard. Toothpaste Smile must be waiting for me. I know he will wait for me. I drive down the asphalt driveway. The gate is still open. The lights of Avignon below. Echoes of holiday pierce the wind that surrounds me. The body isn't in the car any more, is it? No, the body isn't in the car any more. Do you have to have a passport to cross the Spanish border? Drive to Andalusia, take a boat to Gibraltar. Pretty names, a new life, far away. This time its myself I'm leaving behind. Forever.

He is there. He is wearing a leather jacket over his shirt. He is sitting at a marble table inside the brasserie. There is a package wrapped in brown paper on the seat. His smile as he watches me walk across the room. Stop worrying people. Hold on.

"You haven't had your bandage changed?"

"No. I couldn't find a doctor."

"What did you do? Tell me. Did you go to the cinema? Was it good?"

"Yes. And then I had a walk through the town."

I am holding on. He loaded five tonnes of vegetables with Little Paul. The German tourists who brought down the coat delivered it right here, in front of the station. He took their

185

address so that he could do them "a good turn" one of these days. They were on their way to Corsica. Corsica is terrific, lots of beaches. He is watching me with confident eyes, sitting opposite me. He is catching a train at five past eleven, he is going to meet Little Paul in Lyon. Unfortunately that only leaves him a quarter of an hour.

"You've gone to a lot of trouble."

"I wouldn't have done it if I didn't want to. I'm very glad to see you again. You know, in Pont-Saint-Esprit I couldn't stop thinking about you while I was loading my cases."

"I'm better now. Everything is fine."

He grins and takes a swallow of beer. He asks me to come and sit beside him on the seat. When I am there he puts his hand on my left arm squeezes it gently through the sleeve of my jacket.

"You must have friends, somebody you can talk to?"

"Talk to about what?"

"I don't know. All this."

"There's no one. The only person I'd like to call I can't, it's not possible."

"Why?"

"He has a wife, a life of his own. I promised myself a long time ago that I would leave him alone."

He unwraps the package he has brought and hands me my white coat, carefully folded. He says, "Your memories of what happened on Saturday must have got mixed up, that happens when you're tired. Once, on two hours' sleep, instead of going to Paris, I went the other way. I was with Baptistin at the time. When he woke up I had already driven a hundred kilometres. And I swore up and down that we had already made the trip. After a while he slapped my face to straighten me out. Would you like something to drink?"

I don't want anything to drink. In the pockets of my coat I find the Air France plane ticket, my little pink elephant, five hundred and thirty francs in a pay envelope, the receipt from the garage in Avignon, and some papers of mine. Toothpaste Smile is watching me, and when I look up to thank him, to tell him that all this is really mine, his eyes are friendly and concerned. It is then that over the din of the brasserie and the pounding of my heart, I hear again, awful and wonderful, the voice of Mama Supe.

And Mama Supe is telling me that I did not kill Maurice Kaub, that I am not mad, oh no, Dany, that it really happened the way I thought it did, that this really is the first night of my life that I've been in this town, where suddenly everything seems to light up, where orchestras are beginning to play. The truth about this weekend appears to me so suddenly that it makes me tremble. My thoughts follow each other so quickly that my face must be transfigured. Toothpaste Smile is amazed, he is happy too.

"Hey, what are you thinking about? What is making you so happy?"

I don't know how to tell him. So I kiss him quickly on the cheek, and I take his hand in my bandaged hand, and squeeze it hard, it should hurt but it doesn't. I feel good. I am free. Or almost. My smile freezes. A thought occurs to me, as blinding as the rest: someone is following me, is spying on me right now, someone must have followed me from Paris for everything to make sense.

"Dany, my child" says Mama Supe, "there's a chance that they've lost you, otherwise you'd be dead already. It's your death they want, don't you understand?"

I must get Toothpaste Smile away from me.

"Let's go, shall we? I'll come with you. You're going to miss your train."

He helps me on with my coat. I open my handbag to make sure I am not mistaken. No, this time I'm not mistaken.

187

A new fear. Outside, Toothpaste Smile puts his arm around me confidently and I can't shake the idea that his life is in danger because of me. I can't help turning around, first to the Thunderbird parked near the brasserie, then to that long street beyond the walls, which I drove up this afternoon and which is now studded with lights.

"What's the matter?"

"Nothing. I was just looking."

I put my left arm around his waist, and he laughs. The station waiting room. A visitor's ticket. An underground tunnel. The platform. I keep turning around. Strange travellers preoccupied with their own worries. Toothpaste Smile's train is announced over a loudspeaker. Dance music in the distance. He holds me by the shoulders and says, "Do you know what we're going to do? Tomorrow night I'll be in Paris, in the hotel I always go to, in rue Jean-Lantier. I want you to promise to ring me."

"I promise."

"Do you have my cap?"

It's in my bag. With a biro he writes a phone number on the inside edge and gives it back to me. Then, as the train arrives, whistling, and pulls up along the platform with an ear-splitting din, he says something I can't hear, shakes his head, takes me by the shoulders and squeezes them hard in his big hands. That's all. As he leaves my life, leaning out of the window to give me a last wave, dark, smiling the smile I love, already far away, already gone, I remember the promise I made myself to help him and his buddy Laventure become millionaires. "Don't lose that cap," Mama Supe tells me. "And since you want to destroy the plot against you you'd better hurry."

On the pavement in front of the station I begin with the ticket for that plane I never took. I tear it into little pieces, looking around me at the same time. To keep up my nerve I tell myself that they must have lost track of me long ago, but I'm sure it isn't true. I can even feel upon me the weight of an unflinching, pitiless gaze.

Once again, for the last time, the Thunderbird. "Don't go back there," pleads Mama Supe. I drive through illuminated streets, around squares full of people celebrating. I have to ask the way to Villeneuve again. In the rearview mirror I watch the cars behind me. The crowd and the music calm me. As long as I am with people I am sure I am in no danger.

Dancing in Villeneuve too. I stop in the same coffee bar as before. I buy a big manila envelope and a stamp. I go back to the car and, in the holiday racket, write the few words that will be necessary if I die. I seal the envelope and address it to myself, rue de Grenelle. I put it in a letter box on the square. I am afraid, but no one is following me through the crowd.

The long route de l'Abbaye. Now, along the winding road, I can see two headlights behind me. The gate is still open. I stop the car in the drive. I turn out the lights. The headlights pass and disappear. I wait for my heart to calm down. I drive on. I stop in front of the dark house. I make sure I am leaving nothing that belongs to me in the car. Carefully I wipe the steering wheel and dashboard with my scarf. I leave Bird of Thunder as I took him in Orly, with an apprehension that constricts my throat and slows down all my movements. "Don't go in, Dany, don't go in," begs Mama Supe. But I have to do it, I must at least destroy that picture on the wall, at least take back my clothes. The door. I turn on a lamp in the hall. It's better already. I close the door after me. I give myself five minutes to put everything back in order and leave. I pause for breath.

I am on the threshold of the room with the leather sofa when I hear something move. I do not scream. Even if

I wanted to, no sound would come out of my mouth. The light is behind me. In front of me is a great black void. "The gun!" says Mama Supe. "You left the gun on the sofa. If he is in the dark, he hasn't noticed it yet." I remain paralyzed, mute, with leaden legs. Another sound, nearer. "The gun, Dany, the gun!" Mama Supe yells inside me. Desperately I try to remember where the sofa is in the room. I drop my bag to the floor to free my good hand. Suddenly there is a gasp right beside me, a kind of frenzied panting. I have to reach . . .

The Gun

I got into my car. I went to Villa Montmorency. I did not know the house. Anita let me in. She was crying. She told me she had shot a man with a rifle. She thought he might still be alive. She had not had the courage to look. I went down into the basement. It was a cellar fixed up as a shooting room. There were cork targets. My step was heavy. I am a heavy man. I walk the way I talk, doggedly. People take this for confidence. It is only the rhythm of my blood in my veins.

I saw the man lying on the floor and the rifle beside him. I know a lot about guns. I used to be a good hunter. It was a Winchester rifle, 7·62 calibre, with a grooved barrel. The initial velocity of the bullets is over seven hundred metres a second. He could not be alive. If one of the two shots had hit him in the head, it would have blown his head off.

I looked at the rifle first. I lost all hope of ever living a normal life again. I don't know what normal means any more. If Anita had used an automatic gun, I would have called the police immediately. We would have passed it off as an accident. On the Winchester there is a trigger guard that has to be cocked before every shot. You must have seen it in Westerns, Dany. You must have seen the good guy in the movie picking off his row of Indians. It was probably because she'd seen it in the movies too that Anita was able to work that trigger guard. She fired three times. Nobody would believe it was an accident.

I examined the man. I knew him. His name was Maurice Kaub. I had met him several times socially. He had two bullet holes in the middle of his chest. I opened his dressing gown to look at them. She had fired point-blank. I looked up and found the point of impact of the third bullet. It was just a black scratch on the concrete wall beside him. I found a piece of bent lead in one corner of the room. I put it in my pocket.

Anita was still crying violently. I asked her why she had killed this man. She said that he had finished with her, that he had been her lover for several years. She had known him before our marriage. I hit her in the face. She fell against the wall. She shook her head, in a tangle of red dress and petticoat. I saw her open thighs and between them the strip of her panties. The sight increased my rage. I grabbed her by the hair and the top of her dress. I pulled her to her feet and hit her. She begged me to stop. I picked her up again and hit her with the flat of my hand. I stood for a long time looking at her sprawled at my feet with her face to the floor. She went on crying through her stupor. I grabbed her under the arms and forced her up the stairs. Blood was running from her nose. I dragged her into the room where you did the typing. I shoved her into an armchair and went into the next room to get water. On the wall I saw the nude photograph of Anita. I stood crying against that wall. I was thinking about my little girl. My life revolves around my little girl. You have to understand me, Dany. Since she was born I have finally known an affection that is unlimited, undivided, totally fanatical. I know what they mean by an absolute. It was primarily to protect my daughter that I decided to kill you. Any other explanation is meaningless without that one.

The rest has to do with what I know about you. I have been watching you longer than you think. I have been watching you since the day I first saw you at the agency, the day you were hired. I remember, wrongly perhaps, that you were wearing a dress of very light yellow, the colour of your hair. I found you beautiful, even exciting. I hated you. I am a very well-informed cuckold, Dany. I know all about my wife's premarital adventures in that little apartment in rue de Grenelle where I went the other evening. I know all about the boys – leaner, better-looking than I am – for whom she spread her legs, and I even know that once there were two of them enjoying her in your bed, and satisfying her as I cannot. She did not tell me about this final humiliation until later, under duress, as she always tells me everything in the end. But I knew about your willingness to lend her your apartment and let her degrade herself. This only made me hate you more for acting like a fine, wholesome girl who leads a blameless life. For me you were a constant reminder of what I longed to forget, you were part of the monstrous dreams of jealousy. You were a monster.

I always watched you secretly, Dany. I watched you furtively but avidly. I watched your left hand. I have always thought that left-handed people are mad and evil and treacherous, like people who bite their nails. Whenever you saw me you must have been laughing uproariously to yourself at the thought of all those bastards who screwed Anita and performed other perversions on her. I was the one who was going mad. Undoubtedly, she was still deceiving me and you knew all about it. She must have told you about the disgusting things people do, and that I am nothing but a clumsy oaf who doesn't know the first thing about making love. I had no hold over you, but I would have liked you to be humiliated too, I would have liked to destroy the splendid harmony of your face, your voice, your walk.

Last year I heard about the shameful episode that obliterated everything else. Late one night, in a restaurant,

Anita and I ran into a young man her age who was as puny and conceited as the rest. Since Anita became my mistress, I've hated young men. I would gladly crush them with my bare hands if I could get away with it. Every last one. Or I would force them to be treated like girls by other men. Nothing makes me happier than finding out that some actor, whom Anita or the stupidest typist at the agency finds irresistible, is a fag. I am convinced that to do that kind of work, to sell themselves willingly, they must all be queer. Anita went pale when she saw this boy. The hand she offered him and the few word she said to him trembled. We ordered supper. He sat with friends at another table, laughing, gesturing, sometimes casting a furtive glance towards us, towards Anita. I paid for the food we had not yet eaten and dragged Anita to the car, which was parked in rue Quentin-Bauchard across the road from a cinema where we had just seen a happy movie for sad people, and I beat her. She told me about that evening before we were married when she had had drinks with two boys – one of them the boy in the restaurant – and you. She told me that after midnight, when you came out of a nightclub, you all went to your place for a nightcap. She said that at a certain point with her dress already pulled up, she was kissing one of the bastards – the other one – while this one was trying to do the same to you. She said that you insulted her and ran out of your own apartment, leaving her there. She kept repeating through her tears, and I knew she meant it, "I wasn't in my right mind, I didn't know what I was doing. Dany doesn't drink, she doesn't make love, she prides herself on being perfect and not needing anybody, but the first chance she gets, she leaves you. She didn't think about me for a second, all-right? She was gone, and I was drunk, drunk." I put Anita in a cab. I went back to the restaurant. The boy was still there. I waited for him outside, and later I followed him along the

Champs-Elysées, walking at my normal pace a hundred yards behind him. He did not see me, he was with a blonde girl who was as infatuated as you all are. He walked her to his place in rue La Boétie. They stopped often to laugh in front of an unlit shop window, or to kiss like animals, so anyone who was still on the street could see them. I caught up with them in the hall of his building. I hit him first, then her. Before she had time to recover from her surprise or to scream, I picked her up, unconscious, and I pushed him, reeling, up the stairs. I swore I would strangle him if he called for help. Out of his mind with fear, he let me into a big apartment on the second floor. I put the blonde girl on the floor and closed the door. The boy was beginning to argue, so I hit him again. I held him against the wall by the front of his torn jacket and I hit him as hard as I could with my open hand. Then, beside myself, I tore off his trousers and the flowered material of his undershorts at the same time, and dragged him into the next room to find an instrument with which I might humiliate him further before the eyes of his mistress. I seem to remember that he pleaded with me and called me sir, that he had neither courage nor the slightest reflex of defence, that he was utterly passive, and that it was this weak passivity that calmed my fury. I threw him into a chair, in the kitchen. I lifted his face by the chin. Blood was running out of his ears and nose. I talked to him. I don't know what I said. He couldn't understand anyway. No one can understand. I went back to the girl in the other room. She called me sir too. I closed her mouth with my left hand and tore off the front of her clothes, standing her against the same wall where I had beaten up her lover. She looked at me, her enormous eyes filled with tears. She was sweet and as terrified as a child. I let her go, Dany. No one can understand. Somehow I found myself in my car in rue Quentin-Bauchard, crying, my head in my arms on the steering wheel. I have cried only twice since my adolescence: that night and last Friday, beside that disgusting picture of my wife. Can you understand, Dany?

That same night I found out about your trip to Zurich and some of the other times Anita had betrayed me since our marriage. She didn't tell me about Kaub, though. I stood alone for a long time looking at my sleeping daughter. Then I knocked myself out with sleeping pills, and I went to sleep on the floor by her cradle, dreaming of her. The next day I arranged to meet the boy I had beaten up in a café near his apartment. His face was swollen but he held forth over a revolting glass of tomato juice, because he knew that now it was I who was afraid of him. I wrote him a cheque. He told me that I was mad, that I ought to be behind bars. He laughed between two pieces of adhesive tape. I lowered myself to the point of asking for his version of that night in May. The real horror was that he had only the vaguest memory of the incident, which had bored him. He said that, in other words, I was paying him for screwing my wife. He wondered out loud whether he ought to split the money with his friend.

The rest of that day I couldn't think about work for a second. Sweating from head to foot, I brooded about Anita's confessions. They featured at least one boy whom I knew and whom there was a possibility of punishing. Do you remember that dark-haired craftsman who looked like a bullfighter, Jacques Vitta, who left the agency shortly after a car crash? The truth is that I waited for him, too, that night, in front of the big complex where he lived in Bougival. When I got there it was seven o'clock and the setting sun was flaming over the Seine. Three or four children came and played near me. I picked up their ball. I talked to them. Then I was alone. The hours passed. I smoked, I walked beside a row of street lamps. It was past midnight when Vitta arrived in his Citroën and parked in a car park. He was alone. When he saw me coming, he understood immediately what I was doing there. He did not want to get out of his car, he clung desperately to the door. I pushed against the Citroën with both hands and turned it over. Windows in the nearest buildings flew up. There were voices in the night. I dragged Vitta out of the car. He had much more pride than the other bastard, he tried to punch me in the stomach. I knocked him down, picked him up, and hit him again on a lawn until I realized that I was going to kill him. I went home. That night, too, I slept on the floor beside my little girl. Two or three days later Vitta came into my office with his resignation. He refused my cheque. He made me pay for a new door and bumper for his car, not for the beating. He had gone to a hotel in rue de Passy with my wife five or six times. Making an obscene gesture, he told me that he had treated her like a whore, that he wasn't interested in her any more. Do you understand me, Dany?

After that it was you I hated, more than anyone else. I tried to stop looking at you during the Monday morning meetings. For a while I seriously considered firing you. Two things stopped me: I would have needed an excuse to offer your colleagues, some professional mistake that you would not be likely to commit; then, too, you would immediately have gone to work for another agency, and I would have run into you again, with a better job and more power over life than you have today. I chose to wait.

Months went by. I was keeping an eye on Anita, and I thought I was doing a good job. I thought that the few days I told you about had cured her of hurting us. I loved her. I have always loved her. I know what they think at the agency, that as soon as she got there she decided to get pregnant and marry the boss. Nothing is further from the truth, Dany. She didn't need anybody to get the money and social position she wanted. On the contrary, she rejected my advances, she wasn't interested in me. She went out with me a few times. I took her to dinner. I talked about my childhood, about how the other kids were afraid of me. I tried to impress her with memories that brought out my physical strength. But to her I was just a big oaf, she was bored. When we left the restaurant, which she did not enjoy at all, I did not know what else to do, I can't dance, I don't know any of the chic places to go. I took her back to her mother's on boulevard Suchet. After that I would pick up some whore to satisfy the desire I had for her. I want you to understand me. The first time I took her it was by force; one Saturday afternoon when the two of us had come to work at the agency. It was the best luck I ever had, for Michèle was conceived that day, and eight months later I married Anita. I know that at least before our marriage she felt some kind of attraction for me, even if it was only her obscene delight in discovering that a man of my build is different from other men in every part of his body. The first times she came to my home she undressed with feverish, hesitant gestures, and I don't know what excited her most, pain or pleasure. The livelier and more confident she was the rest of the day, apparently displaying a rare instinct for domination, the more naïve and clumsy were her efforts to recreate the brutal submission of our first embrace. This is the root of all Anita's misery. She is desperately attracted to what hurts her. The secret of her attachment to Maurice Kaub is that he was able to hurt her constantly, to frighten her, to force her to do things she did not want to do. The pictures of you, Dany, are only a small example – he shrank from nothing to keep her in his power. One night while we were making love she gave me a belt and explained in a few miserable words that I was to beat her without paying any attention to her screams, or else kill her, because there was no way out for her. But

I couldn't follow her, I couldn't lend myself to what I did not understand. Who can? Do you understand me, Dany? Those two bullet holes in a man's chest upset me because they were a threat to Michèle's future; I hit Anita in that basement because I discovered that she had another bastard who had taken me for what I am, a cuckold. But that was all. I was glad he was dead, I was glad that to clear ourselves of this murder it would be necessary to kill you, too. I love Anita. I love her the same way I love my little girl, because, contrary to what everyone else thinks, I know that she is really nothing but a miserable little girl herself. I assure you that it has never occurred to me for a second to abandon her, to let her go to jail, to let her suffer alone, and it never will.

When I went back to her on Friday, in that room where I brought you later, she had stopped crying. We talked for a long time, her arms around my neck, her face against mine. In a monotonous voice she told me about her affair with Maurice Kaub, whom she had been seeing sporadically since our marriage, but to whom she always returned. She had fired at him because the gun was within reach during one of their quarrels. He was getting ready to leave for Villeneuve-lès-Avignon where he was expecting a visit from another woman. There was nothing in her story that suggested any way to elude the law. She told me that in her meetings with Kaub she had always taken a great many precautions because of me. They used to meet at his home when his servants were away – as they were that weekend – and when necessary she had used an assumed name: yours. That was it, Dany.

I am a man who speaks and moves heavily, but I think fast. It was four fifteen at the time. It was three o'clock when she had called me at the office, in tears, and told me to come to Villa Montmorency. Kaub had been dead for an hour and a quarter. It took me a few minutes more to invent the plot that could save us, at least in its broad lines. I think I have said enough for you to realize that your fate did not concern me. The only thing I was interested in was time. It says somewhere – in *Alice in Wonderland*, I think – that time is a person. From that moment on, I did everything I could to get him on our side, against you and everyone else. Time became an obsession.

My first thought was to postpone the moment when Kaub had been killed for those who would be in charge of the investigation, to gain a few hours which would be all mine, like white pages on which I could write another truth besides the real one. This depended, in the first place, on their not being able to perform an autopsy for several days. I had to hide Kaub's body until it would be impossible to determine the precise time of his death. Moreover, he would have to stay alive after a fashion before dying for the second time. That was why I shifted the murder from Paris to Villeneuve. Kaub had planned to go there; he would go. I found his plane ticket among his things. He was going to pick up his Thunderbird which had been left in a garage in Avignon. Anita had heard him phone that morning to find out if it would be ready. He would pick it up. I made Anita describe the house in Villeneuve. She had gone there two or three times, telling me lies for which I no longer had the heart to reproach her. She said that the house was rather isolated but that there were other estates on the same road. She was sure that if three rifle shots were fired, not in a concrete basement this time, but in a room with open windows, neighbours would hear them and would testify to that effect afterwards. That was all I needed.

I made a rapid search of the room we were in and the room that Anita indicated as Kaub's bedroom. While I was doing this my ideas fell into place. At the same time I was discovering the personality of this man and what I had to do, step by step, to shift the responsibility for his death, a thousand kilometres away, onto you. I did not say anything to Anita, for I would have lost precious time in convincing her. I let her in on my plan gradually, that night, as I needed her. I did not tell her that you would have to die until the last minute. I gave her the impression of great confidence and of ploughing ahead doggedly, as always. When I left Villa Montmorency, only a few details remained to be solved. The most serious was that, apart from Anita's using your name on a few vague occasions, there was only one link connecting you with Maurice Kaub. I had no way of appreciating what it was worth at the time. When Anita had told me about her affair, she had mentioned certain photographs that she had taken at your apartment, without your knowledge, at Kaub's request, with a camera not much bigger than a cigarette lighter. She told me that he was experienced in "this kind of nonsense," and that he knew how to make the most of a picture taken under bad conditions. She remembered, however, that except for one shot taken in the morning in good light when you weren't wearing glasses and she could take more risks, all the photographs were either underexposed or obviously taken without your knowledge – and therefore unusable and even prejudicial to the plan I was developing. Besides, Kaub had taken them to Villeneuve and Anita was not even sure he had kept them. You had met Kaub once before our marriage, but only casually, in the hall of your apartment building when you were coming home and Anita was leaving with him. He was sufficiently interested in you to persuade her to take those pictures – purely from a need to humiliate her – when she spent the night in your apartment, but as far as she remembered, you had hardly noticed.

I left Kaub's body in the shooting room and locked the door. In his bedroom I made a bundle of the clothes he had worn that day. I kept his wallet and various papers including a prescription for digitalis, the address of the garage in Avignon, and the plane ticket for Marseille-Marignane. I had his telephone disconnected for the weekend. I left Anita in the house, giving her Kaub's keys so she could lock up when she left. I told her that I was going to bring you back there to get you out of the way for the night, and what excuse I was going to give you. I instructed her to hide anything that might make you think this wasn't our house. She was sure you knew our real address. Actually I didn't care what you thought since you would be dead the next day anyway.

I told Anita I would call her at avenue Mozart in half an hour. She was to dress for the commercial film festival, which we had planned to attend. I would describe to her what you were wearing on the phone, so she could pick out similar clothes for herself. She did not understand. She was pale, her tears had left streaks of mascara on her face. She was a mess. I told her that now she had to be beautiful, natural, and brave.

I had left my car in avenue des Trembles fifty yards from Kaub's gate. I went straight to the agency. On the way I had my first cigarette since leaving. It was now almost five. In my office I got rid of Muchet, who wanted to show me a series of ads. It was the easiest okay he ever got in his whole, incompetent career. I practically pushed him out of the door. I found a plane timetable in my desk drawer and noted the departure and arrival times I would need during the night. I called my secretary on the intercom and asked her to have two tickets for the two o'clock Swissair plane to Geneva the next day sent to my house that evening. I asked her to assemble the Milkaby file. Then I had a shot – vodka, I think – and walked upstairs to your office.

It was the first time I had been in that room since you had occupied it. You weren't there, and at first I thought of sending for you. Then I told myself that this would be needlessly drawing attention. I took advantage of your absence to look around. I opened some drawers, then your handbag, which you had left on the desk. I was looking for something that might fit in with my plan, of course, but above all I was trying to find you, through the objects you lived with. The longer it took you to appear, the more nervous I became. I did not know you. I looked at your white coat, hanging on a hanger on the wall. I touched it. It smelled of the perfume Anita uses, which at first surprised and annoyed me, then gave me an idea. If by some remote chance the same perfume were detected at Villa Montmorency, or in Villeneuve – Anita had gone there with Kaub during the week – this could just as easily be attributed to your presence as to hers. But there was something else about that coat in the room, something at once indefinable and very tangible, that concerned me more than all the rest, that even distressed me. I now think, Dany, that it was the foreknowledge of what was going to happen to me despite all my efforts – that long race without sleep, through night and day, to get here, that long race filled with the obsessions that I have always carried with me.

The creature with the blonde hair who suddenly opened the door was a complete stranger to me. Not one of your features, Dany, not one of your gestures, not one tone in your voice, in that sun-filled office where I felt I was taking all the room, tallied with the image I had of you. You were too close, too present, I don't know. You seemed so calm and self-assured that I felt as if everything were unreal. I played with a little hinged elephant. I realized that none of my nervousness escaped your attention, that your mind was buzzing too, in short, that you were alive. To manipulate Maurice Kaub, according to my plan, was simple. I could move him around any way I wanted as if he were an object, and even make him do what I wanted, because he was dead. But you, by an even greater paradox, were a total abstraction, you carried within yourself ten million unforeseeable movements, any one of which could destroy me.

I left. I came back because I had forgotten something important: you must not tell the other girls that you were working at my house that night. I went to the accounting department and took some cash out of the safe. I put a thick wad of notes into my jacket pocket, the way I used to during the war, when I was twenty. It was the war that revealed to me the only talent I possess, namely, the ability to sell anything to anyone, including what people buy most easily and at the highest price: hot air. A new typist – I don't know her name – was watching me with an idiotic expression. I told her to get to work. I called my secretary and told her to take the Milkaby file, a ream of typing paper, and some carbon paper to my car. I saw you go through the hall in your white coat. I went to the copy department, where I heard a familiar uproar. It was Gaucherand distributing the holiday-pay envelopes. I asked for yours. Then I went back to your office. I was sure you had left a note explaining your departure to the others.

When I saw that piece of paper clipped to your light I could not believe my eyes. You announced that you were taking a plane that night, which was exactly what I wanted people to believe. But as I told you, Dany, I think fast, and my joy was short-lived. Already you had made a move which seemed to fit in with my plan beyond all hope, and already it was a move that could ruin everything. I was planning to send the famous telephone message to Orly in your name, indicating your determination to follow Kaub to Villeneuve if he left. The trouble was you could not have decided to leave three hours before finding out that he would ignore your message and leave anyway. Presented with this note which anyone at the agency could see, I could still choose either it or my telephone message, but not both. If I hadn't thought of that, if I hadn't foreseen a discrepancy which would be obvious to the stupidest policeman, you would have won the case, Dany, even dead. I chose my telephone message. I folded your note twice and put it in my pocket. It was not addressed to anyone, and after Kaub's plane had left, I might be able to use it. Time is a person, Dany, and what you and I have been through these last few days has simply been a duel to win his good graces.

I picked you up by the front door. You were tall and statuesque against the light. I drove you to your apartment on the pretext of letting you get your things, but really to study the layout so I could get in again. I remember your calm voice in my car, your short-nosed profile, a sudden shaft of sunlight that set your hair aglow. I did not trust you. The less I talked to you and looked at you, the less material I would be feeding to that strange and unsleeping machine which I sensed behind those dark glasses, that smooth forehead. It was later than I had planned when we walked into your apartment. At first I located all the details of Anita's confessions, all the bad dreams I had had. You had disappeared into the bathroom. I called avenue Mozart. Lowering my voice, I told Anita to wait for us at Villa Montmorency with Michèle. She said in a worried voice, "Michèle? Why Michèle?" I answered that it was better. I could not explain, for I could hear you very distinctly, moving around on the other side of the partition. I thought that you would be more likely to believe it was "our house" if our daughter were there, but this was not the only consideration that motivated me. I needed to have Michèle near me. I was probably afraid that in case things got worse, I might be separated from her when there was still time to get out of the country. This was a good idea, for Anita and Michèle are safe right now.

The worst moment was when you came back into the room. Anita was asking me questions over the phone which I could not answer. I had to describe you to your face without arousing your suspicions. I pretended she had asked me, "I haven't seen Dany for six months, has she changed?" You were sitting on the arm of a chair, putting on some white shoes. The tight skirt of your suit, fashionably short, provided an excellent view of a pair of long legs which I was rather surprised to find myself noticing at a time like this. I talked. I think my voice was the same as usual. My mind was as much of a mess as Anita's makeup a little while earlier. For the first time I realized physically that I would have to kill you, to stop the life in this body so close to mine, not with plans, with ideas, but with my bare hands, like a butcher. A bad moment, Dany. But it passed. I know now that everything they tell you to make you believe the opposite is untrue. It passes, it really does. You feel that physical abhorrence once, only once – the same thing you feel when you think you have to die yourself, no stronger – but then it goes away forever, and what doesn't go away you get used to. It's easy to kill, it's easy to die. Everything is easy. Except, maybe, to console for one minute the child who is still trapped inside of us, who has not grown up, who never will grow up, and who never stops calling for help.

On the road to Auteuil I sent you into a chemist to buy that bottle of digitalis for which I had the prescription. At the time I did it only to create a link between you and Kaub, but when I thought it over while you were gone I realized that when the time came the next morning it might be the weapon I needed to kill you. I had decided to make it look as if, after bringing the body of your lover from Villeneuve to Paris in the boot of his Thunderbird, you finally lost all hope of covering up your crime, and committed suicide. Swallowing a bottle of digitalis seemed a believable way of committing suicide for a woman. It would be simple enough for me. All I would have to do was make you swallow it by force, and you weren't strong enough to prevent me.

At Villa Montmorency you showed no surprise, you walked into Kaub's house apparently believing that it was ours. Anita could not accept this idea when I met her on the second floor. Down below, you were beginning to type on the old Remington belonging to the late master of the house. Michèle was sitting in a high-backed chair on the landing beside us, holding her doll. I felt better now that she was there. Anita said, "I know Dany better than you do. I'm sure she's not taken in. You never know what's going on behind those glasses." I shrugged my shoulders. I was thinking about your white suit. The very fact that it came from a shop that was one of my accounts made it impossible for me to call and have another one sent right over. The one Anita had, although also white, was quite different. She said she would examine yours and find a solution. She had white shoes and could comb her hair the way you did. I told her what she had to do: take the little girl to her mother's house; buy plane tickets at the Aéroport des Invalides; go to the festival where we were expected and tell people I was there; then go to avenue Mozart, change her clothes, take a taxi to Orly, and catch an eleven o'clock Air France plane for Lyon where we were to meet. When we had settled the details of this meeting, we discussed your evening alone in this house.

The typewriter was clattering down below. Anita said that if she knew you, you wouldn't stop typing until your eyes got tired, and that you weren't the type to snoop around in a strange house. Nevertheless, I preferred to be on the safe side.

We spiked the wine that she later served with your cold supper with some of Maurice Kaub's sleeping capsules. We had to use several, for Anita said that you would never drink more than one glass. I guessed at the number. We did this in the kitchen, after you thought I was gone. Actually, while Anita was showing you the room where you were to sleep, I went back into the big room, opened your handbag, and took your keys, your driving licence and – on impulse – your turquoise silk scarf. Gently I kissed Michèle, who had fallen asleep in the kitchen. I took a suitcase of Kaub's which I had packed upstairs with the clothes he had worn that day and went down into the basement.

He looked like a fallen statue, absurd under a harsh light. I told him silently that now I had the last laugh on him. Anita and I were fighting for a single life – ours and Michèle's. Never had she been so truly my wife. What could he do about that? A miserable piece of shit, that's all he was now. I took the Winchester and laid it across the suitcase. I found a box of 30 × 30 cartridges on a shelf, and I took that along too. I had already picked up the two shells Anita had ejected, after making sure the third was still in the magazine. I locked the room and went out the back way, down into the garden. Anita was leaning against the wall waiting for me. I gave her some money. I kept all of Kaub's keys. I did not have time to pick out the ones to the house in Villeneuve. Anita kissed me passionately. She told me that I could depend on her, that I was a loyal man, and that she loved me.

It was after six thirty when I got into the Citroën. My last memory of the house that night was a lighted window on the ground floor and behind it the blurred image of your face and your blonde hair. I went to your apartment in rue de Grenelle. I did not meet anyone on the stairs. I opened the door to your apartment and closed it behind me. I immediately phoned the message to Orly. In Kaub's suitcase I put two dresses, a pair of black trousers, some underwear, and some other things I found in your drawers. I also took your white coat and a single earring because the other one fell behind the bureau. It was ten past seven. Kaub's plane left at seven forty-five. But I stopped to look into the bathroom. The dress you had worn today was still there. I took your perfume bottle.

After that it was the autoroute du Sud, the hand of the clock racing towards seven thirty and the needle of the speedometer pointing to 160. I left the Citroën with a car park attendant in front of the airport. I checked in my suitcase with apologies and a tip. I ran as fast as I could. As I was going through the gate to the runway a man handed me "your" telephone message. I gave him a thousand-franc note so he would remember me. They did not ask me my name on the Caravelle, but twice on some harmless pretext I told the stewardess that my name was Kaub, Maurice Kaub, and that I was going to Villeneuve-lès-Avignon. I had a vodka and read the newspaper. The flight lasted a little over an hour. I went over my plan. The fact that I did not look like Kaub did not bother me in the least. Nobody would remember the physical appearance of one traveller among so many others. They would vaguely remember the name or certain words that leave an impression, like Avignon; that was enough. It was during the trip, realizing that Anita would also be impersonating someone and would be encountering much more serious difficulties – she would have to create a very precise impression – that I hit upon the gimmick of the bandaged hand. This is the kind of detail you remember: "It was the woman in the Thunderbird with a bandage on her hand." I saw all the advantages that could be derived from this "brand image" if I chose the left hand. Anita would check in at a hotel and openly leave an identity card without having to write it herself, since you were left-handed. And this bandage would not hamper her in any way, since she was not. Besides, your suicide would be interpreted as tantamount to a confession of murder. Nobody would be surprised that you did not leave a formal document.

In Marseille-Marignane it was dark. After claiming my suitcases I bought gauze and adhesive tape in the station chemist and caught a cab for Avignon. I talked to the driver about my alleged profession as a contractor. We agreed about the miserable housing situation, then I fell silent again. He let me out in front of the Cotti garage. I gave him a good tip. He had driven eighty kilometres in fifty minutes. Later I realized that I could not remember a thing about him. I don't even know what colour his hair was. I don't care what they tell you, Dany, nobody really notices anyone else. I counted on that in my effort to deceive those who would be in charge of the investigation, and on that point, at least, I think I was right.

The garage was dimly lit and quiet. A man met me in front of the glassed-in office. I paid him for the repairs to the Thunderbird. He gave me a receipt. I told him I had a house in Villeneuve. He brought out the Thunderbird with its top down, newly washed, and parked it by the door As I took the wheel I tried to figure out how to start it at a glance. It was easy. I think I left without his noticing the slightest hesitation.

I had to ask the way to Villeneuve, which I did not realize was so close to Avignon. It was ten fifteen when I opened the gate of Domaine Saint-Jean. As soon as I was inside this house I took the rifle out of the suitcase and fired three shots, two out of an open window and the third into the wall of the main room. To foil an expert investigator, I collected the shells and replaced them with those from Villa Montmorency, which I threw on the floor under the furniture. I put three fresh bullets into the magazine. Then I listened to the night for a sound. If anybody came, my plan was to run away, leaving Kaub's suit, your things, and the Thunderbird behind. Nobody came. I did what I had to do in a quarter of an hour. I found the mounted enlargement of the nude photograph of you upstairs in that pornographer's studio. I leafed through all the pictures, removing yours – except for two that were acceptable for my plan – and some shocking ones of Anita. For unlike you, Dany, she had posed of her own free will. I tore them up and put them in a big paper bag which I took with me later. I found the negatives in a drawer where they were numbered and catalogued, where you were all reduced to the rank of postage stamps. I also found contact prints. I took the mounted photo of you downstairs and hung it on a wall in place of a picture of a girl in a grotesque crouching position who could have been under twenty. Before going upstairs I looked at you for the first time. I couldn't explain how or why, but suddenly I had the feeling that you were one of us, an object of my compassion.

In that photograph your face expressed an obvious affection for someone who was at that very moment betraying you, taking advantage of the fact that you are almost blind to satisfy the voyeurism of that piece of shit. It was a sudden insight; full of a strange fatality. I left you on the wall, fully realizing what a miserable specimen I am.

I planted your clothes in the right places and sprinkled your perfume onto sheets which may still have held traces of Anita's. The bed was unmade. The leather belt was on the floor, I didn't have to touch it. I think I was beginning to be tired, that my nerves were deadened, for the leather belt had no effect on me at all. I left the house unlocked and took to the car my paper bag, your white coat, and the rug in which you later found Maurice Kaub. Also the cartridge box and the rifle. Behind me I left everything in perfect order for an investigation.

I drove very fast, my mind on the road, my headlights on full, oblivious of the people I passed. I got to the Lyon-Bron airport at about one in the morning, twenty minutes before the departure of the plane I had planned to take. It was the last one that night. Anita was not waiting at the appointed place, but in front of it, beside the road. In the glare of my headlights I saw that she was wearing a white suit. I opened the door for her and drove off. She had been there for over an hour. She was cold and frightened. She shivered constantly. I stopped under some trees and told her what she had to do. I gave her your driving licence, your scarf, and your white coat. I bandaged her left hand. I tore out the inside pages of the unused plane ticket for Marseille-Marignane that she had bought in your name. I put it in the coat pocket along with the receipt from the garage in Avignon and your holiday-pay envelope, from which I subtracted the exact cost of your plane ticket. The suit Anita had on was new, it looked like yours. She had bought it without even trying it on in a shop that stayed open late near the Place de l' Etoile. She showed me the skirt, which was folded over at the waist and held up by two safety pins. I could not help mentioning the unmade bed I had seen in Kaub's house. I asked her if she had been the one who had made love in those rumpled sheets. I had such an irrepressible need for details and so little time that I was stammering. She put her hand over my mouth. She swore that no matter what happened, from now on she belonged only to me. I drove back to the airport. I showed her how the car worked. When I left her I kissed her passionately, and she told me again that she loved me.

Our next appointment was at four thirty in the morning, on the telephone. By then, according to a map of Kaub's, she should be as far as Avallon. I ran into the airport with my paper bag and bought a ticket in the name of Mr Lewis Carroll. Another hour's flight in a propeller plane coming from the Middle East. I dozed, the image of your naked body against a white wall flashing several times across my mind. At Orly I did not take the Citroën but a taxi, which left me at the Porte d'Auteuil a little before three. I walked all around Villa Montmorency without seeing a light in any of the windows. Kaub's house was dark too. When I came in I talked in a loud voice as if I were coming home from a boring evening and Anita were with me. I went to the door of the room where you were and called you softly. You were not asleep. In the big room the wine bottle was gone. I found it in the kitchen with your dishes which, unfortunately, you had washed. Still, there would be plenty of other traces of your presence in this house, and I was relieved to see that the level of the liquid was lower than the mark I had made on the bottle by the equivalent of one glass. No doubt the dose of sleeping medicine had not been strong enough to knock you out right away, but I was sure that it would work eventually.

I waited in the garden in front of the house, since your window looked onto the back. As I smoked, I imagined Anita at the wheel of the Thunderbird, speeding through the night. Mentally I went over everything I had done since Kaub's death, looking for a mistake, an oversight. No, I had done my job well. About four I came to the door of your room and called you in a low voice. This time you did not answer. I went in without making a sound. In the soft light that came in from the big room, you were lying on your back with your eyes closed, your face in profile on the pillow. I was now convinced that you were asleep. I had just enough time to go back to avenue Mozart, but for some reason I could not help taking a few steps towards you, coming so close that I could hear you breathe. It was the first time I had seen you without glasses. You looked even less familiar than you had that afternoon. I stood there for over a minute, studying you. Then something happened that almost stopped my heartbeat. You spoke. You spoke just as distinctly as you do during the day. Without interrupting the rhythm of your sleep, you said, "Kill me, oh please kill me." I retreated slowly to the door without taking my eyes off you. I went out. I walked to avenue Mozart, carrying my paper bag.

When I came into my apartment I put on the same act I had at Kaub's house for the benefit of my servants, who were sleeping at the back of the apartment: I talked in a loud voice to an imaginary Anita. It was time for her call. I waited in the bedroom. I had several things to do, but I forced myself to wait by the phone so I could cut off the ring as soon as it began. Then it was five o'clock. I saw the daylight filter through the Venetian blinds and heard the first noises from the street. Something serious must have happened to Anita. As time passed, I began to realize the folly of our undertaking. Finally the ring shattered the silence, I heard it rumble in the receiver as I picked it up. Yes, it was Anita – far away, so far from the life I wanted for us, so far from what I had imagined for Michèle, for us. She played the game I had instructed her to play to be on the safe side. She said she was Dany Longo, that she was outside Avallon in the car, and she gave the password that meant that everything was going according to plan: "I have a rug in my boot, Mr Caravaille." She also said that she had called Bernard Thorr to get our phone number. I know that this layout man is your best friend after that poor man's Gary Cooper who knocked you up and dropped you.

After I hung up I burned the torn-up photographs and negatives that were in my paper bag. I threw the ashes down the kitchen disposal. Then I hurriedly packed three suitcases, one for Michèle, one for Anita, and one for myself, taking only what seemed indispensable. In Anita's suitcase I put her jewels and a bill for the amount I have in the bank in Paris. Most of my money is deposited in Swiss banks, and Anita's signature is as good as mine. In money and securities I think I have enough so that no matter what happens, my little girl can always live like a princess. Besides, Anita would guard what I left her with her life. As I was about to leave, Marie, our Spanish maid, came out of her room in her wrapper, jabbering like a magpie, and asking whether I needed her. I told her I was spending the weekend in Switzerland with my wife, I sent her back to bed, and excused myself.

I took two of the suitcases in one hand and the third in the other and walked back to Villa Montmorency. It was daytime. Waiters were washing down the little strips of pavement in front of their cafés. I was hungry and thirsty but I did not stop. At the door to your room I did not hear a sound. You must still have been asleep. I took the suitcases upstairs and sat down in an armchair to rest. I was afraid that if I lay down I would fall asleep. By seven thirty I still hadn't heard anything from below. I undressed and gave myself a quick sponge bath. I took a dressing gown out of my suitcase and went downstairs to the kitchen. I made coffee. I drank two cups and poured one for you. It was eight o'clock and the sky was clear. Even if she was behind schedule, Anita must be on the autoroute du Sud by now. It would not take her more than an hour to get here. I was very anxious because I was feeling the lack of sleep and she must be feeling it even more. I went outside and opened the garage door and the gate so she would not have to stop. Then I knocked on your door and you answered.

It was after nine thirty when the Thunderbird arrived. You had been working for some time. I came into the room to distract your attention from the garden. Anita came in by the back door. I found her on the second floor, sitting on the edge of the bath running the taps. She looked tired, of course but much less so than I had expected. She had taken off her bandage and her dark glasses. More than anything else, she wanted a bath. "I want to wash it all off," she said. Her eyes were very large and a little set. She held my hand in both of hers as she told me about her race, which had lasted eight hours. She had left traces of "your" presence in Mâcon, Tournus, Chalon-sur-Saône, Avallon, and also at the beginning of the autoroute du Sud, where she had stopped for petrol. The only unexpected event was being stopped by the motorbike policeman because her back light wasn't working, but even that fitted in perfectly with my plan. I helped her off with her clothes and made her repeat it all while she was in her bath. In Chalon she had taken a room in your name, which she had paid for in advance. She had slipped out of the hotel less than half an hour afterwards without being seen. The unexpected event had occurred about a hundred kilometres further north, just after Saulieu. She said that in the state she was in, and knowing that the Winchester was in the boot, she would certainly have fired on the policeman if he had tried to search the car. We both shuddered at the thought. It was in a village café while waiting for the back light of the Thunderbird to be mended that she had called Bernard Thorr and me, and had left your white coat. I concluded from all this that she had played her part as well as possible.

I got a towel and clean underwear out of her suitcase and dried her back. Clad in her white slip, she asked for a cigarette. She had run out hours ago. We went downstairs. While she was talking to you I took the opportunity to replace the things I had taken from your handbag. I went out to the garage. I wiped the inside of the Thunderbird as well as I could. I took the rug from Villeneuve, the rifle, and the cartridge into the basement. Then I went back to the second floor, shaved and put on a clean shirt and a suit. I took a taxi to the agency. In the deserted studio I found a box of old Milkaby layouts. I went to the accounting department and made out a pay envelope in your name. Inside I put the equivalent of two months' pay, plus the 300 francs I had promised you for the typing. I phoned a few colleagues and talked about the night before in Chaillot. Before going back to Villa Montmorency, I took a cab to rue de Grenelle. I went up to your floor and taped to your door the note you had written informing the others of your departure. I took another taxi to Auteuil, where I went to a café and had a sandwich, two more cups of black coffee, and a cognac. I felt I was nearing the end of this misery. I thought I had already won the race.

It was a little past eleven. Anita was ready to leave, you had finished your work. I gave you that pay envelope, which I planned to recover later when you brought back the Thunderbird. It was absolutely necessary for me to put you at the wheel of that car. Unless I did, my plan would not hold up in the eyes of the investigators. Their first move would be to examine the Thunderbird with methods I don't know about but which I assume are highly effective. It would be obvious that you could not have travelled almost 700 kilometres in it without leaving behind some trace of yourself: a fingerprint; a thread of your white suit; a hair. But, in spite of my hasty cleaning, they would find some trace of another woman. By going over your dead body they could easily confirm the fact that there was nothing on your person from this car, not even a speck of dust. I had a hard time talking you into it, Dany. And when you were there in front of me I hesitated, I even think that for a split second I lost the desire to go on. I did not know where I would find the courage to follow you back here, hurt your hand, make you swallow a bottle of digitalis – above all, to endure your terror and incomprehension for the few minutes it would take you to die. Nevertheless, I went on. We picked up Michèle at my mother-in-law's house on boulevard Suchet. We left you in the Thunderbird at Orly. I had told you that our plane took off at noon, but I had two more hours to follow you, kill you, arrange everything at Kaub's house, and meet Anita and the child in the airport restaurant.

I checked in our luggage. Until the moment I left her in the crowded waiting room, Anita did not know that I was going to kill you. If she had thought of it herself, she had convinced herself that I had another idea and that she had lost her mind. She asked what I was going to do. I answered that I could not leave you behind. She shook her head wordlessly, our little girl in her arms, her eyes suddenly filled with tears. I told her to wait in the restaurant until two o'clock. If I was not back by then, she and Michèle were to take the plane without me. I would meet them in Geneva. She kept shaking her head as I left. It was the moment when you were starting to drive the Thunderbird. I picked up my Citroën from the car park. I lost sight of you for a few moments. Then I saw you again fifty yards away, parked in another place. I watched you walk across the road towards the airport. I did not understand. For the first time, Dany, I did not understand.

I followed you, also on foot. I was afraid you would run into Anita and the little girl in the building. I saw them on the third floor, but you seemed to be in a world of your own. You sat at a table in the bar for a long time. I was twenty yards away behind a passport photo-booth. I had imagined everything that could happen if I left the car in your hands, down to an accident that would attract the police. On the other hand, I knew you were too short-sighted to drive fast and a careful person by nature. I believed that you would bring the

Thunderbird back without a hitch more surely than anyone else. I had foreseen everything, Dany, everything. What I still did not know and what I was to learn until it drove me mad was that not a single one of your reactions can be foreseen. You proceed like that crab under whose sign you were born.

Now do you understand, Dany? You got back into the Thunderbird and I followed you in the Citroën. You were supposed to go towards Paris and you went south. I thought you had made the wrong turn, but not at all, you kept on going. I watched you through the window in that restaurant near Fontainebleau where you had lunch. Now it was I who was becoming petrified with incredulity and rage. I sat in my car waiting for you to come out. The hand on my watch continued to race. I realized that I could not catch the Swissair plane, and that Anita and the little girl would fly alone. Desperately I tried to think of a new plan. I still hoped that after your meal you would go back to Villa Montmorency. This must be a short spree, for the pleasure of driving that car. No such thing; then came that broken carousel on which I was trapped, which would not stop. You went into Fontainebleau. I saw you buy some clothes and a suitcase. The sweat ran down my back. Nothing made sense any more. Suddenly you had completely reversed our roles. All that night I had ignored you, I had directed events without giving you any more thought than a piece of furniture. And now it was you who held the secret of the chase, you who were following your plan without thinking about me. All along the road to Joigny – I was behind you, always keeping 200 yards between us, matching your speed – I constructed the wildest hypotheses. The wildest of all was that Anita had been right last night, that you had never been taken in, and that you knew I was following you. The truth was the only thing that did not occur to me. Besides, you gained confidence with the kilometres and I had to fasten my mind on my driving to keep from losing you. Nobody ever observed you with such total concentration, but you always kept me guessing. At the bar in Joigny I almost did not see you slow down. Later, when you left, I wondered anxiously about the lorry driver who had spoken to you. I still did not know how lucky you are, Dany, but I guessed that that encounter, like all the others, would be turned against me. Then it was the end of the afternoon, and that main road near Auxerre where you drove over 160, inexorably leaving me behind. At that point, I realized that the speed of your driving and your purchases in Fontainebleau could mean only one thing: you had not kept the Thunderbird just for a spree, but for the rest of the weekend, you were heading straight for somewhere, and I had to stop you. At the same time, and this was the most frightening of all, I realized that you were retracing Anita's route in the opposite direction. Once again I came close to missing you – and revealing my presence – as I was driving through that village just after you came off the main road. You were talking to an old woman. I waited for you further on, a hundred yards past a petrol station on which I read the name of the village: Deux-Soirs-lès-Avallon. I thought I had gone completely mad. This was the place where Anita told me she had left your white coat. You were proceeding consciously, fiercely, to destroy everything. When I caught sight of the Thunderbird again and the splash of your turquoise scarf, I no longer doubted it. You stopped at the petrol station. This must be the very garage where Anita had stopped. I had her stamped receipt for repairs in my pocket. I looked to be sure and tore it up with absurd fury, sitting at the wheel. Then I got the bottle of digitalis out of the glove compartment, got out of the car, and walked through grass and trees in the sunlight, making a long detour to get to the back of that white building you had entered. Some men were talking outside by the petrol pumps. All I was thinking about was how to get to you and kill you without being seen or heard. These secluded toilets and the door you had left open were convenient. Suddenly I saw you from behind, white, blonde, and motionless, less than three yards away. You were in front of a mirror. I rushed towards the outside wall, paused barely long enough to catch my breath, and attacked. I grabbed you and pulled you off your feet, holding my hand over your face. Your glasses flew across the narrow room in a disorder that accurately reflected the state of my mind. You clung to the door with your left hand. I saw that hand. I don't think it lasted more than half a second, but that half second was the longest of my life. I understood with perfect clarity that now I was destroying my whole plan. The woman who had been seen on the road was wounded in the left hand. You were not. Killing you would not change that fact. I seized the doorknob and slammed the door on your hand as hard as I could. I felt a kind of silent scream against my own hand, which was clamped over your mouth, and suddenly your body went limp in my arms. I let you slip to the floor. You fell to your knees, strangely balanced, your forehead and hair on the floor. I don't know whether it was the noise I had made, fear of the voices I heard outside, the sight of your left hand, which was swelling with startling rapidity, or the thought that if I killed you right away the simultaneity of your death and the wound on your hand would not escape a medical expert, but I fled. I did not catch my breath until I was back in my car again.

I could have killed you there, Dany, but it would have been a mistake. Either I had to kill you near Kaub's body, or I had to take you there after I killed you. I could not have made you disappear in that petrol station, it was as simple as that. I did the right thing. More than once I have had occasion to regret this moment when I had you at my mercy, but I believe I did the right thing.

I waited until evening. I turned my car so that it was pointing for Paris. I was sure that after this you would go back. I wondered whether you had seen me. I was hungry, thirsty, and tired. A few times I got out of the Citroën and walked around in the dusk. I was not yet acquainted with that obstinacy of yours, or that horrifying faculty for rallying in the very depth of your depressions. I did not yet know how lucky it makes you.

You drove off again, in the direction I was not expecting. It was dark. I made a U-turn. You were driving slowly. Once again, you forced me to go at your speed. The back lights of the Thunderbird blinded me. I lost you at Saulieu, where, without warning, you turned off the main road. I drove through the town several times, looking for you in vain. After stopping for petrol, a glass of wine, and a sandwich, I headed south again. The kilometres ticked by beneath my wheels. I was alone with the most acute sense of abandonment I have ever known.

The Thunderbird was parked by the Saône in Chalon. I stopped fifty yards away on the same side of the street. I think I was laughing. I walked slowly through the night towards the car, which now had its top up. Suddenly the headlights went on. I saw that there was a man with you. And then you started the car. I ran back to the wheel of the Citroën. I told myself that you were doing all these incomprehensible things out of pure sadism, that you had decided to drive me mad before you finished me off. I caught up with you, though; I saw you go into the Hotel La Renaissance with that boy in the grey sweater. There was a bandage on your left hand. I would have gone there anyway, since Anita had told me the name of the hotel where she had taken a room during the night. It was clear now that you were ruining my plan point by point. I let you leave. I let you drive out of Chalon with this character whom you wanted solely because he was the symbol of everything that makes me sick. You cannot know how tired I was, Dany.

I spent a long time in the garden of that other hotel while you sat at a table with him in a deserted dining room. I watched you as I had at lunch, through the window. You were wearing a pair of trousers the same colour as your scarf, the splash of turquoise I had been following all afternoon. I think that at that moment I almost believed that you really had been Kaub's mistress, that I had become the victim of my own hoax. I waited and waited. I saw you go upstairs to give yourself to that bastard. I saw a shaft of light appear at a window whose heavy curtains were drawn across your night of love.

I headed back to Paris. Anger kept me awake for a few more hours. Again I drove with my headlights turned on full, oblivious to others on the road. Three hundred and forty kilometres. I would reach Paris by five o'clock in the morning. Yes. I would do it. I would get Kaub's body, rolled in its rug, and the rifle. I would destroy the picture of Anita that I had forgotten on the wall of the room. I would not sleep. I would be strong, stronger than my fatigue and my regrets. I would return to Chalon through the dawn. I would keep on mowing down the kilometres, I would be back in that hotel garden before you got into the Thunderbird again; say at about ten in the morning. I would have to be back by ten. Sated with filth behind your curtains, you would sleep at least that late, not suspecting that the big oaf was still on his feet. Even in daylight, I would find a way to transfer Kaub's body and the rifle to the boot of the Thunderbird. After that I would kill you anywhere, the bottle of digitalis between your teeth, your heart stopped in my hand like a bird's. I saw some kids kill a bird when I was young. I screamed and beat them all up. At the age of thirteen I was already taller than the average man, and I was fat. They called me names that infuriated me. But I beat them all up. They made fun of my parents, who were poor. But I beat them all up. I wish I could go backwards. I wish – I don't know – that there was no such thing as filth, that everything was clean and reassuring and motionless. I can't stand it any more, Dany. I slowed down on the way to Paris. Time was against me. At Villa Montmorency I no longer had the keys: I had to take the lock off the back door and screw it on again afterwards. I carried Kaub's body in his rug to the boot of the Citroën. I had trouble getting it in. Then I had to go back for the rifle, and again to burn the picture of Anita and to double check, to be sure we had left no trace of our presence. I looked at the bed you had slept in. I lay down on my stomach, promising myself that I would rest only for a few minutes. I went to sleep. I do not know what force woke me up half an hour later. I could have slept the whole day. I splashed water on my face and left.

After Fontainebleau I had to stop by the side of the road. It must have been about eight. It was raining. Cars whizzed right by me, the Citroën moved. I fell asleep again with my head in my arms on the wheel. I slept only a quarter of an hour, maybe less. I could not forgive myself, it was as if I was letting go of Michèle's life every time I closed my eyes. I stopped again for coffee at a bar on the road near Chagny. I jumped every time a new customer walked by the boot of my car.

You had taken off, Dany, it was past noon by the time I reached the garden of that hotel in Chalon. I did not know which way you had gone or how much of a head start you had. I could not take the risk of asking. I kept going south. By Valence I had lost all hope of finding you again. I called

Geneva. Anita cried and talked in a soft voice, she had given up hope too. I told her, "She kept the car, she is going south, but I have the picture with me, there's still hope." She repeated into the instrument, "Who? Who is with you?" I asked her to wait for me, to love me. I told her I would call that evening. I drove on. The sun made my head swim.

I found you again in Salon. The Thunderbird was having its tank filled in a petrol station. The top was down. A little later you came out of a café with that character from the night before. His arm was around your waist. I did not even feel relief. I had only one thought: to get Kaub's body and the rifle off my hands and into the boot of the Thunderbird. I did it half an hour later on that deserted road outside Marseille where you stopped, for what disgusting purposes I could well imagine. I saw the two of you disappear among the trees on the hill. Without even thinking, I brought the Citroën up beside the Thunderbird. I opened both of our car boots in broad daylight. I had long since taken off my jacket. My shirt was soaked with sweat. I felt as if my head were about to burst. After this transfer, I drove through a din of grasshoppers to a bend that hid my car, and turned around. I told myself that after your picnic you would get back onto the main road for Marseille. I got out of the Citroën and waited beside the road. For a moment I considered going back and killing both of you any way I could, with my bare hands. and letting the police make of it whatever they could, but I told myself that then they would have someone to look for, that they would find me.

I saw your friend get into the Thunderbird alone, turn around too, and throw your open suitcase beside the road. And so I lost you again. There was that car driving off, loaded with a kind of explosive, and there was you. I did not know whom I should follow, him or you. I decided that since you were on foot I could catch up with you more easily than with the Thunderbird. I followed this boy along the main road, as far as the road that leads to Marseille. Here he picked up speed, going too fast for the Citroën. I kept on anyway. I understood that he was stealing the car. At the entrance to the city he disappeared. There is a cloverleaf there. I went around it several times, aimlessly, attracting the attention of a policeman who was directing the traffic coming off the main road. I got back onto the main road, going the other way. Fatigue was paralyzing my mind and will, I was acting at random, absurdly. I thought, "She must be in the same state as me, I'll find her helpless and stranded. I'll eliminate her, and to hell with that bastard and the Thunderbird." I still didn't know you, Dany. All I found on that hill was the message you had left, those few words written with your right hand: TONIGHT 10 PM IN FRONT OF 10 CANBIÈRE. At least I still had one hope of finding you. I tore up the note. Slowly I drove back to Marseille, my mind completely occupied by you. I think I was beginning to understand the meaning of your mysterious behaviour but it was shadowy, I had to get some sleep before the truth could emerge. I took a room in a hotel near Gare Saint-Charles. I fell into a dead sleep with all my clothes on.

The desk called me a little after nine, as I had asked them to do. I ordered some supper and took a bath. I had two days' growth of beard and my shirt was foul, but I was rested and my mind was clear. I realized at last that you knew nothing about the murder or about my following you, that you had kept the Thunderbird on an impulse, and that was all. The papers were in the name of Kaub's business, R.B.C., which stood for Real-Estate-Building-Contracting. You probably had not even noticed. Somehow or other you had run into one or two of the clues Anita had left the night before, but obviously you had not understood why you were attacked in the toilets at the petrol station, or why your left hand had been hurt. And at the moment your only concern must be to get the car back. Perhaps you had some way I did not know about of finding your con man again. That, besides your courage, would explain why you reacted so quickly on the hill.

I called Anita from the hotel phone booth. She had given up. Distinctly, right over the phone so any operator could hear her, she said that it would be better to go to the police and confess the murder. I tried to persuade her to get hold of herself. I told her that I had a solution, that everything would work out. I heard Michèle's voice asking, "Is it Daddy? Is it Daddy?" I promised Anita I would join them in Geneva the next day.

At ten o'clock I was standing across the road from 10 Canebière. Half an hour later I followed you and your gigolo at a distance, trying to guess what was going on in your heads. I understood only one thing, that you both knew there was a body in the boot of the Thunderbird. I had expected to find you alone, on foot, or not to find you at all, since he did not know about your message on the hill. I was even more disconcerted when I saw him put his arm around you again and you walked back towards La Canebière. I had parked the Citroën in a side street. I had to go and get it when I saw you standing in front of the Thunderbird. When I did that, of course, I lost you for good.

I drove through the city at random, with no hope even of finding you again, just for something to do. I thought about you, anxious, with your hand bandaged, in that white muslin dress with the boy's jacket over your shoulders. Later I realized that you had not told the police about the body because the car did not belong to you, because you had kept it without my knowledge. Little by little I succeeded in putting myself

227

in your place. I was sure that that night or the next day you would call Geneva to ask for help. Another solution was to get rid of the body without trying to find out who had put it in the boot. Either way, the trap I had set was closing in. I had planted the telephone message from Orly in the pocket of Kaub's dressing gown. This piece of paper would lead the investigators to you. Anita and I would only have to deny having seen you on Friday. We would seem to be telling the truth, since neither the house at Villa Montmorency nor the Thunderbird belonged to us. I slept in my hotel room until noon the next day. I asked a bellhop to get me an electric razor and the local newspapers. While shaving, I looked through them to make sure there was nothing about Kaub's murder, and that no unidentified body had been discovered in the area. I rang Anita. I told her I was going to wait until evening, because there was a chance that you would ring her. I told her that no matter what happened, we knew nothing about any of this business, that she had to stick to that story. I gave her the number of my hotel so she could get hold of me if anything happened. We were taking a big risk using the telephone this way, but I did not see any alternative. After lunch I walked through Marseille. I bought this shirt, which I wore out of the shop. I threw the other one down a sewer. As I was standing up again I caught sight of my image in a shop window mirror. Yes, it was really me, Michel Caravaille; successful advertising man, head of an up-and-coming young agency, model husband and father, man about town, in short, this person you see before you, Dany, whom you do not recognize, who does not recognize himself. Who is anyone, after all?

Anita rang me at about eight. You had just called her in Geneva. She was out of her head. She was crying. She said, "Please, don't harm her. She really believes she killed Kaub, do you understand? I don't want to be part of this horror.

You must tell her, you must explain to her." I don't know where her thoughts and anxieties led her during those two days and nights without me. I don't know, Dany. I heard Michèle crying, she was probably frightened by seeing her mother like this. I promised over and over again that I would not hurt you. She did not believe me. She said, "I want Dany to call me back, I want her to tell me that she is all right. Michel, I swear to you, if you go through with your plan I'll kill myself too. I'll kill myself, do you understand? I swear I'll do it!" I promised everything she wanted, to calm her down, to gain a few hours.

I drove to this place through the gathering dusk, like a madman. I was driving up the route de l'Abbaye just as you were coming down. I followed you to that brasserie by Avignon station. I saw that lorry driver, and then your white coat, whose presence belonged to the realm of pure magic. I still did not understand what stubborn logic had brought you to this moment. But what difference did it make? I saw you go through the pockets of that coat and take out that pay envelope, when the other one, the one I was planning to take back, was probably in your handbag. I had come into the room, once again I was aware of that brain ticking away behind your glasses. You were beautiful, Dany, when you kissed your friend's cheek, when in one blinding flash you knew everything that had happened, for the simple reason that there could not be two envelopes in your name for the same two weeks' pay. Yes, you were beautiful, but for me you were again the most dangerous person alive. Instinctively I drew back, out of your range of vision.

I watched you while you went into the station with the lorry driver, but I did not follow you. There was a chance that you would get on the train with him, leaving the Thunderbird in front of the brasserie. I gave you that chance. I opened the boot of the car a crack, just enough to see that Kaub was no longer there. I walked back to my Citroën on the other side of the ramparts. Later, from a distance, I saw you leave the station and look around for me. I watched you go by in the Thunderbird. Then I got into my own car. When I was sure you were going back to Villeneuve, I took a short cut to get here ahead of you.

I waited for you in the dark longer than I expected. The Winchester, which you had left on the sofa, was in my hands. You came in and turned on the light in the hall. I must have made a sudden movement. You froze. I saw you silhouetted against the light, you did not see me. But I had to get close to you, I had to fire that shot from very near if they were to think it was suicide. I took another step. At the same time I tried to imagine what your defence reflex would be. I was sure you would go to the sofa and try to grab the gun that was no longer there. I moved forward to bar your passage. To the very end, Dany, not one of your reactions was predictable. Just as I reached you I realized too late that you were not going towards the sofa, but straight for the hall light. Suddenly I heard a bulb burst, and everything went black. I ran and groped in vain for a switch. I heard a sound that I did not understand, at first, and then your voice. It was as clear and crisp as ever. You said, "Don't move, Monsieur Caravaille. I have just posted a letter enclosing the two pay envelopes and explaining everything. I addressed it to myself, but they will open it if I die. I did not address it to anyone else because Anita is my friend. I love her, and I want to help her. Now don't bother to turn on the light in this barn, I took out the fuses." Am I forgetting anything, Dany? Yes. You asked me to drop "my gun", because you "didn't want to have to force me to do it." I did not even ask myself how. I could depend on your already having thought of some fantastic idea. But it was because of something else you had said that I dropped the

Winchester. I came and sat down on this sofa. Later, as I talked to you, my eyes became accustomed to the darkness, and I saw you sit down on the arm of a chair across from me, a vague white shape.

You have listened to me without interrupting, Dany. I want you to tell me where Kaub's body is. Then you will take your things and go home. I want you to act with other people as if no part of this business ever concerned you. I want you to say nothing, I want you to tear up those two envelopes. As for myself, I shall choose the lesser of two evils. I shall arrange everything and turn myself over to the police. I'll take the blame. This murder will cost me much less than it would Anita, you understand. I will be the rejected husband who ruins his life in a fit of despair when he discovers his misfortune. I will have gone through a weekend of confusion, but in the end I will have confessed everything of my own free will. I will hire the best lawyers; this time I will do everything I can to sell my story. Believe me, I will be a good salesman, I don't doubt I'll wangle a suspended sentence.

That's all. I have tried, Dany, to give you the most honest picture of myself I could. Even if it is an ugly one, I hope it suggests the idea that good and evil are merely two aspects of a single fascination. I have watched you a great deal. In the end, I do not know who you are. But you must understand me since, for a moment, you believed yourself capable of doing what Anita did. I want you to give me those fuses, I want the lights to go on again in this barn, I want you to call Geneva and tell Anita that everything is fine. Tell her to wait for me, that I'll do my best not to be late. That's all, Dany. Turn on the lights. Thanks for the weekend.

The young woman with the bandage on her left hand stayed in Room 18 at the Hotel Noailles. She ordered coffee and all the Marseille papers. She read from beginning to end the articles telling how a well-known advertising man had killed his wife's lover and turned himself in to the Avignon police during the night. Then she took a taxi to quai de la Joliette, waited by the gate for a passenger for Cairo via Alexandria, grabbed him by the arm, told him that she was a good egg but that enough was enough, got back her money, and said goodbye. She took the bus to Cassis, picked up her suitcase at the Hotel Bella Vista, paid for her room, and took the opportunity to try out a bright yellow bikini in the swimming pool. Before getting dressed she had lunch on the terrace, sunning herself and looking at the sea through her dark glasses. In the early afternoon, while waiting for the bus to Marseille, she ran into a little boy she knew on the port who was shaking hands with his father. She kissed him and called him Titou. At the age of four boys have even shorter memories than they do later, for Titou did not recognize her. She could not help following him down the street for a moment, twenty yards behind. She liked that, just following him, but an old woman who never left her called her a little goose and said that she was hurting herself and that she should pull herself together. She stopped and took a red-checked cap out of her bag, put it on, slightly back on her blonde head, and strolled calmly back along the port carrying her suitcase. Two hours later, at Marseille-Marignane, she took the first plane she'd ever taken. She was afraid the whole time. The sun was shining in Paris, too. The streets were decorated with flags. She went to her apartment and immediately phoned a layout man she knew and asked him to keep his mouth shut, no matter what he read in the papers. Then she fixed her makeup and called a number that was written on the inside of her cap. About five months later she was married in Marseille, not, as anyone would have predicted, to a lorry driver who stole violets – he was her best man and became a brother to her – but to his best friend, the most wonderful, best-looking, most intelligent, funniest, most adorable, most killing, most everything person she had ever met, a heart-throb who drove a Berliet and planned to become a millionaire because he thought it was a good idea, and whose name was Baptistin Laventure. Thus she became Dany Laventure, so that on the trousseau she had embroidered at the orphanage with hope and wonderful eyes, she did not even have to change her initials.

PARIS, APRIL 1966